Read
K.C. ...

Under the Covers

"It is pure romance and intimacy. Just so sweet."

—Love Bytes

On the Same Page

"*On the Same Page* is yet another example of their strength in writing plots and characters that draw the reader in and are entertaining throughout."

—Jessie G Books

"I highly recommend this to lovers of MM romance, especially those who like a little kink in their stories."

—Scattered Thoughts and Rogue Words

Roots of Evil

"It's a good mystery, but with fun, snark and sassiness that only K.C. can provide in her way."

—Love Bytes

"A good mystery, a murder, a list of potential killers, and Mike's and Jonathon's minds. It was captivating and funny."

—OptimuMM

By K.C. Wells

BFF
Bromantically Yours
First
Love Lessons Learned
Step by Step
Waiting For You

DREAMSPUN DESIRES
The Senator's Secret
Out of the Shadows
My Fair Brady
Under the Covers

LEARNING TO LOVE
Michael & Sean
Evan & Daniel
Josh & Chris
Final Exam

LIONS & TIGERS & BEARS
A Growl, a Roar, and a Purr

LOVE, UNEXPECTED
Debt
Burden

MERRYCHURCH
MYSTERIES
Truth Will Out
Roots of Evil
A Novel Murder

SENSUAL BONDS
A Bond of Three
A Bond of Truth

With Parker Williams

COLLARS & CUFFS
An Unlocked Heart
Trusting Thomas
Someone to Keep Me
A Dance with Domination
Damian's Discipline
Make Me Soar
Dom of Ages
Endings and Beginnings

SECRETS
Before You Break
An Unlocked Mind
Threepeat
On the Same Page

Published by DREAMSPINNER PRESS
www.dreamspinnerpress.com

A GROWL, A ROAR, AND A PURR

K.C. WELLS

Published by

DREAMSPINNER PRESS

5032 Capital Circle SW, Suite 2, PMB# 279, Tallahassee, FL 32305-7886 USA
www.dreamspinnerpress.com

A Growl, a Roar, and a Purr
© 2020 K.C. Wells

Cover Art
© 2020 Paul Richmond
http://www.paulrichmondstudio.com
Cover Photo
© 2020 Wander Aguiar
Cover content is for illustrative purposes only and any person depicted on the cover is a model.

Trade Paperback ISBN: 978-1-64405-865-7
Digital ISBN: 978-1-64405-864-0
Library of Congress Control Number: 2020940945
Trade Paperback published October 2020
v. 1.0

Printed in the United States of America

This paper meets the requirements of
ANSI/NISO Z39.48-1992 (Permanence of Paper).

This is for Parker Williams. Who told me I could write this—*then* told me it would be a series. Smart arse.

ACKNOWLEDGMENTS

THANK YOU to my wonderful beta team, as always.

CHAPTER ONE

RAEL PARTON caught sight of his reflection in the glass door of the building and sighed internally.

I knew I should've gotten a haircut this week.

Not that it would have done a damn thing. Five minutes after sitting in his barber's chair, Rael reverted to looking a mess. It didn't matter what his long-suffering barber did to try to tame Rael's unruly mop of blond hair. The result was always the same.

No wonder I'm single. Who'd want to wake up next to that?

Except that was bullshit, and he knew it. Staying single meant *not* having to share the fact that he could turn into a lion in the twinkling of an eye. There were definite drawbacks to being considered a myth.

Rael blamed it on his lion. It was his default. Of course, he *might* have looked better if he'd gone straight to bed the previous night—except it had been more like early morning—when he arrived at his hotel. *That's what I get for taking a later flight.* A lack of sleep sure wasn't helping matters either. Then again, the location of his hotel had made for a noisy night, and sleep really hadn't been an option.

And I wanted to make a good impression too.

Then he reconsidered. He was a photojournalist who'd made a name for himself by getting into places no one else had reached. Who was going to care if his hair wasn't slicked down and neat and he seemed a little rumpled? He looked the part, dammit.

Rael crossed the marble floor to the wide desk occupied by two security guards. As he drew closer, he reached into his capacious bag for the email invitation.

The larger of the two guards gave him a polite smile. "Good morning." The other looked him up and down, his gaze narrowed.

Rael pulled himself up to his full height of five feet eight and did his best to look professional. "Good morning. My name is Rael Parton. I'm here to interview Mr. Anson Prescott. I am expected." Rael handed the invitation to the first guard.

"Your ID, sir?" Rael gave it to him, and the guard scrutinized it carefully before returning it. "Thank you."

The second guard frowned. "You sure Mr. Prescott is expecting you? Because he hasn't come in yet."

"Unless he flew in by helicopter," the first guard added. "He does that a lot." He scanned the invitation before handing it back with the same polite smile. "Take the elevator to the top floor. Mr. Prescott's private office is up there." He pointed to the rear of the entrance hall. "The last elevator on the right is the only one that goes up that far. You'll have to buzz to be let in, but I'll let his secretary know you're on your way."

Rael replaced the letter in his bag. "Thank you. You've been very helpful." Well, *one* of them had. The other had peered at Rael like he expected him to pull a gun at any moment. He gave the men a cheerful nod, then headed for the five elevators. Around him, people were scurrying like ants, the air buzzing with chatter as employees began their working day. Rael pressed the button for the last elevator, his phone in his hand. He'd made sure it was fully charged before leaving the hotel, ready for recording the interview. His camera was in his bag, along with his list of questions, and he patted it reassuringly as he got onto the elevator.

This was only the third such interview Rael had conducted in his latest project, A New Breed, a series of articles on corporate America. He'd identified ten rising companies that were experiencing great success under the direction of young CEOs. Getting in to see them so far hadn't proved problematic; it appeared this new breed of rising stars were keen to talk about themselves.

What made his heart race was the thought of interviewing Anson Prescott. Global Bio-Tech was at the top of Rael's list, and it had taken him three months to tie Anson down to an interview date.

The twenty-two-year-old CEO, although happy to talk to him, was apparently supremely busy.

Twenty-two. Christ. What was I *doing at twenty-two?* Hell, Rael was thirty-five, and he still didn't have shit figured out.

The elevator came to a smooth halt, and the doors slid open, revealing a wall of glass emblazoned with the words Global Bio-Tech in gold lettering. Rael smiled to himself. *No one can say they don't know which company this is.* He located the green button set into the glass and pressed it. About a minute later, an immaculately dressed woman appeared. She smiled as she approached, pointing a remote at the glass wall. One of the panels slid open.

"Mr. Parton? I'm Veronica Brading, Mr. Prescott's secretary. My apologies, but Mr. Prescott is running a little late this morning. Unavoidable, I'm afraid. Please come this way. May I get you something while you wait? Coffee, tea, bottled water, or a soda perhaps? If you haven't had breakfast, I can have something sent up."

Rael smiled warmly. "Thank you, but I'm fine." She gave him a single nod before walking back the way she'd come. Rael followed her along a hallway, the floor covered with a deep blue carpet. At the far end was a door. She opened it and stood to one side to let him enter. As soon as he did so, Rael caught his breath.

"Oh my God," he said softly.

"That's usually people's first reaction. Although there *have* been a few who screamed."

Rael turned his head to look at her. "Gee. I wonder why." Then he returned his gaze to the sight before him. A glass cage took up the entire width of one wall. He estimated it had to be at least seventy feet long, twenty feet high, and ten feet deep, reaching up to the ceiling. At each end stood a tree, both of them sturdy looking, almost reaching the top of the cage. In one of the front corners was a pool of water, and tall grasses sprang up over the floor of the cage. Rael couldn't believe it. A complete habitat housed in a glass cage.

But what made his heart hammer was the tiger.

It lay stretched out on a low branch of one of the trees, its left front leg curved around the thick limb as if hugging it, its head resting on the branch—and its bright eyes focused on Rael.

Breathing had never been such a chore.

"What a magnificent animal," Rael murmured. The tiger didn't move, but its gaze didn't falter. It lay so still Rael could hardly believe it was real, until he looked along its flanks to see the gentle movement of its body as it inhaled and exhaled.

He scanned the cage walls. "How do you get into it?" He couldn't see a door.

"There are hatches behind the trees, big enough for someone to crawl through."

Rael gave a chuckle. "Wait—so its dinner crawls inside?"

Veronica laughed. "No, those are for when the cage needs maintaining." She pointed to the ceiling. "There's a wire grille that covers the cage. It slides back so food can be dropped through."

Rael wiped his forehead. "Even so, *I* wouldn't crawl into a cage with a tiger in it." He peered up at the grille. "You'd need a tall set of ladders to even get up there." He couldn't resist. "Do *you* ever get to feed it?"

Veronica put her hand to her chest. "It makes my heart pound just thinking about it. I leave that to braver souls than me."

"Still, it's taking a chance." Rael had only ever seen tigers at the zoo, and each time his lion had roared at the sight of the captives. Which led him back to this tiger. "How does it come to be here?" He hated the idea of someone keeping such a beautiful predator as a pet, a rich man's mere accessory.

"Mr. Prescott rescued it. Someone had smuggled it into the country as a cub and kept it in a basement."

Rael's pulse sped up, and blood pounded in his ears. "A basement?" It was a horrifying thought.

"I know. Apparently, he was a drug dealer who thought it amusing to keep a tiger. But when the police raided his house, they found the tiger, fully grown by then, chained up. It would have been destroyed, but Mr. Prescott spoke with a friend of his who happens to be a judge and got the necessary paperwork so he could save the poor creature."

Rael breathed a little easier. He studied the cage again. "This is a well-thought-out environment," he admitted. The temperature in the room was comfortable, so what with the grille on top, Rael guessed it was the same inside the cage.

"Mr. Prescott went to a good deal of trouble to make sure the tiger has everything it needs."

Except the open air. And space. And freedom to move. To run.

The lion within him growled.

Rael turned to her. "But why keep it here? Why not turn it over to an animal sanctuary or a zoo? Surely that would be better than keeping it captive in a cage. No matter how luxurious or spacious it is." Nothing could compare to the feeling of running through wide-open spaces. Then he realized what had surprised him most.

There had been no mention anywhere in his research of a tiger.

"You'd think having a tiger in his office would be a talking point," he noted. "I can't think why there haven't been double-page spreads about Mr. Prescott and his efforts to save a poor imprisoned tiger."

She gave a graceful shrug. "You'll have to ask Mr. Prescott. The tiger belongs to him, after all." At that moment a phone rang. "Excuse me." She pointed to two couches that took up what space was left in the room. "Have a seat. I'll be right back." Veronica hurried toward a door at the rear of the room.

Rael had no intention of sitting.

He walked slowly toward the cage, careful not to make any sudden movements, conscious of the tiger's scrutiny. He could hear Veronica talking in a low voice in the other room. When he reached the glass, he crouched down, making himself small, unable to tear his gaze away from the glorious predator stretched out languidly on the other side of the glass.

"You're so beautiful," Rael said softly. His lion wanted to flatten himself to the floor, to roll onto his back, making himself vulnerable.

He'd always thought of himself as dominant, but there was something about this tiger that made him want to submit.

Something Rael couldn't fathom.

A wave of nausea rolled over him, and in his head he heard a faint voice. *Help me.* A male voice, kind of weak.

What the fuck?

His stomach clenching, Rael swallowed. "Either I'm going crazy or I just heard you in my head." He placed his hand flat to the glass. His heart pounded as the tiger dropped down gracefully from its perch on the branch and leisurely sauntered toward him, its muscles moving in sinuous harmony. When it reached Rael, the tiger pressed its nose against the glass covered by Rael's hand.

And there it was again, the overpowering urge to submit. Then such impulses were flung aside when he heard the voice again. *Help me.* The nausea wasn't as bad as before, but the voice was just as weak.

Ice crawled its way down Rael's spine. *Oh God. I'm not going crazy, am I?*

As if in response, the tiger lifted its regal head and locked gazes with him. *Help me?*

Before Rael could react, Veronica came back into the room, and he rose hastily to his feet. Out of the corner of his eye, he noticed the tiger's retreat to its former perch, and its departure caused Rael's chest to tighten.

"I'm so sorry, Mr. Parton. That was Mr. Prescott on the phone. He's been unavoidably detained and won't be able to see you today."

Rael's heart sank. "Then it seems I've come a long way for nothing." He mentally calculated the time he'd wasted. A three-hour drive through the snow to the airport. Six hours in transit, including the stop in Salt Lake City. Not to mention the cheap and definitely *un*comfortable hotel in downtown Chicago.

"I was *about* to say, Mr. Prescott assures you he will be here tomorrow. And as recompense for letting you down like this, he's asked me to book you into the Langham Hotel tonight as his guest." Veronica smiled. "I've taken the liberty of reserving you a suite with a view of the river."

6

Rael did his best not to let his jaw drop. "That's very kind of you." A five-star luxury hotel beat the pants off the roach motel he was staying in. He'd seen photos of the Langham when he was looking for a place to stay—seen, then dismissed. He might make a comfortable living, but that didn't mean he was about to throw *that* much money around.

She waved her hand. "It's the least we could do, especially after you've flown here from Idaho." She inclined her head toward the cage. "It's awesome, isn't it? I could sit and watch it for hours. Except then I'd get no work done, and I'd be out of a job."

Rael gave the polite chuckle he was sure she expected. "In that case, I won't keep you any longer. I'll see you tomorrow. The same time?"

She nodded. "And thank you for being so understanding. I'll see you out."

And that was that. Rael gave the cage one last lingering glance. The tiger was once again stretched out on its branch, but its gaze was still fixed on Rael.

I didn't imagine that, did I? Then he caught his breath when the tiger slowly raised its head.

Help. The single word was barely audible but laced with so much pain and anguish it shook Rael to his core.

"Mr. Parton?"

With a shiver Rael zapped back into the moment. Veronica was staring at him. He forced out a wry chuckle. "Sorry about that. I must have zoned out for a sec."

She smiled. "Easy to do when you're faced with a tiger."

He walked with her to the glass wall, where she pointed again with the remote. Once on the other side, he gave her a smile. "Until tomorrow, then."

She nodded before heading back to her office.

Rael waited until she'd closed the door behind her before leaning weakly against the glass.

What the fuck just happened?

It wasn't as if he didn't come across a lot of creatures during his monthly shift in the Salmon-Challis National Forest. Most tended to run like crazy when he showed up, understandably. He'd never had one speak to him, however. That was definitely a first.

How did he do that? How did he get inside my head? Because if that voice was accurate, the tiger was male. *Never mind that. How could I understand him?*

For the life of him, Rael had no idea. All he did know was that the incident had shaken him badly. His heartbeat was nowhere near its normal rhythm, and there was a fluttery feeling in his belly that wouldn't go away. The iciness that had slithered down his spine seemed to have found its way into his very core. But the thought of that tiger, his gaze focused so totally on Rael, sent a tingling sensation all over his skin that wasn't exactly unpleasant. What made it all the stranger was the sudden urge to shift. Never before had he encountered such a strong inclination.

I don't understand any of this.

He called for the elevator, his head in a spin. Maybe he needed to go to his new hotel and rest. Maybe sleep would help him think more clearly.

And if it happens again tomorrow?

Rael couldn't think about that right then. Especially when part of him badly wanted to hear that voice again, to be near the tiger.

What the hell was going on?

CHAPTER TWO

I COULD get used to this.

The Langham Hotel was the epitome of luxury, from its vaulted ceilings and chandeliers right down to the white leather couches in the lobby. Rael checked in, then went up to his room. He whistled as he took in the wide windows that looked out over the river.

"She wasn't kidding about the view."

He dropped his bags and jacket onto the bed. He'd planned on two nights in Chicago, and checking out of his previous hotel had been a pleasure. But now that he was done for the day, he found he couldn't relax.

He hadn't been able to shake the tiger from his thoughts.

Did I miss it in my notes? Rael pulled the folder from his bag and then grabbed one of the complimentary bottles of water. He sat on the couch, opened the file, and read through his findings.

By the time he finished, he'd found a couple of mentions of Anson's exotic pet, but no pictures. There was, however, plenty of information about Anson Prescott's father. Tom Prescott had been a genius. He'd founded Global Bio-Tech, which right from the get-go had been a high-flying pharmaceutical company. He would still have been in charge if cancer hadn't reared its ugly head a few years previously. Anson had been almost twenty-one at that point. But it hadn't been in young Anson's hands that Tom Prescott had left his company. No, he'd entrusted it to his stepson, Dellan Carson, sixteen years older than Anson and, from what Rael could glean, Tom's right-hand man for several years.

Makes sense, I suppose. Anson was too young to be running a company.

Then why was he running it now? And why was Dellan no longer on the scene?

Rael booted up his laptop and opened a search engine. After half an hour, he was no better off. There was no mention of Dellan once Anson had taken over the company.

Did something happen to him? And if so, why isn't it out there? Because people didn't vanish into thin air. There had to be *some* record somewhere.

Rael reached for his phone. There was one route he could take that might prove useful. He scrolled through his contacts until he came to Kyle. Rael mentally prepared himself for Kyle's reaction to his call.

Kyle didn't disappoint.

"Hey, gorgeous. So you've finally come to your senses, huh?"

Rael chuckled. "No, Kyle, I am *not* going on a date with you." They'd worked together on the same newspaper when Rael was starting out. Kyle was an experience not easily forgotten.

"Why the hell not? I'm witty, charming, sexy, devastatingly handsome…."

"You forgot modest," Rael added.

"Yeah, that too."

Rael laughed. Sarcasm went right over Kyle's head. "Listen, I'm calling because I need your help. You still have your contacts in the police department in Chicago, right?"

"Honey, I have a *zillion* contacts, but yeah, I do. What do you need?"

"I'm after anything you can find on a Dellan Carson. Stepson of Tom Prescott. About thirty-eight years old. Was the acting manager of Global Bio-Tech in Chicago until Tom Prescott died a year ago, leaving him in charge. Since then he's disappeared off the radar."

"Okay, I got all that. Gimme a while to get back to you, all right?"

"Sure." Rael glanced around the luxurious suite. "I'm chilling in an awesome Chicago hotel for the night."

"Alone?" Rael didn't miss the hopeful note in Kyle's voice.

"Yes, I'm alone. And I *still* don't want to go on a date with you." It wasn't that Kyle was unattractive. Rael would fuck him in a heartbeat, it had been that long since he'd gotten laid. It was just….

You know exactly why you won't go on a date with him. Kyle wouldn't be happy with a one-night stand. And that was all Rael had to offer. Anything more and there were consequences.

"I could come over, and we could have a drink for old times' sake," Kyle wheedled.

Rael let out a heavy sigh. He really didn't want to hurt Kyle, but....

"Hey, it's okay," Kyle said softly. "I know how I get around guys. I cling. I obsess. After two dates, I'd be proposing. After a week, I'd be turning up at your place with a U-Haul containing all my worldly goods." Kyle laughed, but Rael knew how much truth lay behind his words.

"Someday you're gonna find the perfect guy. You know that, right?"

Kyle snickered. "From your mouth to God's ears. Lemme go see what I can find." And with that he disconnected.

Rael picked up the dining card and checked out the menu. *Hey, if Anson's picking up the tab....* He shook his head. That wasn't Rael's style. Besides, it was way too early to be thinking about dinner. He'd only just grabbed a sub after leaving his no-show interview.

And there he was, back to the tiger again. Okay, seeing a tiger in such a setting was impressive, not to mention bizarre, but that voice had really shaken him. He kept replaying those words over and over. *Did I imagine it?* Too little sleep and too much coffee might explain it, but....

In his heart, Rael knew it had been real. Because it wasn't only the voice. There was the way he'd felt when the tiger had gazed into his eyes, the way Rael had wanted to lie at its feet in submission.

It all added up to one damn big mystery.

Rael kicked off his shoes and stretched out on the couch, a pillow stuffed under his head. *A little nap couldn't hurt, right?* Who knew when Kyle would be getting back to him? He closed his eyes and breathed deeply, focusing on the rise and fall of his chest as he sometimes did when he needed to relax. He was succumbing to the warm fuzzy feeling that preceded falling asleep when his phone vibrated its way across the coffee table.

Blinking, Rael answered it without glancing at the caller. "'Lo?"

"Hey. You sound drowsy. Did I wake you?"

Rael struggled into an upright position. "Damn, you work fast."

Kyle laughed. "That's me, a regular Speedy Gonzales. Okay, you ready for this?"

"Hit me."

"Dellan Carson is listed as missing."

That woke him up. "Say what?"

"And it gets better. So is his dad. Well, sort of."

Rael snorted. "*Sort of* missing?"

"Jake Carson disappeared when Dellan was seven. Seven years after that, Dellan's mom had him declared dead. I guess she figured he wasn't coming back. Not long after *that*, she married Tom Prescott. She met him when she was working as a barista. One of *three* jobs, mind you. Hardworking lady. Then two years later, Anson is born."

"Who had Dellan declared missing? His mom?"

"Uh-uh. She died about a month before Dellan disappeared. Anson had him declared missing. The word is he's running the company until Dellan shows up again."

"And from the look of things, he's running it very successfully." Rael tried to piece it all together. Dellan was in charge of the company, then disappeared, leaving Anson to oversee it in his stead.

"To have one Carson disappear is unfortunate. But *two* Carsons?" Kyle chuckled. "If I was a suspicious kinda guy, I might smell a rat."

Something smelled rotten, that was for sure. Rael frowned. "Wait a sec. How come there's nothing online about Dellan being missing?"

"Beats me. It's in the police records, but it's not being made public. Maybe someone is pulling some strings. And it would have to be someone pretty rich or powerful—or both—to quash the story. Put it this way. I had to call in a few favors to get my source to even tell *me*."

"What kind of favors?" Then Rael reconsidered. "Wait. Don't answer that."

Kyle laughed. "Is that it? Is that all you wanted?"

"You did good," Rael told him.

"Anytime, honey. You know that. Now get off the phone and enjoy your awesome hotel—alone." He paused. "I'll bet you've got a king bed too. Sure you won't get too lonesome all alone in that big ol' bed?"

"Nice try. Thanks, Kyle. Talk soon." Rael disconnected the call, then made a few notes. *Looks like I'll have something else to talk about tomorrow.* He yawned. Time for a nap. With the phone on silent.

Except he couldn't sleep. His stomach was in knots, and his brain wouldn't quit. After half an hour of restlessness on the couch, he gave up and went to the bed. Maybe that would prove more conducive to sleep. He closed his eyes, forcing himself to breathe deeply and slowly, willing himself to fall asleep.

Eventually, sleep came, and he sank into it, only to find himself standing inside the glass cage. What shocked him was that he wasn't afraid, not even when the tiger dropped down from its branch as it had done that morning. It stilled, its gaze locked on Rael. Then it launched into the air, a graceful arc of stripes and sinew, and landed right in front of him, its heavy paws connecting with a dull thud as it hit the ground.

Rael couldn't resist. He knelt on the floor of the cage, his pulse racing, and reached out to bury his hands in soft fur, stroking the noble head, the tiger's breath warm against his own face. He ran a single finger down one curved incisor, feeling its sharp point but still without fear. Next Rael ran his hands over the tiger's flanks, aware of the heart beating beneath the fur. He pressed his face into it, breathing in the tiger's scent.

It was glorious.

Then the fur was gone, and Rael was left holding a naked man. A beautiful man with rich brown hair, tinted with bronze. And God, his eyes. They were green, but with amber flecks around the iris. A short, stubbly beard, peppered with gray, covered his jawline and chin. The man was thin, and Rael swore he could feel every one of his ribs. The man clung to him, gazing up at him, those gorgeous eyes locked on his.

13

"Help me."

Oh fuck. That voice. It was the same as before—only now it pulled at Rael, tugging at his heart.

"Who are you?" Rael demanded. Before the man was able to reply, Rael drew him closer and kissed him, unable to stop himself from responding to that voice. The moment the man's lips met his, a warmth rushed through him, spreading to every part of his body.

They parted, and the man frowned. "I have a name?"

Rael smiled. "Of course you do. Everyone has a name. What's yours?"

The man's frown deepened. "It's... so difficult to remember."

"Try," Rael urged him.

"Kiss me again," the man implored.

Rael pulled him until he was in Rael's lap, Rael's arms around the thin body. The man looped his arms around Rael's neck, and Rael leaned in to kiss him, leisurely, aware for one brief moment of an odd taste. Something... chemical, almost.

Then the man pulled back and smiled, and an overwhelming feeling of happiness surged through Rael, bringing tears to Rael's eyes.

"I remember now! I'm Dellan."

With a shock, Rael found himself awake and cold in a dark room. Shivering, he switched on the bedside light and glanced at his phone.

Fuck. It was one in the morning.

He touched his face, disturbed to find tears there. Rael shivered again, unable to shake the dream. *But was it a dream?* He could still remember how the tiger's fur had felt. The significance of the tiger becoming human wasn't lost on him. Clearly, Rael was imagining him as a shifter. But as for it being Dellan?

He sat up and shoved pillows behind him. He needed to talk to someone, and there was only one person who fit the bill. *Thank God she's still a night owl.* He speed-dialed, listening as it rang once, twice, three times....

"What's wrong?"

He breathed more easily at the sound of his mom's voice. "Can we talk?"

She laughed. "That is why you called me at this hour, right?" Then her voice softened. "What is it, sweetheart? You sound... strange."

He told her about his meeting that day. The tiger in the cage. Dellan's disappearance. The dream. And when he was done, he waited for her to respond, to tell him everything would be okay and there was nothing to worry about.

He wasn't prepared to hear her crying.

"Mom?" he said in alarm. "Mom, what's wrong?" He waited as she got herself under control, hiccupping as she tried to stop her tears.

"Oh, Rael. You don't get it, do you?"

"Get what? That I'm dreaming about a tiger shifter?"

She drew in a deep breath. "Think about it. Think about how you reacted when you heard his voice. How you felt when you stroked his fur. When you kissed. When you touched each other. When he smiled." Laughter bubbled out of her. "Oh, my sweet boy. He isn't just *any* shifter. He's your mate. Your *fated* mate."

"My—" Whatever words he was about to say died in his throat. *I have a mate?*

CHAPTER THREE

THIS MADE no sense. For one thing, if mates were even a *thing*, she would've told him about them when he hit puberty. When they first had "the Talk" about what was coming up fast—his first shift.

Then it hit him. Mom obviously hadn't told him everything.

"Mom?"

She sighed. "I know what you're going to say, and I should have mentioned it before now. But sweetheart, I never, ever thought it would happen."

"Why not?" Rael was trying to digest this new information, but it kept sticking in his throat.

"Rael… mates are rare. Like, unbelievably rare."

"And how rare is that, exactly?"

Mom sighed. "The odds of winning the Powerball jackpot are 1 in 292,000,000. Finding your mate? You have a better chance of winning Powerball, trust me."

"Is that why you didn't tell me about them?"

There was a pause. "Why should I tell you about something that is so rare among our kind, it's almost a myth?"

He stilled. "But… then, Dad isn't your mate?"

Another soft sigh filled his ears. "I love your father very much. I know he loves me. But no, honey, we aren't mates. I just happened to meet another lion shifter who was this gorgeous guy with eyes that made me melt, and we fell in love. And to be honest, I'd have still fallen in love with him if he hadn't been a shifter."

"So how do you know Dellan is my mate?" Rael's chest tightened, and that fluttering sensation in his stomach was back.

"Because you heard him in your head."

"And how do you know that makes him my mate, if they're so rare?" Rael's head was reeling.

"I listened, that's all. Every chance I got to be around shifters, I listened. I guess you pick up stuff. Well, I picked up enough to know that between mates, there's supposed to be some kind of telepathic communication. A psychic link. Maybe that's how he got to be in your dream. I'm just guessing, of course." He caught the expelled breath. "You need to talk to someone who knows about these things. All *I* could tell you was you were a shifter, and as far as humans are concerned, shifters are a myth. They think if we ever did exist, we've all died out. So we let them think that. And as for mates... no one *I* listened to had ever met anyone who'd found their mate."

From puberty, his mom had instilled in him the rule of law for all shifters: in a shifted state, he was not to approach humans or attack them. His prey was to be animals. Then his parents advised him to find a space where he felt safe and to shift there once a month. The Salmon-Challis National Forest was perfect, big enough that he could get about unseen by human eyes.

Then he realized what really bothered him about this whole new state of things.

"Wait a minute. Don't *I* get a say in this? I mean, is that it? He's my mate, so I just *deal* with it?"

There was silence. When she finally spoke, her voice was low but firm. "I don't know how these things work, but I don't think for a moment some... higher power is sitting somewhere, giggling to themselves because they've put two *assholes* together. I'd *like* to think they've put you two together because you complement each other. Because you'd be good for each other. And if *I'd* just found out I had a mate, the *last* thing I'd be doing was complaining."

"What?" He'd never heard her so riled.

"Are you for real?" Her voice grew louder. "I've just finished telling you that what you've experienced is so rare virtually every shifter you've *ever met* would tell you it's not possible, that they've never heard of such a thing, and you want to *complain*?"

"Yes, but—"

"But nothing. Think about your dream for a second. Didn't you feel good when you held him? When you kissed? That's your own *body* telling you who he is. But put that aside for a minute. You know what I'd be thinking if I were in your shoes? I'd be planning how I'm going to get my mate out of there, because this stinks. This feels really… wrong."

"You're forgetting something." Rael swallowed. "I'm not saying you're wrong about him being my mate, but we're kind of overlooking one important question. Why is he in there? What if he's attacked and killed a human? Maybe that's why they're keeping him caged."

There was a pause. "This is your mate. What does your heart tell you?"

Rael stilled. Everything in him was telling him Dellan was a good guy. Scared, maybe. Desperate even. But Rael didn't sense any badness in him at all.

"What you need are answers, and the only way I can see for you to get them is to free him. So what are you going to do about it?"

Her words finally sank in. "Wait—what?"

"Well, you can't leave him there. Maybe he is dangerous, but then again, you're a lion, so you are too. What if they're keeping him against his will?"

"If that was the case, surely he'd just shift and escape." That was what Rael couldn't get his head around.

"So he *chooses* to be in his tiger form and live in a cage? Is that what you believe?"

When she put it like that…? Then common sense took over. "Mom, he's in a cage on the top floor of a skyscraper. How do you propose I get him out of there?" Even as he said the words, he knew how they sounded.

Like he was making excuses. Avoiding the question. Avoiding the solution.

"Hell, you got into that warlord's enclave last year. If you can do that, you can do anything."

"But that was different. Someone else got me in there." Another excuse. *What's wrong with me?*

"Then someone else can get you into that skyscraper. Don't you *know* people?" Then she drew in a long breath. "I'm sorry. I got carried away. It's just that… oh my God, Rael, you have a *mate*. And he needs you. He keeps asking you to help him."

And there it was, the one argument he couldn't ignore. Because… that voice.

He could still hear that voice.

"What about you?" he asked. "Don't *you* have any contacts, someone who might be able to help?"

"As soon as I finish talking to you, I'm going to wake up your father, and we'll put our heads together." She chuckled. "He won't thank me in the morning when he's grumpy and he has to go to work, but it'll be worth it if we come up with something. You're going back there tomorrow?"

"Yes. Though I'm not sure how much of this I can bring up in the interview. What if Anson is the one who's imprisoned him?" Rael still couldn't get over Dellan not being able to shift. It didn't make sense.

"Sounds to me like someone has gone to a lot of trouble to keep Dellan's disappearance out of the news. The last thing you should do is draw attention to yourself by mentioning what you know. Especially if you're going in there at some point to rescue him."

"Let's leave the escape plans until after the interview, okay?" He wanted to see how things felt in the morning. More importantly, he wanted to get an idea of the kind of man Anson Prescott was.

"You're not running away from this for some reason, are you?"

Rael had to be honest. Yes, he'd shied away from the idea initially, but she'd gotten through to him. *Worn me down is nearer the truth.* "No, I'm not," he said sincerely. "But let's see how tomorrow goes, all right?"

"Do you know what time it is?" Rael's dad sounded pissed off and groggy in the background. "I can hear you yelling from the bedroom. For God's sake, tell Rael to go to sleep, then come to bed."

"Not until you and I have talked," Mom said firmly. "Put the coffee on. You're going to need it."

Rael smiled as he caught his dad's mutterings, something about it being a good thing he loved her. "I'll leave you to it. Give Dad my love—and my apologies."

"Sure thing, sweetheart. Get some sleep. Love you."

"Love you too." He disconnected. The thought occurred to him that he hadn't eaten since his late-morning sub, but he was too wound up to think about calling down for food. He got off the bed, rummaged through his bag, and discovered a couple of protein bars. He ate each one in three bites, then headed for the swanky bathroom to brush his teeth.

The alarm set on his phone, Rael climbed into bed and prayed for a dreamless sleep.

VERONICA SMILED as she opened the panel for him. "Hello again. Mr. Prescott is waiting for you. I trust you spent a comfortable night?"

"The hotel was an excellent choice. Thank you again." Rael followed her along the hallway and through the door into the main office. He glanced at the cage as they passed it, dismayed to find the tiger—Dellan—asleep, his back to Rael.

"He's awesome, isn't he?" A man stood in the doorway, sharply dressed, a coffee cup in his hand.

Rael gave him a polite smile. "I was admiring him yesterday." He held out his hand as they drew closer. "Mr. Prescott? I'm Rael Parton."

"Anson, please. Mr. Prescott sounds like you're talking to my dad, God rest his soul." Anson shook the proffered hand. "And my apologies for my absence yesterday. Unfortunately, I was called away on urgent business. Please, come in." He stood aside and gestured to the office beyond the door.

Rael followed him in, Veronica behind him. Anson's office was small compared to the vast space that housed the cage. There were two desks, one significantly larger than the other, a couple of filing cabinets, and a wall on which were several monitors. One other door stood at the rear.

Anson sat behind the larger desk, and Rael got a better look at him. He was of a similar height and build to Rael, but his hair and complexion were darker. Deep brown eyes focused intently on him, and Rael wondered what was going on behind them.

"Coffee? Tea? Water?"

Rael smiled at Veronica. "Coffee would be great, thank you." He reached into his bag and removed his camera, along with his notes.

Anson grinned. "I didn't think it would be long before we saw that. I've seen some of your work, Mr. Parton. Very impressive."

Rael could be just as complimentary. "Not as impressive as what you've accomplished since you took over the running of Global Bio-Tech. You've taken the company to new heights."

Anson gave a modest shrug. "It seems I have a flair for this business."

"That would be a massive understatement. There are many large pharmaceutical companies out there, but few with such a positive reputation."

Anson laughed. "What you *really* mean is, Global Bio-Tech isn't included in all the usual big pharma conspiracy theories." He waved his hand dismissively. "I've heard them all, believe me. How there's a cure for cancer, but it's being suppressed. How pharmaceutical companies are fleecing people for meds that cost cents to produce. Well, not here. If there's a cure for a major disease out there, and we find it, we'll research and develop it, then put it on the market at a fair price. Medicine shouldn't cost the earth."

Despite his concerns, Rael couldn't help but admire Anson's stance. "That's a refreshingly ethical viewpoint nowadays."

Anson picked up a photo frame that stood on his desk. "It's how I was brought up." He gazed at the photo before turning it to reveal the face of Tom Prescott. "I hope wherever my dad is, he's proud of what I'm achieving with the company he left in my care."

His mom's words of warning went right out of Rael's head. That opening was too much to ignore.

"But didn't he leave it to your half brother, Dellan Carson?" Rael asked with as innocent an air as he could muster.

Anson stilled. "I see you've done your homework." He replaced the photo in its former position, then met Rael's gaze. "Yes, my dad left the company to Dellan. I was given a seat on the board. It was felt at the time that I was too young for such a huge responsibility."

"And yet here you are," Rael observed.

Anson smiled broadly, visibly relaxing into his chair. "Here I am indeed. Obviously I'm better equipped to deal with the running of a major company than my youthful appearance would indicate. I may be only twenty-two but as you can see, Global Bio-Tech is flourishing in my tender care."

Rael inhaled deeply, drawing Anson's scent into his nostrils. The man was human, there was no doubt. "So if Dellan was left the company, how did you end up running it? If you don't mind me asking." His pulse sped up, but Rael did his best to appear calm.

Anson quirked his eyebrows. "I thought you were here to discuss what I've achieved, not delve into the family history." Before Rael could respond, he waved his hand again. "It's fine. You're a journalist. Of course you're curious. Who wouldn't be? It's very simple. My brother, Dellan—I do consider him my brother, not my half brother—decided that for the moment, his interests were leading him in other directions. So he took a sabbatical in order to explore those interests. He's in Europe or Asia right now, looking into new ventures, confident that if I should need him at the helm, I would find him and bring him home. Not that I see any need to do such a thing."

Rael had to admire the smoothness with which Anson lied. *Europe or Asia, huh? Dellan is a good deal closer than that.* "He obviously has faith in you."

Anson smiled. "Which is exactly what he said in the letter he wrote to the board before he left."

"It must be good to know you can call on him when—if—you need to. After all, you've lost both parents. At least you still have Dellan."

22

For one brief moment, Anson's eyes glistened, but then he blinked. "As you say. At least I still have Dellan." He clasped his hands on the desk. "Now. How about we get on with the interview. Then you can take all the photos you want of our setup here. I've arranged a little guided tour so you get to see everything."

"That sounds perfect." Rael got out his phone and brought up the voice recorder before referring to his notes. "Okay. Let's do this." He pushed aside the temptation to ask to see Dellan's letter to the board. Not that seeing it would do anything but confirm what Rael's instincts were telling him—Anson was not to be trusted.

And it still left one question unanswered. Why hadn't Dellan shifted back into human form? There could only be one response—something was preventing him from shifting. But what?

That only raised more questions. Did Anson know Dellan was a shifter? Did he know the tiger in his office was his half brother? He'd had Dellan declared missing, sure, but that didn't mean he knew Dellan's current location. *Maybe I'm maligning him. Maybe he's being kept in the dark. Maybe someone else is responsible for keeping Dellan in his shifted form.*

There were far too many maybes. And if Rael was going to make any attempt to free Dellan, he was going to need help.

"THANK YOU again." Rael shook Anson's hand. "I'll send you the link when the article is published."

"I look forward to reading it."

Before Anson could return to his desk, Rael put out his hand to stop him. "One last request before I go? I'd love to get a shot of you and the tiger."

Anson gave him a thin smile. "Sorry, but no. That might seem odd, but I have my reasons."

Rael shrugged. "It was just an idea."

Anson huffed. "That tiger has been exploited enough. Veronica will show you out." Anson returned to his seat behind his desk, already peering at his monitor.

Rael gave a nod, then followed Veronica out of the inner office. As they passed the cage, a sudden movement caught his eyes, and he came to a halt. The tiger had left his tree and was walking toward him, head high.

"I think it likes you," Veronica observed. "Usually it stays put."

"It's a he," Rael corrected, moving toward the glass and crouching down, his palm pressed against the cool surface.

"You're an expert in tigers? I had no idea." Her tone spoke of amusement.

"Mr. Prescott referred to the tiger as he when I arrived here. I figure he should know. It's his tiger, after all." Rael didn't look at her as he spoke but kept his gaze trained on the tiger's noble face, admiring the velvety appearance of his nose, the pale green eyes with those same amber flecks he'd noticed in his dream, and those long, white whiskers.

He took a deep breath. *Hello, Dellan.*

No reaction.

Acutely aware that he didn't have a clue what he was doing, Rael tried again, opening his mind as best he could. *Dellan. That's your name, remember?*

The tiger shuddered, then pressed its nose against the glass. *Yes. Dellan. I'm Dellan.* He pulled back, gave a slow blink, and his pupils enlarged. *You. Who are you?*

Rael wanted to cry and laugh at the same time. Both hands were on the glass now, and Dellan brought a heavy paw up to one of them. Rael focused hard. *I'm Rael. Rael.*

Dellan lowered his paw. *Rael.*

Heat radiated through Rael's chest, and the same tingling he'd experienced the previous day was back, only stronger. Rael couldn't hold back his smile. *Do you know who I am?*

The tiger lay down, his front paws crossed, his gaze still fixed on Rael's face. Then electricity jolted through Rael, and his heart pounded as Dellan projected one word.

Mate.

"Wow." Veronica's softly spoken exclamation broke through, and Rael blinked, the moment lost. Dellan got up, sauntered back to his tree, and climbed it gracefully to settle on his branch.

Rael got to his feet. "Wow?" His heart was still racing, his skin still tingling all over. *It's true. All of it.* He couldn't deny his body's reaction to Dellan's presence or the joy that had surged through him on hearing that simple word.

"I've never seen it—him—so animated."

Rael smiled. "I'm good with animals," he said truthfully. He had to get out of that building to someplace where he could let out his emotions. Where he could call his mom and hear her cry once more.

He had a mate. And he was going to get him out of there. Somehow.

CHAPTER FOUR

RAEL LEFT the building, his mind awash with various scenarios for getting Dellan out of there. Any doubts he'd had previously were washed away, replaced by the steely resolve to act. It wasn't long, however, before he realized he was out of his depth. He couldn't do this on his own. He needed help.

Professional help.

No way was he flying back home. He was going to stay put until this got sorted, one way or another. That meant finding a cheap place to stay, because he sure couldn't afford the Langham's prices. At least he'd checked out of there that morning. His stuff was in an overnight bag over his shoulder.

Rael looked for the nearest coffee shop, and as luck would have it, there was a Starbucks on the corner of the next block. He tugged his coat tightly around him, fending off the cold wind, and headed in that direction. Once inside, he ordered an Americano, then took the stairs to the upper floor, hoping to find a quiet corner. It was less crowded than downstairs, thank goodness, and most of the tables' occupants were engrossed in whatever was on their laptop screens. Perfect.

Rael headed for the farthest corner, put down his coffee, and got out his phone. He scrolled through his contacts until he found Pierce. Rael rummaged through his bag and pulled out his notepad and a pen, then clicked on Call.

"Hey, stranger. Haven't heard from you in a while." Pierce sounded as cheerful as always. "How are things? You got plenty of work on right now?"

"Actually, I'm in the middle of a big project, and something's come up. I need your help."

"Hey, you got it." Pierce's manner went from jovial to brisk in a heartbeat. "Anything, man. You know it."

Rael had met Pierce during a conference for journalists a couple of years ago. They'd gone out for a drink the first night, and when Pierce didn't return from the restroom, Rael went looking for him, concerned. He found him in the alley behind the bar, trying to fight off three drunken guys who'd dragged him there. Rael plunged into the brawl, fists flying, and the guys fled. Pierce was a mess, so Rael took him to the emergency room and got him patched up. They'd remained friends ever since, exchanging news via email and text.

"You remember that kidnapping case you covered?"

Pierce laughed. "You mean *the* kidnapping case, don't you? The one that made my name? How could I ever forget?"

Pierce had gotten information about a kidnapping in which a senator's family was taken from their home at gunpoint. Pierce knew where the kidnappers had taken the wife and three kids and had passed the information on to the senator, who in turn hired an ex-military team to mount a rescue. Pierce had asked to go along, and surprisingly, the leader of the team agreed. The mission was a success, with all the victims returned to safety—and all the bad guys taken out.

"Who was the leader of the rescue team?"

"Horvan Kojik. Not a man you'd easily forget, believe me." Pierce chuckled. "Come to think of it, his whole team was pretty memorable."

"How do you spell that surname?" Rael wrote carefully as Pierce spelled it out. "Do you know where he's based? I need to contact him."

There was silence for a moment. "And if I want to know why you need to see him?"

"Sorry. I can't share that right now." That way too complicated. "Let's just say I've got a missing person case of my own, and I need his help."

"Got it. Let me find his contact details. I didn't have a number for him, but I think he's living in Indiana someplace."

Rael heaved an internal sigh of relief. Close enough to Chicago that Rael could go see this Horvan—assuming he could help. He waited while Pierce sought the details. Based on what he could remember from Pierce's article, the team had comprised several ex-military guys with specific, impressive skills. He also recalled they'd been well paid by the senator.

I wonder how he'd feel about doing this for free. Rael's stomach clenched. This could all be over before it even started.

"Okay, I've found an email address. It's not in his name, but it's the one I used to get in touch initially. I've sent it to you."

"Thanks. I'm sorry I can't tell you more, but—"

"Don't sweat it. I understand. I hope it works out for you." Pierce's voice was warm. "I still owe ya. Seriously."

"I'm just glad I was there."

Pierce snickered. "And *I'm* glad you're so handy with your fists. Let me know if you need anything else, okay?"

Rael thanked him again, then disconnected. Since all he had was an email address, his initial message had better be intriguing as hell if he was going to get this Horvan interested enough to reply. He sipped his coffee and scribbled down a few ideas, adding and deleting phrases. By the time he'd finished his coffee, he had the message as damn near perfect as he could get it.

> *To Horvan Kojik*
> *I hear you're a man who can get into hard places.*
> *Well, I have a challenge for you.*
> *I want you to help me in a near-impossible rescue.*
> *There's a tiger in a glass cage, on the top floor of a Chicago skyscraper, and I want you to help me get it out of there.*
> *If you think you're up to it.*
> *Let's see.*
> *You've got my contact details. Use them.*
>
> *Rael Parton*
> *Photojournalist*

If this *doesn't get him interested, nothing will.*

Rael typed the message, then checked it three times. He added his phone number at the bottom, then hesitated.

Am I crazy doing this?

He pushed the thought aside. Dellan needed him. That left him no other option. Rael hit Send.

He went downstairs and ordered another coffee; only this time he added a pastry. Then he went back upstairs and began the online search for another hotel. He had no idea how long he'd be staying in Chicago. That would depend on the result of his email.

He'd found a couple of possibilities when his phone rang. The screen said Unknown Caller, and his heartbeat sped up. *It can't be. Not that fast.* His finger trembled as he clicked on Answer. "Hello?"

"Okay. You're for real. I'll grant you that. I looked you up. So tell me more about this job. Seriously?" A rich, deep chuckle filled his ears. "You want me to rescue a tiger from the top floor of a Chicago skyscraper? Why in hell would you want to do that? Or are you one of those activist nutjobs who goes around liberating bunnies from testing labs? Not that I have anything against bunnies, you understand. They're very tasty."

Rael couldn't argue that point. "Yes, I'm being serious." He struggled to remain calm, but his heartbeat had quickened for some reason. "And as for why I want to do this, I can't explain that. Not over the phone." He wasn't even sure he could explain it face-to-face. "But this whole conversation is fruitless if you can't do it in the first place."

There was silence for a moment; then Horvan's deep voice rumbled over the line. "*If* I can do it?" He snorted. "I'm going to let that go, because you obviously don't know me, but I promise I can get the job done. I just have this little quirk that I like to know *why* I'm doing something."

"Then we need to meet." Rael had no clue why he was so agitated.

"You're still in Chicago?"

"Yes."

"Okay. I'm about five hours' drive from there. Let's see, it's...." A pause. "Eleven thirty. How about we meet at six this evening?"

"You're... you're coming today?" Rael's chest tightened.

Horvan chuckled. "What can I say? You got me interested. I wanna know more. I've got a place in Chicago. I'll send you the address. You come alone, okay?"

"Who would I bring?" The only person Rael knew in Chicago was Kyle, and he certainly wasn't bringing him.

"Where are you staying in Chicago?"

"Funny you should ask that. I was looking for a hotel when you called."

"Then stop looking. You can bunk with me."

Rael stilled. "But… you don't know a thing about me."

"I know you're a real person. I've seen your articles. And while I would never normally do this, for some reason my gut tells me I can trust you. I always go with my gut. Plus, I know fifty-seven ways to kill a man, so I think I'm more of a danger than you are." He snickered.

Rael couldn't argue with that, especially as his gut was telling him the same thing. "How do I contact you? In case I get held up or something goes wrong?"

"*Nothing* is going to go wrong, but I'll message you from my personal cell, all right? That way you'll have a number. In the meantime, I'm gonna make a few calls. If this goes ahead, I'm gonna need my team, so it's best if I give them a heads-up."

"Wait." Rael's heart pounded. "Don't do that yet."

"Why not? This isn't the kind of job I can do on my own."

"Yeah, I get that, but…." Rael had to be honest. "I can't pay for a whole team. Hell, I'm not even sure if I can pay *you*. I didn't expect you to agree to see me so fast."

Silence.

Fuck. Rael knew he'd blown it. "I guess that means you're not coming, right?"

A heavy sigh greeted him. "What is it about you? If anyone else came out with that, I'd have hung up already. But I so much as *consider* ending this call, and it's like there's this voice in my head yelling at me, saying I'd be crazy to do that." Another pause. "And

30

I find *that* as intriguing as your email, so I guess I'm still coming to Chicago. See you at six." Then he disconnected.

Rael stared at his phone in amazement. *What the fuck?* This was surreal. Then his phone buzzed, and there was a text from Horvan, from his personal number, with an address.

That left Rael with hours to kill. The temptation to go back to Global Bio-Tech to see Dellan one more time was huge, but he knew he couldn't risk doing that. The last thing he wanted was to arouse suspicion.

One option was doing a little sightseeing, and thankfully the predicted rain had been a no-show. The temperature was cool, but at least there was no snow. Rael had left that behind in Salmon, Idaho. And Chicago in March was kind of pretty—the clouds reflecting in the towers of glass and the occasional burst of sunlight sparkling on the river.

Not that Rael was in the mood to play the tourist. He simply wanted the hours to fly by until he got to meet Horvan.

He's not the only one who's intrigued.

Of course, what Rael really wanted was to shift. He'd been aching to do it since seeing Dellan in that cage. It would have to wait. When this was all over and he'd gotten Dellan out of there, he was going to head back home to his forest.

And if fate were with him, he wouldn't be alone, and the Salmon-Challis National Forest would gain a tiger. That brought him a smile. *The two of us, running together, play-fighting, swimming....* Thinking about it made him glow inside.

His phone buzzed, and he swiped the screen. Mom. "Hey."

"How did it go this morning? Did you see Dellan again? Is he all right?"

Rael told her everything he could about the morning's encounter, and as he'd expected, she burst into tears when he related how Dellan had called him mate. "No crying," he said softly. "I have a plan." Well, the germ of one.

That stopped her tears. "You do?"

"Uh-huh. I'm meeting someone tonight who may be able to help me. He's... he's done this sort of thing before."

Mom chuckled. "Oh really? Sounds like a very handy man to have around. But make sure you stay safe, okay?"

Rael said nothing. If Horvan was going into that building, Rael intended accompanying him, and that had the possibility of being distinctly *un*safe.

"Rael Alexander Parton, I know you. What are you up to?"

"Mom—"

"I'm wasting my breath. He's your mate. You're going to do whatever it takes to get him out, and I suppose that might be dangerous. Forget I said anything."

"I promise I'll stay as safe as I possibly can, okay? What about you? Did you come up with any contacts for me?" Not that he'd need them if Horvan was as good as he claimed to be.

"Your dad did have one idea. Wait. He wants to tell you himself." There was a moment's pause before Rael heard his dad's voice.

"Son? From what your mother's told me, it sounds like you might need medical help once you've gotten him out of there. Well, I've been thinking. Do you have any contacts in the military?"

"No, but how about ex-military? Will that do?" The timing of his dad's question was uncanny.

"Yep. Now listen. I knew a guy a few years back. Horse shifter. He said when he was in the military, there was always a medic around who knew about shifters. Maybe it's a thing. Maybe a lot of shifters end up in the military. Stands to reason they'd have to have a doc on call who wouldn't bat an eye if they had an emergency or something."

"An emergency shift? Is there such a thing?" Rael chuckled.

His dad ignored the attempt at humor. "I'm just saying, maybe your ex-military contact might know of a doctor who'd be able to help."

"Yes, they might," Rael said slowly. "But you're forgetting one thing. They'd only know that if they were a shifter themselves."

"Yeah, but—" Dad sighed. "You're right. Sorry. I guess I got carried away."

"What about your horse shifter friend? Wouldn't he know?"

Dad's voice was so soft. "He died, son. Heart attack. Didn't see it coming."

Rael's heart went out to him. This had clearly been a good friend. "I'm sorry, Dad."

His dad cleared his throat. "Now get this straight. When this is all over and Dellan is safe, you bring him to meet us, okay? We want to meet our prospective son-in-law. Well, as good as."

That was the first time the full implication hit Rael. "Oh... oh wow."

Dad let out a soft chuckle. "You hadn't thought about that part, had you? We always hoped you'd meet someone who was perfect for you. We didn't care if he was a shifter or not. We only want you to be happy. Well... I guess you can't find someone more perfect than your mate." In the background, Rael could hear his mom crying again.

"I'll bring him, I promise. As soon as he's able to visit." That was the unknown quantity. Rael had no idea what was going on physically with Dellan.

"You do that. Okay, we won't keep calling you. We'll let you get on with... whatever it is you have to do."

A thought occurred to him. "Dad, are you okay? Why aren't you at work?"

"Well, let's see. *Someone* woke me up at an insane time because she was yelling at you over the phone, and *then* she kept me awake talking about you and your mate. So I took the morning off to see what I could find out for you. I figure you need all the help you can get." His voice softened again. "God be with you, son."

"Love you!" Mom called out.

"I love you both, so much." Rael disconnected, then wiped away the tears that pricked his eyes. He had no idea if Dellan could hear him, but that didn't matter.

Dellan? I'm going to get you out of there. I promise.

Now all Horvan Kojik had to do was live up to Rael's promise.

RAEL LOOKED up at the red brick building on West Nineteenth Street. It stood in a pleasant neighborhood, made prettier by the murals and vibrant coffee shops. He'd strolled up and down the nearby streets, gazing into the windows of eclectic stores and cozy cafes, wishing time would speed up so he could go meet Horvan. When the wind picked up, he'd found sanctuary in a cafe.

Finally, it was almost six o'clock, and he hurried up the stoop to ring the bell. Except…. Apartment 1F wasn't listed. Then he gazed down below the railings in front of the building. Steps led down to a basement, and a brightly painted red arrow, above which was written 1F, pointed to a deep red door. Rael leaped down the steps and rang the doorbell, his heart hammering.

The door opened, and there stood a mountain of a man, with wide, muscled shoulders, short-cropped dark brown hair, and intense dark eyes. His beard extended from a goatee to a thin line of hair along his jawline, accentuating his angular face. His white T-shirt clung to his chest, revealing his bulging pecs, the short sleeves tight around his muscular upper arms.

Horvan Kojik looked him up and down and gave a predatory smile. "Cute. Definitely cute."

Oh my. Rael's heart did a flip-flop. His skin tingled, the sensation spreading down his back and arms, and he knew exactly what had caused that reaction. It was the rich scent emanating from Horvan that filled Rael's nostrils. He breathed Horvan in, and the smell was heavenly.

Shifter. He's a shifter.

Horvan's eyes widened, his smile replaced by a look of utter shock. *Holy fuck.*

The words were as distinct as if he'd spoken them, and the quick burst of nausea was beginning to feel familiar. Rael was stunned into silence, struggling to process what his brain was telling him. Except deep down, he knew.

He just didn't believe it, because…. *What. The. Fuck?*

He drew in a long breath before speaking, trying to appear calmer than he felt. "Holy fuck is right."

Horvan's jaw dropped. "Wait—how the fuck did you do that?"

Rael sighed. "Because—according to my parents—we're mates." *They are not gonna believe this.* He wasn't sure *he* did.

"Stop that." Horvan glared at him. "Why can I hear your thoughts?"

"Because we're mates," Rael repeated patiently. *Another mate? Seriously?* "I have *got* to buy a Powerball ticket," he muttered.

Horvan stood aside. "I think you'd better get in here out of the cold, because I'm freezing my nuts off, and then you can start explaining what the fuck is going on."

As Rael crossed the threshold, he gently patted Horvan's forearm, then opened his mind. *Relax. It isn't as scary as you think, once you get used to the idea.*

"Like I'm gonna get used to hearing someone's voice in my head," Horvan said with a snort.

Rael could tell it was going to be a long night, with quite a few surprises in store—for both of them.

CHAPTER FIVE

HORVAN CLOSED the door behind them before leading Rael into a large living room. There wasn't much in the way of furniture, only a wide leather couch, a small coffee table, a tall cabinet, and a TV. An Oriental rug covered most of the wooden floorboards.

"Nice place," Rael commented, striving to ignore the heat barreling through his body.

"Fuck, you smell good," Horvan murmured as he moved in closer until there was barely an inch between them.

Not that Rael was complaining. Horvan's scent was sending his blood rushing south, and Rael's dick was like a lead pipe in his jeans. "I had the same thought." He'd been around enough shifters to trust his olfactory organs. But no one had ever smelled *this* good.

"Speaking of thoughts…." Horvan lowered his head and nuzzled Rael's neck. *God, I want to fuck you right now.*

Oh fuck, not there. Rael shivered as warm lips kissed his neck. Horvan's instincts were spot-on.

Inside Rael's head, Horvan chuckled. *Hey, I like knowing what you're thinking. Talk about knowing exactly where to touch you to drive you crazy.* He brushed his lips over the sensitive skin again, and Rael shuddered. *You're trembling. I can feel how much you want this.* Horvan stroked a single finger along Rael's stony length that pressed against his zipper. *Oh yeah. You want this.*

Now *that* was a smug thought if ever there was one.

"Hey, wait a minute!" Rael mentally poured cold water on his erection. "You don't even know me."

"You're a shifter, you're hot, you're here, and I'm horny as fuck. What else do I need to know?" Horvan reached around to cup Rael's ass. "Damn, that feels good."

Rael placed both hands on Horvan's broad chest, distracted for a second or two by the firmness of the flesh beneath his palms, and pushed him gently away. "Down, boy. We need to talk."

Horvan grinned. "Fuck first. Talk later."

Rael tried to glare, but it was damned difficult when all he wanted to do was strip off his clothing and find the nearest flat surface. Come to think of it, a wall would do fine. The image that came to mind was that of Horvan, naked, lifting an equally naked Rael into his arms and pinning him against the wall while he thrust up into him, Rael's legs wrapped around him as he clung to him….

Horvan laughed. "Now *that's* what I'm talking about."

Rael's libido was going to be the death of him. He drew in a deep breath. "We still need to talk." He took another whiff of Horvan and then gaped. "What *are* you?"

"Bear." Horvan's eyes glittered. "Wanna see?"

Stupid question. Of *course* he wanted to see. "Show me." Rael took a couple of steps back, giving Horvan room.

Horvan crossed the floor to the windows and closed the blinds. Then he rejoined Rael in the center of the room. Slowly, he pulled his T-shirt over his head, and Rael resisted the urge to drool. His mate was gorgeous, a mass of smooth tanned flesh and rippling muscles. When Horvan unfastened his jeans and tantalizingly lowered the zipper, Rael's heartbeat slipped into a higher gear at the sight of the girthy cock that sprang up, thick enough to make his hole contract. *Yes, please.* Rael licked his lips.

"I thought you wanted to talk first." Horvan was still grinning, the bastard. He pushed his jeans to the floor and stepped out of them. Before Rael could respond to his comment, Horvan's body rippled before him, and in his place was a beautiful black bear. It dropped onto all four paws with a thud, standing about four and a half feet tall at the shoulders. Rael estimated it had to be at least five hundred pounds. *Oh my God, those claws….*

The rich smell of him was overpowering in the small apartment, and it was glorious.

Rael stepped closer, reaching out to bury his hands in the black fur. The bear's muzzle was cream, its snout gray, and there was a touch of gray fur on its brow. But the eyes.... They were bright with intelligence and warmth.

"Look at you," Rael breathed, rubbing his face against the bear's. He smiled. "I thought you'd be a grizzly at least." Horvan uttered a low growl, and Rael stroked his round ears. "Not that I'm complaining, you understand. You're the most beautiful bear I ever saw in my life."

Horvan emitted a strange sort of rumbling noise, and Rael's instincts told him it was a happy sound.

It was no good. He had to shift. Rael took a step back and quickly squirmed out of his clothes. He concentrated, letting his lion emerge until he was standing beside Horvan, about a foot shorter at the shoulder. Rael tossed his head, shaking his mane, and moved closer until their noses touched.

Beautiful kitty. Horvan rubbed his snout against Rael's mane, burying his head in it, and Rael's heart pounded. Instinctively, he dropped down onto the rug, rolling onto his back and exposing his belly, his heavy paws in the air. Horvan nuzzled the long fur, moving lower to where Rael was already erect, before returning to rub his face in Rael's ruff. Rael got up off the floor and leaned into Horvan, pushing against his neck and shoulders, and a wonderful sense of peace flowed through him.

Imagine how amazing it will be when there are three of us.

Then he gave a start as Horvan shifted back abruptly. "What do you mean—three of us?" His voice had a hard edge to it.

Oh fuck.

Rael shifted, ignoring his lion's low roar of disappointment. They stood facing each other, both breathing rapidly, both of them trembling a little with the aftereffects of shifting. Horvan narrowed his gaze. "Up to the point when I opened my front door, I had no idea there was such a thing as a mate. *You*, I get, but that's only because I can't ignore how it felt when we shifted. But now you're talking like there's another. So spill."

"Can we at least put some clothes on first?" Rael pleaded. It was going to be a difficult enough conversation without having to cope with Horvan in all his naked glory. Plus, Rael couldn't hide his own arousal, and he didn't think Horvan needed a distraction.

Horvan grumbled but then pulled on his jeans and T-shirt. "I don't know about you, but I need a drink." He walked over to the cabinet, opened it, and took two squat glasses from a shelf inside. "How about you?"

"Whiskey if you have it." Rael got dressed, his heartbeat returning to normal.

Horvan said nothing but poured the whiskey. He handed a glass to Rael, then indicated the couch. "So… mates?" His brow was furrowed.

Rael held up his hand defensively. "Hey, I'm only marginally ahead of you. I found out about this in the early hours of this morning." He sat down and swallowed a mouthful of whiskey, wincing as the fiery liquid hit the back of his throat.

"But how did you know I was your mate?"

"I didn't!" Rael sighed. "I came here to set up a rescue. Finding out you were both a shifter *and* my mate was as big a surprise to me as it was to you. Believe it or not, mates are incredibly rare."

Horvan stilled. "This tiger you want me to rescue… it's more than just a tiger, isn't it?"

Rael nodded. "He's our mate."

His eyes widened. "*Our* mate?"

"Well, if he's mine, it stands to reason he's yours too. Only don't quote me, because right now I don't have a fucking clue." Inside, he prayed Horvan was going to accept the bombshell Rael had dropped on him.

Dellan's freedom depended on it.

Horvan sagged against the cushions, his glass in his hand. "And why does he need rescuing?"

As succinctly as he could, Rael shared his suspicions. Horvan's face darkened as he listened. When Rael finished, Horvan drained his glass, then got up to pour another.

"You do believe me, don't you?" Rael asked anxiously. Granted, he was asking a lot.

Horvan said nothing for a moment but sat on the edge of the seat cushion, his elbows on his knees, staring into his glass. Finally he raised his head and looked Rael in the eye. "I believe you, because all my senses tell me you're telling the truth. I'm just having a hard time accepting it, that's all. You walked in here and changed my world."

And you think my world hasn't changed?

Horvan gave a wry smile. "That will take some getting used to. At least I don't feel sick now, like I did the first time I heard you inside my head."

Rael gaped. "Me too. Both with you *and* Dellan. It must be a mates thing." He hesitated, but the question was right there on his lips. "Will you help me?"

Horvan rolled his eyes. "What kind of man do you think I am? As if I could say no. I mean, I'm an asshole, but ask anyone who knows me and they'll tell you I'm not *that* much of an asshole."

Relief flooded through Rael. He put his glass on the coffee table, leaned in to Horvan, and kissed him on the mouth.

Oh my God. Rael shivered at that first intimate human contact, and he was close enough to feel Horvan's reaction. Horvan pulled him in, deepening the kiss, and Rael went with it, riding a wave of pleasure, cupping the back of Horvan's head and drawing him closer.

Horvan broke the kiss with a gasp. "If that's how *kissing* you feels, imagine what it's gonna be like when we fuck." Rael caught his breath, and Horvan chuckled. "Yeah. I can see some definite advantages to having mates."

At least he accepts it now.

Horvan arched his eyebrows. "You know I heard that, right?"

Rael sighed. "You're right. That part is going to take some getting used to." Rael's stomach chose that moment to complain, and his face heated. "Sorry about that."

Horvan cupped Rael's cheek in his hand. "Sweetheart, don't sweat it. I'm not the delicate type." Rael gave him a grateful smile, and Horvan's eyes gleamed. "You ain't heard nothing until you've heard a bear fart." He winked. "Not that I would ever do that, of course. At least, not without warning."

Rael rolled his eyes. "Wow. Really feeling the love here."

Horvan patted his knee. "Tell you what. Let me make a few calls. Then we'll go out and grab some dinner. After, we can come back here and talk some more. Maybe we can come up with a few ideas before the boys get here."

"The boys?"

"I meant what I said on the phone. I can't do this alone. We're gonna need more help. And the sooner we get started, the better." He patted Rael's knee again. "Don't worry. They're good guys. Of course, they lack my charm and wit." He got up from the couch and walked out of the room.

Rael bit his lip. *Saying nothing.*

I heard that!

Rael needed to ask someone who knew about such things if there was a way to shield his thoughts. Because having Horvan in his head was one thing, but how on earth would it be when there were two of them? Things could get real noisy inside Rael's head.

And another thing to consider. Over what distance could this... telepathy work? Because surely there had to come a point when they couldn't hear each other.

Then he considered that last thought. *There has to be* someone *we can talk to who knows about shifter mates.* His parents knew next to nothing from the sound of it. *What we need is an expert.* Except how did one go about finding such a person?

Horvan appeared in the doorway. "You're right. We need to know more. And I might be able to help us there." He gazed pointedly at Rael. "While I'm making my calls, isn't there someone *you* need to talk to? I mean, I don't know you all that well—yet—but what about family, friends?"

Rael frowned, perplexed. Then it hit him. "Oh Lord, my parents."

He'd better make sure they were sitting down first.

"THESE ARE really good tacos." Correction—they *were* good tacos. Rael had pretty much demolished them as soon as they were placed in front of him.

"Well, you said you like Mexican. I found this place a couple years ago. It's great when you want a quick bite. And their buffet is awesome." Horvan took a long drink from his bottle of beer, then leaned back in his chair. "So how did you come to hear about me?"

"You did an op a few years ago where you rescued that senator's family who'd been taken and were being kept someplace in the Appalachians. I know Pierce, the journalist who went in there with you."

Horvan beamed. "Pierce. Sure, I remember him. Skinny runt but with a good head on him. *Two* good heads, actually." He leered. "Not to mention a wicked mouth."

Rael stared at him. "Really? You're going to sit there and reminisce about a blow job in front of your mate? How does 'highly inappropriate' sound?"

Horvan frowned. "Hey, I was single at the time. Plus I was horny."

Rael smirked. "Is there ever a time when you're not?" Horvan seemed to be the typical alpha male, not that Rael had a problem with that. But he certainly did *not* want to hear about his mate's sexual conquests. "Tell me about the mission."

Horvan shrugged. "It was pretty straightforward. Textbook, really. I don't think they were expecting the senator to react the way he did." He smiled. "We were a complete surprise." Then he laughed. "Oh God. There was one morning before we raided their camp when I just had to shift. Must have been the surroundings. They reminded me of home."

"And where's that?" Rael inquired.

"New Albany, Indiana. Right on the border with Kentucky. Forests as far as the eye can see. That's where I go to shift. Anyhow, that morning I got up early, before everyone else, went a distance from the camp, undressed, and shifted." He sighed. "It was so good. Only, when I got back to camp, all hell had broken loose. Someone else had gotten up early too, and had gone for a morning walk. Trouble was, he'd found my pile of clothing. Plus he'd seen my bear. They were all convinced I'd been eaten or something." Horvan snickered. "As if a bear was gonna eat *me*."

"I take it they don't know about you. Your team, that is."

Horvan shook his head. "I figure what they don't know won't hurt 'em. Let them go around blissfully ignorant of us, like the rest of humanity."

"So how did you explain the clothing?"

He grinned. "I told them a tale about how I was a secret nudist and liked to go for naked rambles. They bought it, thank God."

There was one question Rael had been burning to ask ever since their phone conversation. "I have to ask…. Do you *really* know fifty-seven ways to kill a man?"

Horvan chuckled. "More, but I had a bottle of Heinz sauce on the table in front of me when I was talking to you." He smirked. His phone buzzed, and he picked it up, peering at the screen. "Great. Roadkill will be with us in the morning. He's catching a late flight." Horvan peered at Rael's plate. "You done?"

Rael chuckled. "Why—aren't you?" He had to admit, Horvan's appetite was impressive.

Horvan shrugged. "I got snacks at the apartment if I get the munchies. But I really think we need to head back there. Tomorrow's gonna be a busy day by the look of it, and we need our sleep." Another grin. "And other things."

Oh Lord. Rael had a feeling he knew *exactly* what Horvan was referring to. Only thing was, Rael had ideas on that subject too.

Ideas he was keeping quiet about.

HORVAN'S PHONE buzzed as he let them back into the apartment. "And that should be Crank," he commented as he closed the door. He removed his phone from his pocket and smiled as he gazed at the screen. "Yup. That makes all of them. They'll be here tomorrow."

Rael chuckled. "Your boys have some weird names. So far you've mentioned Crank, Roadkill, and Hashtag." The efficient way Horvan was dealing with the situation instilled confidence.

Horvan went through the archway into the kitchen. "Their names are practical. Crank flies anything that *can* fly. Great chopper pilot. Roadkill—"

"Let me guess. He's the driver," Rael surmised. "So Hashtag is your tech guy?"

Horvan stuck his head around the corner and beamed. "You're smart. I like that. Yeah, Hashtag's the man when it comes to tech. I'm making coffee. You want some?"

Rael nodded, and Horvan went back into the kitchen area. As Rael sat down, his phone vibrated, and he took it from his pocket.

Okay, your mother has stopped crying now. I'm still stunned. And both of us can't wait to meet them. THEM.

Yep. Still can't take it in. You don't do things by halves, do you?

OH. Your mother says she's going shopping tomorrow for the biggest bed she can find for the guest bedroom.

Rael couldn't even think about that part. It got him *way* too hot under the collar.

"We didn't come up with many ideas," he called out to Horvan.

"That's because we were too busy eating," Horvan called back. "For some reason I was starving." He popped his head around the corner again and grinned. "I was obviously anticipating tonight's… exercise." Then he disappeared from view.

Rael hadn't stopped thinking about that ever since Horvan's comment in the restaurant. He had a feeling Horvan was not going to like what he'd decided, but Rael refused to be moved on this. Provided he could resist Horvan's charms.

Of course, for all Rael knew, Horvan could already have seen his decision right there in Rael's head. Hopefully there were limits to how much his mate could see.

"How many bedrooms does this place have?"

Horvan leaned against the wall. "One." His eyes sparkled. "What a pity. You'll have to share my bed." He inclined his head toward the kitchen. "Coffee's ready."

Rael got up and followed him into the adjacent area. "Listen, about the sleeping arrangements. We have to talk." His pulse quickened.

Before he could say more, Horvan took him by the shoulders, spun him around, and pushed him gently up against the wall. Rael groaned inwardly at the feel of Horvan's hard cock at his ass. "Uh-uh. No more talking. Now we fuck." He slid his large hands down Rael's body to his butt, squeezing his cheeks.

"We… we can't," Rael gasped.

Horvan froze. "Why the fuck not? We're mates, aren't we?" He leaned in until his breath tickled Rael's neck. "You telling me you don't want to fuck? Because…." He slid his hand around and down to cup Rael's hard-on. "Pants on fire." He gently squeezed it, and a soft moan spilled from Rael's lips. Horvan chuckled. "Uh-huh. *That* doesn't lie." He undulated his body, his dick pressing against the seam of Rael's jeans. "Because I know where *this* wants to go," he whispered.

Fuck. Rael wanted it there too, but this wasn't the time.

He turned around, looped his arms around Horvan's neck, and kissed him, taking his time. Horvan quickly warmed to the kiss, his tongue exploring Rael's mouth, his hands going around Rael's waist.

Rael carefully broke the kiss. "Of course I want you. Right now, I feel like a cat in heat." He chuckled. "Which, of course, I am. But… not yet, okay?"

He felt Horvan's shock in his mind before a word escaped his lips. Horvan blinked. "When, then?"

Rael took a deep breath. "When it's all three of us. I'm sorry, but I really feel our first time should be together." He locked gazes with Horvan. "Try to set aside your raging lust and rampaging libido for a minute and you'll know I'm right."

Horvan stared at him in silence for a moment, then sighed heavily, his shoulders sagging. "You're right. Not that I like it, and I'm not even sure it makes sense, but yeah, you're right."

A wave of thankfulness crashed over Rael, and he kissed Horvan again before leading him by the hand into the living room. He pointed to the couch. "Then that's where I'll sleep tonight."

Horvan uttered a low growl but finally nodded. "Okay. But I can see me taking several cold showers while you're here." He nodded toward the couch. "Sit. I'll bring the coffee."

Rael sank thankfully onto the couch. Thank God Horvan responded to reason.

Although there is *one thing you should be aware of, sweetheart.*

Rael jerked his head toward the kitchen. "And what's that?"

Horvan appeared, carrying two mugs. He handed one to Rael. "If you're gonna play hard to get, you need to remember what you wrote in that email." Rael frowned, trying to recall his words, and Horvan grinned. "And I quote, 'I hear you're a man who can get into hard places.'" His eyes gleamed. "Challenge accepted." He nodded toward Rael's coffee. "Drink before it gets cold. Because then it's bedtime."

Rael realized his first thought had been correct.

It was going to be a *very* long night.

"Baby, you got *that* right." Horvan snickered.

Rael sighed. He was going to have to work on this whole "not thinking" thing.

RAEL KNEW it was a dream, but it was so real. He was back in the cage again, only this time, Dellan hadn't come to him. He lay on his branch, his head resting against it, his leg hanging down limply.

Dellan. It's me, Rael. Your mate.

Dellan didn't move. He gave no sign he'd even heard Rael.

Please, Dellan. Show me you can hear me.

At last the tiger slowly raised his head and stared at him. *Mate. Need you. So tired.* He lowered his head.

46

Is something wrong? Rael's heart pounded. He strode over to Dellan and stroked his fur.

It was cold.

Can you shift? Dellan, can you shift back?

The tiger blinked. *Shift?*

Rael nodded. *Shift back into a human. Like me.*

Dellan closed his eyes. *Not like you. Tiger. Dellan tiger. Not human like mate.*

His speech patterns were beginning to scare Rael. It was as if he'd forgotten *how* to speak. Rael held Dellan's head in his hands and stared into those tired eyes that had lost all their luster. *Listen to me. You are human. Somewhere deep inside you know this. Find that spark, Dellan. Find the human part of you and hold on to it. Because I'm coming—we're coming—to save you.*

Dellan pushed his nose into Rael's hand. *Save me. Please.* And then something snapped, and Rael was pulled from the dream to awaken with a cry, tears pouring out of him. He sat bolt upright, unable to contain the violent sobs shaking him.

"Hey. Hey." Horvan was there, his hands so gentle on Rael's back. "Easy. You were having a bad dream. I could feel it from my bedroom." He scooped Rael up into his arms like he was made of feathers and carried him out of the living room into the dark bedroom.

"What… what are you doing?" Rael blurted out between the sobs that still shook him.

"I'm taking you to my bed. You're sleeping with me." Horvan laid him gently on the bed. "Get in."

"But… I thought we agreed—"

Horvan silenced him with a finger to Rael's lips. "Hush now. I'm just going to hold you, okay? Nothing else, I swear. You're going to sleep in my arms."

With a final sob, Rael realized it was exactly what he needed. "Yes," he managed to get out. He got beneath the sheets, and Horvan climbed in beside him. He gathered Rael to him and held him close, his arms around Rael's body, Rael's back pressed against Horvan's warm chest.

Horvan kissed his hair. "Go to sleep, sweetheart."

"But the dream… it was so real." Rael's heart quaked. "It was like we were losing him."

"Then we'll work as fast as we can to get him out of there, all right? Tomorrow. Wait and see what tomorrow brings." Another kiss, but this time it was unexpectedly tender. "Sleep, sweetheart."

Rael closed his eyes and lost himself in Horvan's warmth and strength. That wonderful feeling of peace washed over him again, and he knew it came from the connection with his mate.

Tomorrow, then.

He prayed it wouldn't be too late.

CHAPTER SIX

MATE. FUCK. I have a mate. Scratch that. Two of 'em. And both needed his help.

Horvan stood beside the bed, gazing at his sleeping mate and holding a mug of steaming coffee. Rael's distress the previous night had left Horvan unsettled initially. What assaulted him was guilt that he hadn't shared Rael's dream. Then he realized Rael had an advantage—he'd met Dellan in the flesh. *Maybe that's what's needed to connect us psychically.* For all Horvan knew, the first time he laid eyes on the tiger, he'd have the same experience as Rael.

How the fuck is this going to work? He'd always been a "love 'em and leave 'em satisfied" kinda guy, but the man currently curled on his side in Horvan's bed, snuffling into the pillow, had gotten under his skin in a matter of hours. Except it was more than that. Rael was already inching his way into Horvan's heart. *And when we rescue Dellan? What then? Can a heart love two people at the same time?*

Horvan had always experienced enough difficulty loving *one*.

It still seemed like some weird dream.

Bang—there are mates.

Bang—I have a lion for a mate.

Bang—there's a tiger who needs rescuing.

Bang—and by the way, he's my mate too.

He knew he should be scared shitless—this was all new territory, after all—and he wasn't sure why his brain was accepting all this so calmly, but some instinct told him it would work out. Theirs couldn't be the only case of three mates, right? This had to have happened before, right?

Then he chuckled inwardly. *What the fuck do I know?* All he did know was from the moment he'd awoken with Rael in his arms, all he'd wanted to do was snuggle, to wake Rael with a kiss. Of course, there was a lot *more* he wanted to do, but that wasn't gonna happen. Despite his grumbling the previous night, he knew Rael was right.

It has to be the three of us. Only problem was, them finally getting together was looking like it might be a long way off. Horvan glanced down at his dick pushing against the soft cotton of his shorts and sighed internally. *You're gonna have to make do with my hand for a while.*

Then he stilled. *I can't believe I thought that.* Because that simply wasn't him. If Horvan had an itch, he made sure it got well and truly scratched. There was always a willing hole somewhere, right?

Apparently that way of thinking was now wrong, and the fact that Horvan was even contemplating monogamy was all the proof he needed that his world had been turned upside down.

"That for me?" Pale, sleepy blue eyes, barely visible beneath a mop of tousled blond hair, gazed up at him, and Horvan pushed his thoughts aside.

Horvan grinned. "Well, that depends what *that* refers to." And whether or not Rael had heard his thought. "Did anyone ever tell you how cute you are when you've just woken up? I think it's that whole bedhead thing you've got going on."

"My hair is a curse," Rael groused as he sat up and leaned back against Horvan's mountain of pillows. "I guess it must be part and parcel of being a lion, because it always looks like my mane no matter what I do with it." He smiled. "You have the same eyes when you shift, do you know that? They're this lovely warm brown."

Horvan was usually pretty good at accepting compliments, but for once he was at a loss for words.

"Please, tell me that *is* my coffee."

Laughing, Horvan handed him the mug. "It wasn't, but I can go pour another. Looks like you need this."

Rael wrapped his hands around it. "Trust me, you do *not* want to get between me and my first cup of coffee." He glanced around the room. "What time is it?"

"After nine, but I let you sleep. You had a rough night." Horvan perched on the edge of the bed.

50

"Sorry for disturbing you last night, but that dream...." Rael shivered.

Horvan nodded. "I get it." He might not have shared the dream, but Rael's reaction to it had permeated his slumber. "How did you sleep once you were in here?" Horvan had slept like the proverbial log.

There was that adorable flush again. "Great, thanks. It's a comfy bed."

Horvan nodded, smiling. "Was I comfy too?"

Rael smirked. "You were okay. A bit lumpy in places."

"Hey, one of those *lumps* was all your fault." He cocked his head to one side. "Can I ask you something? What's Dellan like?"

Rael took a sip of coffee before responding. "I think he's about my height. Brown hair, a lovely bronze shade, actually. A bit of a beard that isn't much more than stubble, with a little gray in it. And the most beautiful green eyes."

Horvan liked the sound of Dellan already. "How old is he?"

"Thirty-eight." Rael smiled. "And I'm thirty-five, in case you're interested."

Horvan shrugged. "I'm not. Age is just a number." He bit back a smile. "And before you ask, no, I'm not sharing *my* number."

Rael widened his eyes. "Oh come on. I'm your mate. You can tell me."

"Nope."

Rael smirked. "But it's okay to ask how old Dellan is, right?"

Horvan couldn't hold back a second longer. He leaned in and kissed Rael on the lips.

Rael made a disapproving noise and broke the kiss. "Hell no. Morning *and* coffee breath? Are you nuts?"

Horvan chuckled. "I don't give a fuck." He pulled back, however, and let Rael drink his coffee. The boys would be there soon, and once Horvan had treated them to breakfast, they could get the ball rolling.

"By the way." Rael's eyes glittered. "Since you were wondering... I *was* referring to your dick."

Horvan scowled. "Hey, no fair when we can't play. I can see you're gonna be a handful."

"Oh, I already *know* you're more than a handful," Rael replied with a chuckle.

"And when we've got Dellan out of there and he's human again?" Horvan cupped his package and gave it a squeeze. "You can have as much of this handful as you can take."

Rael grinned. "You forget. I've already seen it. And I think I can take all of it."

Horvan narrowed his gaze. "Stop that." His head was filled with images of Rael on all fours on the bed, legs spread wide, while Horvan plowed into him, burying his dick up to the hilt in that tight, hot hole.

"It is, by the way."

Horvan frowned. "What is?"

Rael's eyes danced with mischief. "My hole. Tight."

With a groan, Horvan lurched up off the bed, and at that moment the doorbell chimed. *Saved by the bell.* "Looks like we've got company." He headed for the door.

"Horvan?"

He came to a halt and turned back to look at Rael, whose face was flushed, no trace of amusement there. "I'm sorry. You're right. I shouldn't mess with your head, not when we've both agreed to keep our hands off each other until Dellan's with us."

Horvan couldn't miss the sincerity in Rael's voice, and warmth filled him. *Thank you.* His mate was an honorable man. Then it struck him. Maybe that was why some unknown power had brought them together. Rael was perfect for him.

"But teasing is so much fun," Rael added, his eyes glinting.

Horvan gave him a mock glare before hurrying out of the bedroom, aware of Rael's soft chuckles. "Put some clothes on," he fired back over his shoulder. "I do *not* want my mate walking around naked in front of these guys." *I'm the only one who gets to see that cute little ass.*

I heard that!

The doorbell chimed again, and Horvan laughed. "You always were an impatient bastard, Crank," he called out as he reached the door. He unbolted it and flung it open. Crank stood there, his hand in the air.

Crank gaped. "How'd you know it was me?" Then he grinned. "Hey, you. Good to see ya. Now let me the fuck in. I'm freezin' my ass off out here."

Horvan tugged him across the threshold, shut the door, then seized him in a tight hug. When he released him, Horvan looked Crank up and down. "You've put on weight. Suits you." It was the same dirty-blond buzzcut, however. The day Crank changed *that*, the earth would come to a standstill.

Crank rolled his eyes. "I swear. You and my mom, you must exchange notes. I think I'm getting tubby, *she* thinks I look great." He gave the apartment a cursory glance. "Nice. Minimalist. I approve."

"Why thank you for the interior decorating comments." Horvan laced his tone with sarcasm. "Coffee's on. We'll eat when the other two get here."

"Roadkill messaged me he'd just landed as I got into a taxi. He shouldn't be long. As for Hashtag, when he gets here will depend on how much interest TSA takes in his luggage." Crank's eyes gleamed. "Is that all of us?"

"For the time being."

Crank widened his eyes. "I was intrigued enough by your call yesterday. Now? I can't wait to hear more."

"And you will." Horvan's heartbeat raced. If his buddies were going to do this, they had to know everything. *It's not going to change things—is it?*

It'll be fine. Trust me. They sound like they're good guys. Even in Horvan's head, Rael's voice came across as reassuring.

Crank stilled, his gaze fixed on a point behind Horvan. Crank snickered. "Looks like nothing's changed."

Oh, I see how it is. He thinks I'm only another of your booty calls.

Horvan turned to face Rael, who stood in the doorway, his hair still tousled, looking cute in jeans and a dark green T-shirt. Horvan fixed him with a firm stare. *Except there will be no more booty calls, baby. Just you, me, and Dellan.* That had been Horvan's last thought as he'd fallen asleep, and the realization was having less and less of an impact. He'd done the whole "fuck everything that moves" thing. Maybe it *was* time for a change.

Rael's lips parted, and his eyes shone. *Oh wow.* Horvan tried not to stare at the sparkle in Rael's eyes before he wiped them.

He gestured to Rael. "This is Rael, my… partner." The words were enough to quicken his pulse. *Never thought I'd be saying that.* He didn't miss Crank's exaggerated, overly dramatic gasp.

"Holy fuck. We've reached the end times. Because I'm pretty sure Horvan Kojik settling for one guy has to be one of the signs of the coming Apocalypse."

Inside his head, Rael chuckled. *Wait till he hears about Dellan.*

Horvan rolled his eyes. "Rael, this is my buddy, Crank. He thinks he's funny."

Rael came over, one hand extended, the other holding his mug of coffee. "Hey. Good to meet you. Horvan's told me a lot about you."

Crank snorted as they shook. "Whereas *you* are a complete surprise." He rubbed his hands together gleefully. "Wait until they get a load of you."

Horvan cackled. "Oh, believe me, there are bigger surprises to come." Rael bit his lip, his eyes twinkling. From outside, Horvan caught the sound of lively chatter and loud laughter drawing closer. He met Rael's gaze. "Showtime."

Food before revelations. Shocks were always best on a full stomach.

HORVAN KNEW it wouldn't be long once they got back to the apartment. The boys chatted with Rael while Horvan made fresh coffee, wondering who was going to get the ball rolling. Horvan's money was on Crank.

"So *now* do we get to hear why we're gonna rescue a tiger?" Crank hollered from the living area. "Because unless you've gone all eco-warrior on us, it doesn't make a whole lotta sense."

"Horvan, an eco-warrior." Hashtag guffawed. "Yeah, right."

"Hey, he likes taking off his clothes and strutting around naked outdoors, remember?" Roadkill snickered. "Maybe eco-warrior is the next stage in his evolution."

Horvan walked into the room carrying a tray laden with mugs. Rael, Hashtag, and Roadkill were on the couch, and Crank was sitting on the floor facing the front door. Horvan placed the tray on the table and assessed the available space. He could do it at a pinch.

"And another thing. Not once have you mentioned terms," Roadkill piped up. "So unless we're now working pro bono...."

Horvan had known pay was going to come up.

"Maybe I should explain, seeing as this is all my idea," Rael said suddenly, looking up at Horvan before addressing the others. "You see, the first thing you need to know is that it isn't really a tiger."

"Well, you've not got *this* team together to rescue a plushy, so if it isn't a tiger, what is it?" Hashtag folded his arms, looking smug.

Before Rael could answer, Horvan muttered, "Oh for God's sake," and started stripping off his clothes.

Roadkill chuckled. "Uh, Horvan? If you're trying to convince us to go on this mission with you, that's fine. But you should know most—wait, no, *all*—of us have seen your equipment at some point, so it's not like you getting naked is going to be much of a surprise."

Horvan glanced around him as he unfastened his jeans. "You might wanna move back. This'll take up some room."

Crank snorted. "For Christ's sake, H, it ain't *that* big. Talk about delusions of grandeur."

His gasped "Holy *fuck*!" as Horvan stepped out of his puddled jeans and shifted was so gratifying. Horvan stood in the middle of the living room, waiting for the rest of them to react.

Rael got up from the couch, came over to him, and stroked his head and shoulders. "Hey, beautiful," he said softly. Horvan pushed his nose into Rael's hand, letting out a low, happy growl from the back of his throat.

Hashtag was up next, approaching Horvan with obvious caution. "Whoa. Okay, mind officially blown." He stretched out a hand toward Horvan, who lifted his head to meet Hashtag's touch. Hashtag laughed, a bright sound that echoed around the room. "Well, I'll be fucked."

Roadkill joined him, caressing Horvan's flank with less caution than his buddy. "It's real. I'm stroking a goddamn bear in a basement apartment in fucking Chicago."

Rael chuckled. "I think you've made your point, Horvan."

He agreed and concentrated on shifting back into human form. Rael handed him his clothes, and Horvan got dressed. As he pulled his T-shirt over his head, he noticed Crank was still staring at him. Horvan glared. "Problem?"

"Hmm?" Crank's furrowed brow smoothed. "Oh, not a problem as such. More a question." He held his hand above his head. "This is you." Then he held his hand a distance away from the floor. "And the bear is like this. So… when you become a bear, where does the rest of you go?"

Horvan blinked. "Really? That's your question? You find out shifters are real, and that's the first thing you wanna ask?"

"Now wait a minute." Hashtag moved to stand at Crank's side. "To be honest, I was wondering too."

Roadkill shook his head. "With all the shit we've seen and done, do you honestly think this is going to faze us?"

Crank groaned and smacked his hand against his forehead. "Fuck. That bear… the one I thought had had you for breakfast. That was *you*, wasn't it?"

Roadkill snorted. "Gee, you just worked that out?" Horvan and Hashtag laughed.

Rael laughed too. "See? I told you it would be okay. And they reacted better than the one and only person I ever shifted in front of. He fainted."

Hashtag's eyes widened. "Wait—you're a shifter too? What kind?"

"A lion." Horvan loved the hint of pride in Rael's voice.

Crank turned to Horvan. "Now see?" he declared triumphantly. "If *he'd* shifted, that would've scared the shit out of me. He's king of the beasts, whereas you? You're more like a... cuddly teddy bear." His lips twitched.

Horvan was fighting the urge to shift right back and let Crank feel how fucking *un*-teddy-bear-like his claws *really* were. Roadkill got there first. He stabbed his finger in the middle of Crank's chest.

"You? Sit down and be quiet." Then he pointed at Hashtag. "And the same goes for you. How long have we four known each other? For over a fucking *decade*. And yet he's never let us in on this before now. That tells me this is fucking important. So let's listen to why we're doing this." He glanced at Horvan. "Your move." Roadkill sat down before reaching over for a mug of coffee.

Rael's eyes glittered with approval. "I like him."

Horvan laughed. "Yeah, I'm pretty fond of him too." He faced the three men. "This tiger... he's... trapped, somehow. He can't shift back. We don't know what happened to him, but—"

"But we suspect dirty dealings are at the root of it," Rael interjected.

Horvan nodded. "So we have to get him out of there. Because if we don't help him, we're gonna lose him. And neither of us know what that will do to us."

Crank stilled. "What do you mean?"

Rael sighed. "The simplest explanation is... imagine that from birth you have someone out there who fits you so completely you're not whole without them. And when you meet them, they click into place like they were always meant to be there. They're not just a boyfriend or girlfriend—they're your mate." He glanced at Horvan and swallowed. "And Dellan is ours."

Silence fell in the room. Horvan held a hand out to Rael, who took it, lacing their fingers. His hand felt so small in Horvan's large mitt.

"Oh my God." Roadkill gazed at them with a pained expression. "You have to get him out of there."

"And we're gonna help you do it," Crank added in a grim tone.

"So what's the plan?" Hashtag leaned forward. "You *do* have one, right?"

Fuck.

CHAPTER SEVEN

HORVAN LAUGHED. "I was kinda hoping we were all going to come up with something as a team." He knew from experience that once they got their heads together, the ideas would come thick and fast.

"Fine." Roadkill glanced at Crank and Hashtag. "Well, that answers my question about pay. This one's for free, right, guys? Either of you got a problem with that?" Both shook their heads, and Roadkill gave a satisfied smile. "Good job. Now that we've got *that* out of the way, let's talk intel." Roadkill glanced at Hashtag. "How long are you gonna need for your surveillance?"

Hashtag shrugged. "For this kinda mission, usually about a week. I really could do with more, but we haven't got time for that. I think a week is pushing it as it is."

Horvan's chest tightened. Judging by Rael's expression, he was feeling the same. "A week?" Rael stared at Horvan, clearly aghast. "Dellan could be dead in a week."

Horvan's stomach turned over. He couldn't afford to think like that. "We can't go in without good intel. We need to know a whole load of shit before we even set foot in that building." He met Hashtag's gaze. "Is there any way you can hack into their system so we can see their video feed here on a laptop?" He was assuming there was a system of cameras in the building.

Hashtag stroked his jaw. "It might be possible. It depends how strong their system's defenses are." He cocked his head to one side. "Why is this important?"

"Because *that* way, we can see how Dellan is doing at any given hour." Horvan glanced at Rael. "You can't go back in there, as much as you'd like to. You'll only arouse their suspicions."

The anguish in Rael's eyes was almost too much to bear.

"I think I'd better get started right away." Hashtag grabbed his bag. "Give me the address and I'll carry out my first recon."

Crank placed his hand on Hashtag's arm. "You want some company?"

"Nah. I'll do this first one on my own. I'll be back later to let you know what I found out." Hashtag met Horvan's gaze. "I'll be here for dinner." He grinned. "An address would be good."

Rael got out his phone. "Put your number in here. I'll send it to you."

Hashtag quickly typed in his cell number. "There." His eyes sparkled. "Send me loads of memes and you're a dead man. I hate that shit." Then he patted Rael's cheek. "Don't you worry. We're gonna get your mate out of there," he said quietly. "And you never know. I might go there and find out all I need real quick."

Horvan smiled to himself. For all Hashtag's brash manner and talk, he was a sensitive soul. Horvan walked with him to the front door. "Be safe."

Hashtag held out his fist, and Horvan bumped it. "You know it. So point me in the right direction."

Horvan snickered. "Head for the skyscrapers. The Global Bio-Tech building is one of those."

Hashtag blinked. "You weren't kidding. Your mate is on the top floor of a skyscraper?" His lips twitched. "Piece of cake, then." His expression grew more somber. "You know you can rely on me. I might be a bit of a joker, but when the chips are down…."

Horvan knew it. "Go find out all you can."

Hashtag nodded. He clasped hands with Horvan before heading up the steps to the street. When he was out of sight, Horvan came back inside.

"When we have a better idea of what's going on, we'll take turns doing the surveillance with Hashtag, if we need to," Roadkill told him.

"So what do I do?" Rael demanded.

"Right now? There's nothing you can do. And I know that feels awful, but we have to wait." Horvan hated the weariness that stole over Rael's face. "You really didn't sleep that well last night, did you? Why don't you go take a nap?" He indicated Crank and Roadkill. "These two are probably gonna play cards until Hashtag gets back. It's not as if you're missing anything."

Rael nodded wearily. "A nap might be good."

Horvan walked over to him and kissed him tenderly on the lips. "I'll wake you if there's any news or when it's time to eat, whichever comes first."

Rael smiled. *You'd better.* He headed for the bedroom.

As the door closed with a snick behind Rael, Roadkill cleared his throat. "Okay, can we talk? Because you gotta know we have a shitload of questions."

Like Horvan hadn't seen *that* coming. "Sure." He joined Roadkill on the couch, and Crank sat on the coffee table facing them. "Fire away."

"So how come you never told us?" Crank demanded. "Why keep it a secret? Have you always been able to do this?"

"How come nobody knows about shifters?" Roadkill chimed in.

Horvan held up his hands defensively. "Whoa, there. How about one question at a time?" He leaned back against the cushions. "As for how come no one knows about us, I was always told we were viewed as a myth. Maybe we should stay like that."

"For God's sake, why? I think it's freaking awesome." Crank chuckled. "Scary as hell, but awesome."

Horvan shook his head. "Think about it for a second. Think how people react to things that frighten them. Other races, gays, et cetera. Mankind doesn't have a good record when it comes to dealing with stuff that's out of the ordinary. Sure, they *might* understand, but let's be honest—who wants to test that theory?"

Roadkill gave him a speculative glance. "Have you met other shifters?"

"Sure. Not that many, but yeah."

He smiled. "But how do you know they're a shifter? Is there some secret handshake or something? A code sign you give each other?"

60

Horvan laughed. "We do it by smell."

Crank wrinkled his nose. "Yeah, I can understand that. I can still smell that bear." Roadkill whacked him on the leg, and he scowled. "Come on, don't tell me you weren't thinking the same thing."

Roadkill ignored him. "What about kids?"

"What about them?"

"Well… if you had kids, would they be bears?"

"You only get shifter babies when you mate with a shifter. If I mated with a human, the babies would be human too. And as for whether or not they'd be bears, that would depend on who had the dominant gene."

"Wait." Crank's eyes widened. "Shifters mate with humans?"

Horvan nodded. "A buddy of mine—he's a bunny shifter—he mated with a human. A woman," he added for clarity.

"A *bunny* shifter? For real?" Crank shook his head. "Now I've heard everything."

Horvan chuckled. "They have eight kids."

"She *does* know, right? That he's a shifter?"

Horvan laughed. "Of course she does. Otherwise it might be difficult to explain why he disappears from time to time to go shift."

Crank snorted. "Or why they've got eight kids."

"Is that what you do? Shift now and again?" Roadkill asked.

Before Horvan could respond, Crank grinned. "*Now* I know why you live in that piddling little town. You've got all that space to shift in."

Horvan nodded. "I have to be careful. There aren't that many black bear sightings in Indiana." He glared at Crank. "And watch what you say. I happen to *like* that 'piddling little town.'"

Roadkill gazed at him thoughtfully. "When did you first shift?" He smiled. "Because I have visions of this cute little bear cub running around."

"At the onset of puberty. That's when I found out what I was. My parents are both bears. They took me on vacation to some god-awful remote spot. I'd been grousing the entire time about how there was nothing to do. Then I learned why we were there." Horvan smiled.

"It was the best vacation ever. Dad taught me to fish in the lake, and I spent most of the time in bear form. When it came time to go home, I didn't want to go."

"When you say he taught you to fish...." Roadkill laughed. "Suddenly I'm envisioning every bit of footage I've ever seen about bears catching salmon."

Horvan chuckled. "Yup. Although we fished for trout, not salmon." He smacked his lips. "Delicious."

"I hate to stop you in full reminiscing mode, but you still haven't answered my question." Crank looked him in the eye. "Why didn't you tell us?"

Horvan had known that one was coming. "If I'm honest? I was scared. I didn't want you to look at me differently. I... I didn't want to lose your trust."

Roadkill smiled. "As if that was gonna happen." He inclined his head toward the bedroom door. "So when did you meet Rael?"

Horvan grinned. "Yesterday."

Crank's jaw dropped. "Seriously? From the look of you two, anyone would think you'd been together ages."

Horvan shrugged. "Maybe that's because we're mates. But like Rael says, don't quote me. The first I knew about mates was when he turned up on my doorstep." He glanced at the bedroom door. "Feels like I've known him a lot longer." A feeling he couldn't account for logically.

"So that's it? You just accept that he's your mate? You don't question it? He fits into your life, and you assume everything is going to be hunky-dory?"

Horvan turned his head slowly to face Crank. "How can I explain this to you? Yes, he's my mate, but... I don't know him—yet. I look forward to finding stuff out about him. I know I'm gonna love him—that's a given—but I have the rest of my life to work out *why* he's perfect for me."

"Wait—you *know* you're gonna love him?" Crank gaped. "Whoa. This is—"

"Tell me about it." This whole state of affairs was still making Horvan's head spin. "And as for accepting the situation and not questioning it...." He smiled. "It's pretty difficult to doubt it when I can hear his thoughts in my head, and he can hear mine." He could imagine how *that* was going to go down.

Roadkill gaped. "Seriously? There's some kind of telepathic link between you?" His eyes widened. "That is so freaking cool." Then his expression softened. "You're really worried about Dellan, aren't you?"

Horvan let out a heavy sigh. "Yeah, I am. We both are." He told them about Rael's nightmare. "If he's right, Dellan is getting weaker. I think what Rael fears most is that Dellan might totally lose the ability to shift. Worse, he might lose his humanity, and we'd never get him back."

"Do you have any idea as to why he's stuck as a tiger?" Crank asked.

"None whatsoever. But once we get him out of there, I want answers." Horvan glanced at Roadkill. "I'll need you for that part."

Roadkill frowned. "Me?"

Horvan nodded. "To fetch Doc Tranter. He might know what's wrong."

Roadkill gaped at him. "Doc Tranter." He expelled a breath. "Oh my God. The doc is a shifter too, isn't he? How many of you are there?"

"I have no idea. My parents didn't know much either, beyond the basics. I had so many questions growing up. Where do we come from? How long have we been around? How many different kinds of shifters are there? Only there were no answers." It felt like there was a gaping hole in his life. Horvan hated knowing nothing of his origins.

Roadkill coughed. "Can I be practical for a moment? If Rael turned up yesterday, and it looks like we're going to be here for at least a week.... You didn't plan on having four guys to stay, did you? So maybe while we've got the time, I should go do some grocery shopping."

Horvan nodded. "That would be great." Supplies had been the last thing on his mind.

"And I'll start looking into transport options. Because you *know* what my first thought was when your message said skyscraper." Crank grinned. "We're gonna need a chopper. I'd better see what's available."

A wave of gratitude washed over Horvan. "Thanks, guys." He pulled them up to their feet and grabbed them both in a hug.

Roadkill cupped the back of his head and looked him in the eye. "Anything for you. Because you'd do the same for us." His eyes twinkled. "Hell, we were gonna go hunt the bear that ate you."

Horvan laughed as he released them. "Wow. That might've been awkward."

Crank patted his back. "I know you're not gonna pay me any attention when I say this, but… try not to worry, please? We're gonna do all we can to get your mate out of there."

"What he said." Roadkill placed his hand on Horvan's shoulder. "When Hashtag gets back, you'll see. The ideas will start flowing, and before you know it, we'll have a plan."

God, Horvan prayed they could carry out this rescue before it was too late.

CHAPTER EIGHT

HORVAN WAS removing the pasta dish Crank had concocted from the oven when the doorbell rang. "Hey, Hashtag's timing is spot-on as usual."

Rael laughed as he filled a platter with chunks of garlic bread. "I can't tell if you're being sarcastic or not."

"Oh, I mean it. If Hashtag says he'll have something done by a certain time, you can bet your bottom dollar it'll be done." He inclined his head toward the living room. "Go tell 'em to get their asses in here. They can help themselves." The plates were already warming in the bottom oven.

Rael disappeared from sight. Horvan placed the dish on a metal rack. Hashtag's text had filled him with hope.

I think I've got it. Back soon with news. Get those beers chilled!

The others filed into the kitchen, chatting loudly.

"This isn't anything like that chicken dish you made for us, is it, Crank?" Roadkill asked, eyeing the pasta with suspicion. "You know, the one that gave us all food poisoning."

Crank glared at him. "That was a perfectly fine meal. Don't blame me because you reheated the leftovers twice. You gotta be careful with chicken."

Roadkill rolled his eyes. "Yes, Mom."

"I think we're safe," Horvan said with a grin. "This one's only got vegetables and tofu in it."

"Tofu?" Hashtag seemed horrified. "Since when do you eat tofu?"

"Since he met that girl last year. The one who was vegan. Ain't that right, Crank?" Horvan shook his head. "The things we do for love."

"Say what you like, you bastards. Tofu is a healthy option." Crank helped himself to a large portion before adding a couple of chunks of garlic bread. Horvan made sure everyone had plenty before helping himself. In the living room, Rael, Crank and Roadkill had taken the couch, with Hashtag sitting on the floor, his plate on the coffee table, his laptop open beside it.

"Eat first," Horvan instructed him, perching on the table, his plate balanced on his knee. "You can tell us what you've learned later. Because I'll bet you haven't eaten since breakfast."

Hashtag rolled his eyes. "Yes, Mom." He dug his fork into the cheese-covered pasta. "And never mind what Roadkill says, Crank. This looks fucking amazing."

"Tastes pretty good too," Rael added.

For about five minutes there was no talking but plenty of appreciative noises. Horvan got up briefly to go into the kitchen when he realized he'd forgotten the beers. By the time all the plates were empty, he was buzzing with anticipation. "Okay. *Now* you can tell us."

Hashtag pushed his plate aside and peered at the laptop screen. "Like I said, I think I've got a plan, but I'll need time to set it up. However—" He tapped on the keyboard. "—important stuff first." He turned the laptop so Horvan could see the monitor. "Your mate, I believe."

Horvan caught his breath at the sight. The image was in black and white. A lean, magnificent tiger was pacing slowly up and down along the front of the cage, its head bobbing now and again. "He's beautiful."

Rael was at his side in a heartbeat. "Oh God, that's not good." His face paled in the light from the monitor.

"What do you mean?" Hashtag demanded. The other two got off the couch and crowded behind Horvan and Rael to see.

"Oh my God, look at that," Crank said in an awed tone. "Look at the size of him."

Horvan ignored him, his attention focused on Rael, his pulse racing. "What's not good?"

"Him pacing like that? It's a form of neurosis. It means he's under a lot of stress. Animals in zoos or confined environments go cage-crazy after a while. It's usually a sign they need to be released back into the wild." Rael touched the screen, caressing the tiger, his eyes filled with anguish. He turned to Horvan. "We have to move fast."

Horvan couldn't agree more. "Okay, Hashtag. What's your plan?"

Hashtag swallowed a mouthful of beer before speaking. "The good news is, we won't need to do a week of surveillance. I found out all I need today, which is a good thing seeing as tomorrow is Saturday. The bad news? We're still gonna need a week to set things up."

"But have you worked out how we're going to get him out?" Horvan demanded.

"Sure. We're gonna take him out through the roof," Hashtag replied with obvious confidence.

Crank blinked. "What are we gonna do—cut a hole in it with a can opener?"

Hashtag raised his eyes heavenward before continuing. "I've seen the layout of the building. There's a staircase that goes from the top floor to the roof. They've got a helicopter pad up there. The CEO uses it. So... we'll go out that way. Crank, we'll need a military chopper, something big enough for all of us *and* the tiger."

"Wait a minute." Horvan focused on Hashtag. "Define 'us.'" His heartbeat sped up.

"You, me, Roadkill, and Rael, plus any other guys we get in on this. Crank will be flying it, of course." Hashtag regarded him mildly. "Is there a problem?"

Horvan nodded. "Rael's not going with us." There was no way he was about to endanger his mate.

"Hey, don't I get a say in this?" Rael yelled, his face reddening.

"We need him!" Roadkill shouted.

Crank shook his head. "You can't tell him what to do, mate or no mate."

"Hold it!" They all fell silent at Hashtag's holler. He stared pointedly at Horvan. "Rael *has* to go. As far as we know, he's the only one of us who can communicate with Dellan." He peered at Rael. "That's right, isn't it? You already have a rapport with him?" Rael nodded, and Hashtag turned back to Horvan. "No offense, H, but you and Dellan don't have that yet. Obviously you will, once you guys get together, but for now? We *need* to go in there and have Dellan cooperate with us. He has to know what's going on. From the look of things, he's already stressed. Imagine what his reaction will be if all these strange guys turn up and try to take him from his cage." He paused, his gaze locked on Horvan's. "We *need* him, H."

Horvan looked from Hashtag's earnest expression to Rael's tortured one, his heart quaking. Finally he nodded. "You're right, of course." He knew in his heart that Rael would be protected, but it didn't stop him from worrying.

Hashtag expelled a breath. "Thank God for that. Now, you wanna hear how we're going to get him out without anyone noticing?"

"I do," Crank chimed in. Everyone sat down again, only this time Rael sat at Horvan's feet, his gaze still trained on the laptop's screen.

"This is going to be carried out early in the day. The building opens at six for the cleaning staff, but the CEO and his secretary normally get there at eight or later."

Roadkill chuckled. "How do you know all this?"

Hashtag preened. "It's amazing what you can find out over a smoke break with one of the security guards. And speaking of which… they monitor the top floor with CCTV. I'm gonna hack into their system. I gotta say, it's a pretty shit system for such a hi-tech building. Anyhow, what *they'll* be seeing is a loop, showing Dellan doing tiger stuff in his cage."

"And you think they won't notice a military helicopter landing on the roof? What if we set off an alarm?"

"We won't. I'll make sure of that. And security is gonna be too busy to see *us*, because they'll have their hands full dealing with the protesters."

Horvan frowned. "Protesters?" He had to hand it to Hashtag. The guy had clearly been thinking this through.

Hashtag nodded. "That's what's going to take the time. I need to set myself up with fake accounts on Twitter and Facebook, describing myself as an animal rights activist. *Then* I leak the story of the tiger to as many animal rights groups as I can find. I email them, spreading a tale of the rich CEO who keeps a caged wild animal in his office. I share footage of the tiger. In short, I use social media to whip all the animal lovers out there into a frenzy."

"Isn't that a bit risky?" Rael frowned. "You use social media, and Anson's tech people could pick up on it."

Hashtag shook his head. "Once these groups take a bite, we go quiet. Email, messaging, private groups on Facebook, et cetera. I'm not putting the video of Dellan out in public. Like you said, that's way too risky. No, I'll do a little fishing first; then when I've got their interest— bam." He gave Rael a reassuring smile. "That work for ya?"

Rael nodded. "I should've thought before I opened my mouth."

Horvan squeezed his shoulder. "You ask all the questions you want, okay?"

Hashtag continued, "When I've gotten a big enough response— and let's face it, with social media, that won't take long these days—I set a date for the protest, which gets shared secretly to keep prying eyes away." He folded his arms. "The day in question, the protesters turn up en masse, primed with printed signs. So while *they're* on the first floor, chanting slogans, sitting on the ground, painting graffiti on the windows and the walls, *we* will be on the top floor, getting Dellan out."

"Hey, isn't this *Lethal Weapon II*?" Crank was nodding. "You know, where all the protesters are outside the South African embassy, and Riggs slips in under the door to go—"

"Crank." Horvan glared at him. "Not the time, okay?" Crank immediately mimed zipping his lips.

"Sounds like we might need a few more guys on the ground," Roadkill commented. "Have them in among the protesters, making sure they stay on track." He smiled. "You know who'd be perfect for this? Jase. He's a great little rabble-rouser."

"Good thinking. Get onto him, ASAP. Let's see if he's available." Horvan knew they'd need more men. He hoped the ones they wanted were in the country. Some did a lot of work overseas in Europe and Asia.

"Then what?" Rael asked. "Once we've got him out, I mean."

"We fly a short distance to an arranged meeting point. It can't be a long trip, because of Dellan. We have a guy waiting for us with a motor home. We take it, and he flies the chopper away. Whichever direction we take, he'll fly the opposite way."

"And what direction will we be taking?" Crank inquired.

"That's as far as I got," Hashtag admitted. "But it'll need to be someplace remote, with accommodation big enough for all of us plus a tiger. Of course," he added, "we're hoping he won't stay a tiger for long."

It was the right thing to say. Horvan nodded. "Once we're wherever we end up, I'll be sending Roadkill to pick up Doc Tranter. Maybe he'll be able to help."

Hashtag gave him an inquiring glance. "What does the doc know about tigers?"

Roadkill laughed. "See what happens when you miss a briefing?" He leaned toward Hashtag and whispered, "Another shifter."

"Holy Christ, they're everywhere." Hashtag shook his head. "This mission is certainly turning into an eye-opener."

"I might have an idea where we can take him," Rael said suddenly. All heads turned in his direction. "I live in Salmon, Idaho. It's a little place with only around three thousand inhabitants. But I chose to live there because the Salmon-Challis National Forest is right on my doorstep. That's where I go to shift. But there are cabins in the forest that you can rent. Some of them are pretty big. Plus it's kinda isolated in places."

Horvan considered the proposal. "Wherever we change vehicles, we're talking about a day's drive to Idaho if we intend avoiding tolls. That works. They won't be looking for a motor home."

"They? Who is 'they'?" Crank inquired.

Horvan sighed. "Someone has gone to a lot of trouble with Dellan. You think they're just going to let him go?" He shook his head. "I think it's likely they'll pursue us. And we have to be prepared for that." He couldn't help noticing how Rael's gaze kept returning to the laptop.

Apparently, Hashtag had noticed it too. "Rael?" When he had Rael's attention, Hashtag tapped the laptop. "I'm going leave this logged in to their video feed, all right? Anytime you wanna look at it, day or night, it'll be here. I'll put my log-in details right by the laptop so you can get back in if it logs you out." His eyes were warm.

Rael swallowed. "Thanks." He got to his feet. "I'm gonna make some coffee. Anyone interested? Or do you want to stick with beer?" A chorus of voices clamored for coffee, and he went into the kitchen area.

Roadkill met Horvan's gaze. "Well, go after him. I might not be his mate, but even *I* know he's upset right now."

Horvan didn't need telling—Rael's distress was coming off him in waves. He walked into the kitchen to find Rael leaning against the sink, head bowed. Horvan went over to him and put his arms around Rael's waist. "Hey," he said softly. "It's going to be okay."

"You don't know that." Rael didn't turn to look at him. "What if… what if we're too late?"

Gently but firmly, Horvan turned him around. He put his hand under Rael's chin and lifted that sweet face to look Rael in the eye. "We have to stay positive, sweetheart. We have to trust this is going to work."

Rael smiled. "I do like it when you call me that."

Horvan chuckled. "You're the first guy I ever called sweetheart. And I guess you'll be the last, with one important exception."

"Hey, there's something we haven't discussed," Crank called out from the living area. "Something fairly major, so get your bear butt in here."

Horvan sighed. "Make the coffee. I'll go see what His Majesty wants."

Rael laughed quietly. "I do like your friends. They're good guys."

Horvan kissed him on the mouth, a chaste, lingering kiss that warmed him. Then he walked back into the living area. "Which bear butt were you referring to?" He unfastened his jeans and turned around, waggling his ass.

"Don't you dare," Crank warned. "There isn't enough room in the whole damn apartment for *that* ass." Horvan glared at him, but Crank merely huffed. "I get that Rael will be sleeping with you, but what about the rest of us? Because all I see is one couch."

"And you can fight it out for who gets it, because the other two will be on the floor. I got plenty of blankets and pillows." He peered intently at Crank. "Besides, weren't *you* the one who was always telling us you could fall asleep on a rope?" Cackles erupted from the others. "Granted, my floor might be a little uncomfortable, but it beats sleeping on the hard ground. Something we four have done a lot of in our past."

"He's got you there, Crank." Roadkill snickered. "And I vote Hashtag gets the couch. He's earned it." Hashtag bumped fists with him.

"Fine," Crank grumbled. "We'll take it in turns. But I am *not* sleeping in the tub. Had to do that once after a date, and I swore I'd never do it again."

Roadkill arched his eyebrows. "Doesn't sound like it was all that good a date."

Rael walked in with the tray of mugs. "I've been thinking. What if I want to look at the laptop during the night? I might disturb you guys if you're in here."

Hashtag smiled. "Then take it with you to the bedroom. I'm not gonna need it tonight."

Rael's look of gratitude made Horvan's chest tighten. Horvan mouthed *thank you* to Hashtag, who merely nodded.

"Okay, what are we playing?" Crank picked up the pack of cards he and Roadkill had been playing with earlier. "I vote for strip poker."

Roadkill snorted. "Hell no. You always play to lose, and I for one do *not* wanna see your dick again. Or your bubble butt, for that matter." He peered closely at Crank. "You sure you're not bi? 'Cause you seem awful fond of getting nekkid in front of us."

In Horvan's head, Rael laughed, and the sound made him feel a little lighter.

Maybe a game or two is just what we need. You know, to keep our mind off... things. Horvan knew Crank was trying to keep the tone light to help bolster their spirits. He'd worried Rael might be upset by the jocularity from his friends, but it seemed he was concerned over nothing.

No, I'm not upset, not at all. I understand why he's doing it. I might not show it, but I really appreciate the way he's looking out for you. Well, us. Rael's eyes sparkled. *As long as I don't end up naked. They do not get to see my bits and bobs.*

Horvan chuckled. *But you have such lovely bits and bobs.* Then reality hit home. *Hey. Maybe I don't want you seeing their bits and bobs.*

Rael's lips twitched. *You forget. I've already seen what you're packing. They can't even begin to compete.*

Damn, that made him feel good.

"Does anyone here get the feeling we're missing out on something?" Roadkill was regarding him and Rael with obvious amusement. "I mean, please, don't let *us* interrupt your mental sexy shenanigans."

"Yeah, if you two lovebirds wanna go somewhere and... *commune*, that's fine by us," Crank added with a grin.

"I think you mean *mate*, don't you?" Hashtag was grinning too.

Horvan rolled his eyes. "Deal the cards."

Don't worry. We can commune *later.* Rael flashed him a smile. *When we're alone.*

Horvan knew it wouldn't amount to more than cuddling and caressing, but damn, that sounded good. *You know it.* Then Rael's smile faded, and an image flashed through Horvan's mind.

Dellan in his cage... pacing.

Horvan would hold Rael all night if it would keep his mate from being distressed.

CHAPTER NINE

RAEL HAD no idea what had awoken him so abruptly, but his chest felt constricted and his breathing labored. His heart was racing too. Beside him, Horvan slept soundly. Rael sat up, running his fingers through his hair.

Dellan. Something's wrong with Dellan. Not that he had any idea if their link extended over so great a distance, but it was the most likely explanation. At least Rael had the means to check on him.

He eased himself carefully out of the bed, trying not to disturb Horvan. Through the closed door, he could hear snoring. Rael crept over to where he'd left the laptop on the chair. He grabbed Horvan's robe from its hook on the back of the door and put it on. *Lord, it drowns me.* He snuggled it around him, sat in the wicker chair, and opened the laptop, glancing over to see if its light bothered Horvan. When it became obvious nothing short of a nuclear bomb was going to wake his mate, Rael logged in, straining to read the password Hashtag had given him.

The sight that awaited him stole his breath. Dellan was not alone.

Rael lurched out of the chair and scrambled onto the bed, the laptop held precariously in one hand. He shook Horvan's shoulder. "Wake up!"

"Whaaa?" Horvan blinked and rubbed his eyes. Within seconds he was alert. He sat up quickly. "What's wrong?" Voices from the living room told Rael he'd woken the others too.

Good. They need to see this. "Get in here, all of you," he yelled.

"I do *not* wanna watch, okay?" Crank grumbled groggily. The door opened, and the three men stood there, blinking, wearing nothing but shorts. "What time is it?"

"You need to see this. There's something going on," Rael said urgently.

The men piled onto the bed, everyone peering at the laptop.

"Wait—who the fuck are they?" Roadkill demanded.

Beside Rael, Horvan stared at the screen. "What's going on in there?"

Rael had no clue. Two men stood at one end of the cage, outside the glass, holding on to a naked girl who was struggling, clearly extremely reluctant to be there. She threw back her head, her mouth wide, her long hair flying. Rael caught his breath when one of the men opened a small tin the size of a tablet and removed a hypodermic needle. Another man appeared from off-camera, grabbed the girl's arm, and held it out, keeping it immobile.

"What the fuck?" Horvan sounded as agitated as Rael felt.

The man with the needle removed a tiny vial from the tin, then slowly transferred the liquid to the hypo. The girl was held fast by the other two, and, disconcertingly, her legs were shaking.

Rael couldn't tear his gaze away from the screen. Around him, the voices of the others rose in alarm.

"What is that stuff?"

"Never mind that—what the hell are they doing there? And why is she naked?"

"What sick fuckery is this?"

Dellan was at the far end of the cage, watching the proceedings, crouched by the pool of water, his tail thrashing from side to side, his head low.

"Is he scared?" Horvan asked.

"I can't tell!" Rael felt so fucking useless. Then he gasped as the man wiped the girl's wrist before emptying the contents of the vial into her arm. She was still struggling, but the other two held on to her tightly. "Dear Lord."

"God, I wish we had sound," Hashtag complained.

"Why? *Watching* this is bad enough."

Rael had to agree with Roadkill. The man with the small tin put it away in his pocket, his gaze focused on the girl.

"He's waiting for whatever they've injected her with to take effect," Horvan said quietly. Roadkill murmured in agreement.

Fuck, this was agony, staring at the screen, rigid with suspense. All Rael could hear was the others' breathing, so loud in the quiet room. No one spoke for what seemed like ages, all of them seemingly waiting for something to happen.

"How long has it been?" Crank asked.

"About ten minutes," Roadkill replied. "But I don't think—"

"Look!" Crank shouted. "Look at the girl. She's gone really still."

A horrible thought slowly dawned in Rael's mind, and when he heard the hitch in Horvan's breathing, he knew he was right.

"She's naked because they're waiting for her to shift," Rael said in a monotone.

Seconds later, the man with the needle opened the cage door, and together, the three men roughly shoved the girl inside. Dellan's mouth opened, his sharp teeth gleaming in the light, and Rael knew with every fiber of his being that their mate was roaring. The girl dropped to all fours, and moments later, there stood a tiger, its eyes locked on Dellan.

"They forced a shift. Whatever they gave her forced her to shift," Horvan concluded. His voice quavered.

"Is that even possible?" Crank demanded.

"If you'd asked me that yesterday? I'd have said no. But what else could it be?"

Dellan and the tiger circled each other, and the hairs stood up on the back of Rael's neck. "I know why they've put her in there. They want them to mate." Ice slid down his spine. Rael buried his head in Horvan's chest. "I can't watch this." Yet he was unable to stop himself. He twisted his head to watch Dellan follow the tiger around the cage, never more than a couple of inches from her. She lay down and rolled onto her back, four heavy paws in the air, and Dellan nuzzled her exposed belly and neck. And when she rolled over again to lie facedown, her back legs stretched out, her body submissive, Rael knew he was right.

Dellan stood over her, straddling her body, licking at the scruff on the back of her neck with long flicks of his tongue.

Don't! Rael screamed in his head. *Don't do it! Fight it. She's not your mate.*

He thought he'd gotten through when Dellan stiffened, his head raised, the female apparently forgotten. Dellan sniffed the air, glancing around the cage. Then he went back to licking the female.

When he lowered his backside, his legs trembling slightly, Rael knew whatever connection they'd had was broken. He looked away. "No. I don't have to watch this." Horvan's strong arm tightened around him, and Rael inhaled his comforting scent.

Horvan stroked his hair gently. "All over now," he said in a low voice.

Rael jerked his head to stare at the screen. Sure enough, Dellan had retreated back to his tree, and the female tiger headed for the cage door. The men were clearly shouting at her, and it wasn't long before she shifted back. Quickly, they opened the door and pulled her from the cage. One man threw a garment at her, and when it became clear she wasn't capable of dressing herself, another man did it for her, pulling the robe over her head and covering her body. All of them disappeared from view, out of the camera's range, and it was all over. Even Dellan casually licked the pad of his left paw like nothing had happened.

"We've gotta get him out *now*," Rael said through gritted teeth. The others stared at him like he'd lost his mind. Horvan's expression resembled theirs.

Rael lost it. "Fine. If you won't help me, I'll fucking do it myself." He went to clamber off the bed, but several hands stopped him.

"Hey, easy now," Crank soothed.

"You're not thinking straight," Roadkill said in a gentle voice.

Rael. Rael! Horvan's voice rose in his mind, blotting out the others. Rael stilled, conscious of Horvan's arms around him, the others retreating. *You can't help him right now.*

I tried to reach him. I thought I had, but then he just.... Words failed him.

Horvan kissed his head. Rael caught the murmur of something about coffee, and the others left the room. Horvan cradled Rael with a gentle rocking motion, and far from making him feel immature, it soothed and comforted him.

"Better?"

Rael nodded, his head pressed against Horvan's wide chest.

"Okay. Put some clothes on, and then we'll go out there and talk about this. I don't think any of us could get back to sleep right now. Does that sound okay?"

Rael gave another nod.

"By the way—" Horvan kissed his forehead. "—you're really cute in my robe."

Rael whacked him on the arm. He knew Horvan was trying to distract him. He had to be as frustrated as Rael. Of course, with his training, he could compartmentalize things better.

Once he'd pulled on his jeans and a sweater, Rael joined the others in the living room. Roadkill handed him a mug. Rael ignored the space in the middle of the couch and went over to where Horvan was sitting on pillows on the floor, leaning against the wall. Rael sat with his back against Horvan's chest, knees bent, hands wrapped around the mug. Horvan's arms went around him once more, their physical connection restored.

"Okay," Hashtag said after a moment. "About what you said in there. You—*we*—can't help Dellan right now. Yes, we *could* go in there, all guns blazing. We could get him out of the cage, but then what?" He gazed earnestly at Rael. "Think it through. Are we gonna waltz him through the lobby? No, of course we're not. We have a plan, and we have to stick to it. You need to trust us, because getting jobs like this done? It's what we do."

"Although, truth be told, we have *never* had a job like this," Crank commented wryly.

Hashtag glared at him. "You know what I mean. I'm trying to instill some confidence in him."

Rael sighed. "I do trust you, honest. But…." He went with the truth. "I tried to reach out to Dellan psychically. To stop him."

"Is that why he paused? Before he... you know...." Roadkill expelled a breath.

"Look, we need to talk about what we saw," Crank interjected. "And I don't mean the mating thing. If you're right and they injected something to make her shift, it raises some questions. One, why would anyone make a drug that does that? Why would they need it? Two, if that's what it was, why didn't it last long? Because she was able to shift back once the deed was done. Surely whatever they gave her would still be in her system."

"Unless they only gave her a tiny amount. Or not full strength," Roadkill suggested. "Hell, we can only guess, right?"

"Why did she collapse like that?" Hashtag demanded.

"Shifting normally takes its toll on a body," Horvan explained. "It takes a lot of energy, especially if you shift for any great length of time, and when we shift back after such a time period, we're usually ravenous."

"You know what I don't get? A little slip of a thing like her, and she turns into a four-hundred-pound tiger." His eyes gleamed. "*Horvan* shifts into a wee little teddy bear."

Roadkill smacked him upside the head. "Firstly, I'd hardly call five hundred pounds of black bear a 'wee little teddy bear,' and secondly, you do *not* want to piss off said black bear. He might be smaller than a grizzly, but he has claws the size of steak knives, remember?"

"Horvan didn't go all weak when he shifted back," Hashtag observed.

Horvan snorted. "As if I'd let you guys see me looking weak."

Rael had his own theory as to why she'd collapsed. "I think her state was more to do with what they were doing. You know...."

Crank snorted. "Yeah. Sex wipes you out, right?" He blinked at the silence that followed. "What?"

Roadkill let out an exaggerated sigh. "In the dictionary next to 'insensitive fucker,' it says, 'See Crank.'"

"Yeah, way to fucking go, Crank." Hashtag inclined his head in Rael's direction. "I really don't think he needs reminding, all right?"

Rael huffed out a breath impatiently. "I think we're all missing a point here. What if this happens all the time? What if these guys are bringing shifters to Dellan's cage, drugging them, then shoving them in there to mate? Why the fuck is this happening? Who is doing this?"

Horvan's hand was on his waist, stroking him. "All good questions, and ones to which we don't have the answers right now. Speculating is only going to drive you nuts."

"Horvan is right," Roadkill agreed. "And going over and over this is not gonna help. Let's concentrate on the plan. In the morning, Hashtag will start work on his online campaign, and Crank will sort out the transport. I'll get more guys in on this. And you?" He stared at Rael. "You are gonna find us a place to stay in that forest."

Rael nodded. "You're right. Let's focus on action rather than reaction."

That's my mate. Horvan kissed his shoulder.

"I gotta say, I'm really liking this all-new, lovey-dovey Horvan." Crank's eyes glittered. "I could get used to this." He batted his lashes. "Where's my kiss?" Crank puckered up, his eyes closed.

Hashtag snorted. "If you're real lucky, the bear has one for ya." Crank's eyes popped open, and everyone laughed at his startled expression.

"Thank you, Crank," Rael said sincerely. He knew exactly what Crank was doing.

Crank shrugged. "Just trying to lighten the load, you know?"

"And on that note...." Roadkill glanced at the wall clock. "I think it's time we all get some sleep. Or try to, at least." There were murmurs of agreement.

Horvan got to his feet, pulling Rael with him. "Let's give these guys their bedroom back." He curled his hand around Rael's and led him out of the room to cries of good night. Rael caught Crank's last comment.

"Bedroom? We got no bed. Tomorrow, go to Walmart and buy some air mattresses."

Once inside the bedroom, Horvan slowly undressed Rael down to his shorts, then pulled him gently toward the bed. He removed his own clothing and got in, his arms wide in a clear invitation.

Rael climbed in beside him and snuggled up against Horvan's muscular body with a sigh. "You feel good."

Horvan wrapped his arms around Rael and held him close. "And I'm going to feel good for the rest of the night." He pressed his lips to Rael's forehead in a sweet kiss. "Now close your eyes and go back to sleep."

His earlier horror and rage finally having subsided, Rael closed his eyes and concentrated on the sound of Horvan's breathing, regular and low. It wasn't long before he was sinking into a deep, thankfully dreamless, sleep. His last conscious thought was of Dellan.

Good night, mate. Hold on. We'll be there soon.

Hopefully before it was too late.

CHAPTER TEN

RAEL STIRRED, dimly aware of daylight filtering through his eyelids. Then he sighed happily as a warm hand stroked his belly.

I've been waiting for you to wake up.

Soft lips pressed against his neck, and Rael stifled a moan. *Hey, no fair. That really turns me on.* He gasped as Horvan slid his hand lower, his fingertips brushing over Rael's pubes, not stopping but continuing his exploration, trailing his fingers down Rael's morning wood.

So I see. Or should that be feel? Horvan's mental chuckle filled his head.

Then Rael became aware of Horvan's hard cock against his hip. *Oh fuck. We... we agreed we wouldn't, remember?* He moaned as Horvan curled his fingers around Rael's dick, pulling gently on it. Rael arched his back instinctively. *No... don't do that. I haven't jerked off for a few days. I'll come like a geyser if you do that.*

Thankfully, Horvan released his cock, and Rael shivered. He opened his eyes and looked into Horvan's. "I know it's hard, but—"

"It sure is," Horvan said with a chuckle.

"Difficult! I meant, it's *difficult*, but you know it's right." Rael swallowed. "I want you, okay? I'd like nothing more than to draw my knees up to my ears and have you balls-deep inside me, but—"

"Did you *have* to put it like that? Talk about painting pictures in my brain. And it doesn't help that you're *thinking* about it too. Christ." Horvan sat up in bed, his breathing rapid.

Rael joined him, his arm across Horvan's broad back. "Sorry. I'll try to keep a lid on my thoughts, okay?" He cupped Horvan's cheek and gently turned his face toward Rael's. "You do think we're right about this, don't you? Waiting, I mean."

Horvan expelled a long, shuddering breath. "Yeah." He glanced down with a rueful smile. "I know part of me would like to argue the point. But I don't want to mess this up. I want everything to be just right. And that includes the first time I get to make love to my mates."

Rael blinked. "Make love. Not fuck. Now *there's* a change right there."

Horvan snorted. "Yeah, I know. Don't spread it around, okay? I got a reputation to keep." He sniffed the air. "Do you smell coffee?"

Rael's stomach growled. "And bacon." He threw back the sheets and launched himself out of the bed and into the bathroom.

Horvan cackled. "Well, I guess I know where *I* stand on your list of priorities." But he did the same, reaching for his toothbrush. "I need a shower, but that can wait. With five guys in the house, we're gonna need a lot of hot water."

Rael blinked. "You're going to stand there while I pee?"

Horvan rolled his eyes. "Lord, I never knew a lion could be so dainty."

Rael laughed. "I suppose I can get used to it." He shook, flushed, then washed his hands.

Horvan peered at Rael. "Did you get some decent sleep?"

That was all Rael needed to recall what had occurred to him in the early hours of the morning. He paused, his toothbrush in his hand. "I had an idea—several, actually—and I think we need to discuss them."

Horvan stilled. "That sounds serious."

Rael sighed. "It could be deadly serious. I'll wait until we're all together." He put down the toothbrush, moved closer, and wrapped his arms around Horvan's waist. "In case I haven't told you already? I'm so glad I've got you for a mate." He smiled. "The mate I never knew I needed—until I did."

Horvan bent lower and kissed him, enfolding Rael in his arms. "Ditto, sweetheart." He released Rael and grinned. "Now brush those teeth so I can kiss you properly. Then we'll go see if Crank has cremated the bacon yet."

The ablutions finished, they left the bedroom and walked into the living room. Mugs sat on the coffee table, and from the kitchen area came laughter.

"What's so funny?" Horvan called out.

Roadkill stuck his head around the corner. "And good morning to you too. We were tossing a few ideas back and forth, that's all." He smiled kindly at Rael. "Did you get any sleep?"

Rael shrugged. "A little." He craned his neck to see into the kitchen. "You guys are making breakfast?"

Roadkill nodded. "There's bacon in the oven, Hashtag is doing the eggs, and Crank is burning the toast."

"Hey!" Crank's voice rose indignantly.

Roadkill disappeared from view. "Don't take your eyes off that toaster, you doof. That's how the first lot of toast ended up as charcoal."

Beside Rael, Horvan laughed. "Ah, this feels like old times."

Rael envied him a little. He didn't have any friends who were as close to him as these guys obviously were to Horvan. Having said that, they'd been through a lot together by the sound of things.

Horvan's hand was at Rael's back. *They're your friends now too, sweetheart.*

It was a comforting thought.

Once breakfast had been demolished and another pot of coffee was percolating, the men gathered in the living room. Rael couldn't wait any longer. "I've been thinking…."

"Did it hurt?" Crank said with a cackle. Horvan glared at him, and he held up his hands. "Okay, okay, I'll shut up."

"That drug they gave the girl to force her to shift…. Maybe that's what's keeping Dellan in his tiger form." Rael gazed at their faces. "What do you think?"

"I don't know. She shifted back awful fast," Hashtag commented, stroking his stubbled chin. "They'd have to have Dellan on an IV of the stuff to keep him from shifting back."

"Not if it's in his food. In his water. In the air he breathes." Rael's heart sank as he uttered the words. "I know I'm guessing, but it's the only thing that makes sense. And there's something else. That first dream I had, when Dellan came to me and shifted? Well, I'm thinking now that it was… more than a dream."

"What do you mean?" Roadkill got up to fetch the second pot of coffee.

"We kissed, okay? But there was something odd about it." Horvan's hand curled around his, and Rael laced their fingers. Rael struggled to recall what had struck him at the time. "When our lips met, there was a taste. A chemical sort of taste."

Crank stared at him. "Like, a drug?" Rael nodded. Crank's face darkened. "Those bastards." His gaze met Hashtag's. "We gotta make this happen fast, dude. As fast as you can pull it together."

Hashtag nodded, his expression somber. "What day is it? Saturday? Okay. I'll spend the whole weekend on my laptop if I have to. Let's aim to make our move on Friday. Earlier if I can generate enough support out there. That means you've gotta have our transport ready to go at a minute's notice, buddy."

Crank nodded gravely. "I'm on it."

Roadkill cocked his head to one side. "If we're right and they *are* drugging him, how long is it gonna take for the drugs to work themselves out of his body?"

"How long is a piece of string?" Horvan groaned. "We get him off the drugs, and it could be fast or slow, depending on how long he's been on them and how much is still in his system."

"You think I'm right, don't you?" Rael demanded.

Unfortunately, yes. Horvan squeezed his hand. "Yeah," he said aloud.

"As for how long he's been on them?" Rael had already considered this. "Worst-case scenario, he's been in tiger form ever since Anson Prescott took over the running of the company. Maybe more than a year."

"Holy fuck." Roadkill's normally ruddy complexion paled. "Okay. We are gonna get Dellan out. Then we are gonna fucking *nail* those bastards. You with me?" He stuck out his hand, and in silence, four more covered it.

Horvan got to his feet. "Okay. I have to go out, but I won't be long. Sounds to me like you all have something to do while I'm gone." His remark was met with nods all round.

"I thought you wanted a shower." Rael bit his lip. "But I guess you don't smell *too* bad."

"Yeah, only like a five-hundred-pound bear stuffed into a two-hundred-pound human," Crank said, grinning.

"Maybe I *like* the smell of bear," Rael retorted. He got up too and gave Horvan a hug. "Be safe?"

Horvan chuckled. "I'm only going to Walmart. I think I'll be safe enough." He grabbed his jacket. "I'll bring subs back with me for lunch. I know what *you* lot like, so that only leaves Rael."

"Meatball sub, please," Rael said quickly. "With lots of cheese."

"Yeah, he's a meat eater, after all," Crank added, his eyes twinkling.

Rael walked with Horvan to the door. "I'll find us a cabin, okay?"

Horvan nodded. "Play nice with the kids."

As he climbed the steps, Rael said in a stage whisper, "I'll try not to eat them."

Horvan laughed. "Roadkill would need too much tenderizing. He might be a little tough." With that, he gave a wave and strode off.

Rael closed the door. *And now to work.*

RAEL LOOKED up from his laptop and glanced at the bedroom door. "Has anyone checked if he needs anything?" Hashtag had commandeered the room as soon as Horvan left, saying he'd concentrate better with a little peace and quiet. No one had seen him since.

"He's got water, sodas, and snacks. He's fine," Roadkill assured him. It was the two of them in the living room; Crank had gone outside for a smoke and to make a phone call. "How are you doing with the cabin situation?"

Rael smiled. "I think I've found the perfect one. Want a look?"

Roadkill shifted closer and peered at the screen. "Pretty."

"I wasn't looking for pretty," Rael said with a chuckle. "This one is set on seven acres. It sleeps ten—not that I see us needing *that* many beds, but you never know—and it's roomy inside. Plus, it looks like it's in a fairly remote spot."

Roadkill scrolled through the details. "Rustic. Basic kitchen. Lots of space. There's a store not that far away too." He leaned back, smiling. "You're right. It looks perfect. Is it available now?"

Rael nodded. "The season doesn't really start until April."

"Now here's a question for you." Roadkill gazed at him thoughtfully. "How long are you gonna rent it for?"

"Like Horvan said, how long is a piece of string? Initially, I'll rent it for as long as they'll let me. If we have to move to another place, so be it." If he could rent it for the remainder of March, that would be a plus.

Crank came into the apartment, shivering. "It's cold out there." Roadkill got up off the couch and went into the kitchen.

Rael laughed. "Wait till you get to Idaho."

Crank eyed him suspiciously. "We're not talking… snow, are we?"

"Right now? We most certainly are." Rael was enjoying the look of horror on Crank's face. "Aw, what's wrong with a little snow?"

Crank gaped. "It's fucking *freezing*, that's what's wrong with it." Roadkill walked over to him, holding out a mug of coffee, and Crank took it with noises of gratitude.

"Any luck?" Roadkill asked him.

Crank nodded after slurping his coffee. "We've got us a 1964 Huey."

"How did you manage that so fast?" Rael was seriously impressed.

Crank narrowed his gaze. "I have friends you don't even wanna know about. I called in more than a few favors and got what we needed. Be happy with that."

"1964?" Roadkill speared Crank with a hard stare. "You sure that bird isn't going to fall apart midair?" Crank merely returned his stare. "Fine. So we're in business." Roadkill rubbed his hands together. "Excellent."

"Are we any clearer where we're flying it to?" Crank asked. "Because I'll need to organize someone to fly it on once we get into the motor home."

"I've already done that." Roadkill glanced at his phone. "Pickle is going to meet us in Gary, Indiana."

Crank laughed. "Good ol' Pickle." When he caught Rael's inquiring glance, he smiled. "So called because he spends most of his life pickled. He loves his booze, that one."

"And he flies?" Rael was horrified. "I wouldn't be drunk in charge of a *motorcycle*, let alone a helicopter."

Crank chuckled, then glanced at Roadkill. "How far along are you with the motor home?"

"I was waiting on you to agree on the departure point, but I've researched southern Illinois and northern Indiana, based on what Horvan said. We have several options."

Rael loved their confidence.

Crank inclined his head toward the bedroom door. "He's still at it?"

Roadkill nodded. "But Horvan should be back soon, and he'll make sure Hashtag stops to eat. You *know* what Horvan's like." Crank's lips twitched.

"What *is* he like?" The exchange intrigued Rael.

Crank snickered. "A mother hen. Not that we'd have him any other way."

Roadkill widened his eyes. "Oh my God. Even better." He grinned. "Mama Bear." The pair of them burst out laughing, and Rael had to fight the urge to join in.

Horvan was going to *hate* that.

"While we've got you alone…." Crank lowered his voice. "Can we ask you something?"

"Depends on what you want to know." Rael was curious to see where this was leading.

Crank looked at Roadkill, who leaned forward. "What does it feel like when you shift?"

Rael smiled. "It's the most exhilarating feeling ever."

"Does it hurt?" Crank asked. "Because I remember watching a werewolf movie once, and it looked fucking painful. His snout grew out, then his hind legs, and oh my God, watching his spine—"

Roadkill whacked his arm hard. "Did you *see* any of that when they shifted? No, you did not. So obviously we can forget werewolf movies." He rolled his eyes.

"It doesn't hurt," Rael assured Crank. "You just... concentrate, and it happens. And as you might have noticed, it helps to be naked first. Otherwise it gets messy."

"Have you ever shifted by accident?" Roadkill asked.

Rael bit his lip. "Once. I was young, barely out of puberty. Me and my best friend were in my bedroom, and I think we were arguing about something. Anyhow, he got me so pissed, I shifted. I guess it was the heightened emotions or something. I shifted right back, but the damage was done."

Crank's mouth opened. "Was he the one who fainted?"

Rael nodded. "When he came round, he was shaking like a leaf. Finally I got him to calm down. I had to tell him what I was."

"Isn't that dangerous? What if he tells people?" Roadkill shook his head. "I'm not sure how I would have reacted at that age."

"He never told a soul back then. And I'm certain he won't now."

"Why?"

"Because his wife would kill him," Rael said with a chuckle.

"Huh?" Both Roadkill and Crank stared at him, clearly perplexed.

"We lost track of each other once we went to college. But years later he got back in touch. Turns out the girl he was dating? She was a shifter." Rael laughed. "I wish I could've seen her face when she saw his lack of reaction to her revelation. She must've expected him to freak out."

"What kind of shifter is she?" Crank seemed fascinated.

"Puma. Wes tells me about nights when they're on the couch and she lies on her back so he can give her belly rubs. And there's this thing he does with a flashlight? Drives her crazy. She's just a big kitty, after all. Like me."

"My turn." Roadkill regarded him with interest. "Are you aware of your lion when you're human? Can you feel it?"

Rael shrugged. "Sure. I can always feel it. It's like a comforting presence in the back of my mind." He grinned. "At least until someone drives stupid or gets into the ten items or less lane with a couple dozen items. Then I have to keep a tight rein on him because we both want to rip their throat out."

Roadkill became very still. "You wanna rip out their... please, tell me you're joking."

Rael burst into a peal of laughter. "Yes, I'm kidding." Roadkill and Crank joined him, although their chuckles had a distinctly relieved quality. "My lion is always there, content to stay quiet until I can get away to the forest or, if by chance, I feel threatened."

"Okay, let's get onto the real important stuff." Crank lowered his voice. "Shifter sex. Have you ever fucked in your lion form?"

Hoo boy. Rael took a deep breath. "I've never had sex with a shifter."

"Wait—but... Horvan...." Roadkill's brow furrowed. "You and he haven't...?"

"We're not complete yet. When we've got Dellan? *Then....*" That was as much as Rael was willing to say, and he had a feeling it had been too much.

"Wow," Crank said in an awed tone. "Horvan's not getting any. I'm surprised he's not cranky as hell twenty-four seven." He snorted. "Pun intended. I was right when I said it before. We've reached the end times."

Before Rael could question him further, the front door opened and Horvan entered, laden with bags.

"What have you been buying?" Rael stood and went over to relieve him of some of them.

"Air mattresses and pillows, what else?" Horvan gave him a peck on the lips before Rael took the bags to the bedroom door and left them there, out of the way.

"Aw. You listened." Crank blew Horvan a kiss.

Horvan blew one right back, and the others laughed. He glanced at the laptops on view. "You guys got a lot done?"

"Yup, we've been very productive." Roadkill took the bag of subs from Horvan. "I'll get these unwrapped and put out chips and stuff."

Horvan thanked him, then came over to where Rael stood. "Pleased to see me?"

"You know it," Rael said quietly, before kissing him on the mouth. Horvan instantly put his arms around him and drew him closer.

"Put him down. There's plenty of time for that later—Mama Bear."

Slowly, Horvan turned his head to glare at Crank. "What?"

Crank shrugged. "If the shoe fits…."

Rael had a feeling this was *not* going to end well.

"Hey!" Crank's eyes gleamed mischievously. "If he's Mama Bear, does that make Rael Goldilocks?"

"Shut up, Crank," Roadkill said loudly.

"No, come on. It's perfect. I mean, look at all that blond hair. I'm right, aren't I?" Crank looked at them for agreement.

"*Shut up, Crank!*" Roadkill and Horvan shouted in unison.

Crank pouted. "Geez, you guys are no fun."

Rael had to disagree. And right then, this was just what he needed to distract him from thoughts of Dellan.

No easy task.

We're going to do this. Hashtag's on the case, and God willing, we'll get everything organized ASAP. Dellan's going to be all right. He's got to be all right.

CHAPTER ELEVEN

HASHTAG CAME out of the bedroom, looking tired. "What day is it?" he joked.

"Sunday. Except Sunday is almost over." Horvan peered at him. "You haven't stopped all day."

Hashtag scrubbed a hand over his face. "I couldn't. I kept thinking of what else they could do to Dellan, and that made me even more determined to sort this out." He walked over to the couch and flopped onto it. "Where are Roadkill and Crank?" Then he held up a hand. "Stupid question. Smoke break. I could do with one myself. I'll wait till they're back inside. I have stuff to tell you all."

"That sounds promising."

Hashtag covered his mouth as he yawned. "Sorry. I'm bushed." He glanced around expectantly. "Anything to eat?"

Rael got up from the couch and headed for the kitchen. "I'll find you something."

Hashtag gave a contented smile. "I like him."

Horvan chuckled. "Because he's feeding you?"

"Nah, it's because he's an okay guy. Whoever picked him certainly knew you. He's a good fit." Hashtag gave another smile. "Hard to imagine a few days ago, I was blissfully ignorant that shifters even existed, let alone that there was such a thing as fated mates." He peered at Horvan. "That is how you'd describe it? Someone destined to be with you?"

Horvan nodded. "And I was as ignorant as you, until he turned up on my doorstep." At that moment, the front door opened and the guys came in, shivering. "A little cold out there?"

Crank gave an exaggerated shudder. "I suppose I'd better not complain, seeing as it's gonna be worse in Idaho. Whenever we get there."

"That would be early to midday Thursday, by my estimate," Hashtag announced.

There was a brief silence as all eyes focused on him. Rael stood in the archway, a bowl of popcorn in one hand and a bag of chips in the other. "What?"

Hashtag nodded. "We're on for Wednesday."

"You got it all organized that fast?" Horvan was impressed.

"And we have the video of Dellan pacing up and down in his cage to thank for that." Hashtag ran his hand over his closely cropped hair. "These animal rights people get seriously wound up about this shit. Not to mention there are a ton of them out there. As soon as I shared the video clip, it started getting a lot of attention. I even got to talk to activists on the phone." He sagged against the seat cushions. "It's happening, guys."

Horvan leaned over and gripped Hashtag's shoulder. "*You* made it happen, dude."

Hashtag gave a modest shrug. "It's what I do, right?"

"Can you be ready with the tech by then?" Roadkill asked, sitting on the floor by the coffee table and helping himself to a huge handful of popcorn from the bowl Rael had placed there.

Hashtag lurched forward and grabbed the bowl, hugging it to his chest. "Mine. I've earned it. And yeah, I'm ready to rock 'n' roll. I've recorded their video feed, making sure it shows only Dellan. Then I'll make it into a loop. I hack into their surveillance system, and bingo, they see what we want them to see."

"And you're sure you can do that remotely?" Horvan inquired.

Hashtag smirked. "I'll ignore that note of doubt. After all, you have your skills, I have mine."

Horvan grinned. "Yes, I remember being on the receiving end of those skills. That thing you did with your tongue? Awesome." Then he noticed Rael's incredulous expression. "Oops."

Rael put his hands on his hips. "Was *every* guy you served with gay?"

"Hey!" Crank yelled indignantly. "Straight guy here. I date girls, remember? Leave me outta this."

"The lady doth protest too much, methinks," Roadkill said with a wink. That earned him a growl from Crank.

Horvan chuckled. "Who said they were all gay? Some had to find out if my rep was true. And they were never dissatisfied," he added with a hint of pride.

Rael folded his arms, his jaw set, his blue eyes flinty.

"Aw, honey, that was in the past. I'm a changed man, remember?" Horvan pleaded. "You *know* there's only gonna be you and Dellan from now on, right?"

Crank cackled. "Now I've seen it all. Horvan metaphorically on his knees to another guy. That's what I call being truly pussy whipped." He did a series of bows to Rael. "King of beasts. The master." He snuck a peek at Horvan. "Someone's in the bearhouse," he sang.

Horvan had the sinking feeling he was really in trouble, until Rael's lips twitched and his eyes sparkled with humor. Horvan gave a low growl. "You little shit."

"When you've quite finished," Hashtag interjected, staring pointedly at Horvan and Crank. "Can we get back to this mission? Because there are things we need to discuss."

Horvan slipped back into work mode. "Go for it." He sat on the arm of the couch and gestured for Rael to join him.

"I've got a plan for once we're safely on the ground," Hashtag told them. "Eight or so of my contacts will post on social media, at a given signal from me, that *they* have the tiger, and he's being taken to an animal sanctuary. Now, these are going to be from legitimate animal rights groups, and all posted from around the Chicago area."

"Eight different groups are gonna claim responsibility for taking Dellan?" Crank beamed. "Genius."

Hashtag gave a half bow. "I thank you. Now for details of the day. Early start, boys. This all kicks off at 7:00 a.m."

"Why at that time?" Roadkill asked. "Why not at night? Surely there'll be fewer people around at night. We're talking a skeleton crew compared with possibly hundreds of people going to work."

"Actually? I'm counting on the crowd. The ensuing chaos could work to our advantage. Besides, why have the protesters turn up at night? There'll be no one around to see them protest, and that is sort of the point, right?" Hashtag helped himself to a mouthful of popcorn before continuing. "I'll be in the chopper on my laptop, monitoring the action in the lobby. We'll have Jase and Finn on the ground, keeping things moving with the protesters. Horvan, Roadkill, and Rael will go in with them, then make their way up to the top floor. You'll give Crank the go-ahead to land on the roof. Once he's down, we'll have to move fast."

"Question." Roadkill cocked his head to one side. "This all works on the assumption that Rael will be able to communicate with Dellan. What if he can't?" He gave Rael an apologetic glance. "Sorry, but we have to be prepared for all eventualities. And you said it yourself—you couldn't get through to him."

"It's okay," Rael said resignedly. "I've been thinking the same thing myself."

"Why is no one asking if *I* can get through to Dellan?" Horvan's chest tightened. "He's my mate too, remember?"

There was an uncomfortable silence.

Roadkill cleared his throat. "In all probability, you will. After all, you and Rael have that link, right? So there's every reason to expect you and Dellan will have it too. But... Dellan has never met you. He's met Rael. Twice. They've communicated. So we've got a much better chance of letting Rael try first." Roadkill peered intently at Horvan. "Okay?"

Roadkill was right, of course. Horvan nodded. He glanced at Hashtag. "You got a plan?"

He nodded. "Though you might not like part of it. Worst-case scenario—we have a wild cat on our hands, and we're breaking into his cage. We'll have to sedate him."

"And how do you propose to do that?" Rael was so still.

Hashtag sighed. "By shooting him with a tranquilizer dart. Then when he's out, we get him into a sling that we can carry out of there with poles balanced on our shoulders."

"A sling... up a flight of stairs and onto the roof?" Crank pressed his lips together, his face tightening.

"Like I said, worst-case scenario. And if it comes to that, we just do the best we can. They won't see us on the top floor. And I'll disable what alarms I can. I'll also be able to see what you see via your cameras."

"How fast are we talking? From landing to taking off?" Rael demanded.

Hashtag's brow creased. "This is where it gets tricky. If we have to use a tranquilizer dart, that could alter things. For one, we don't know how long it will take to put Dellan out. That's why we'd have to wait until he's out before signaling to Crank."

"And the longer that takes, the more likely the police will interrupt us," Horvan added.

Hashtag nodded. "That's why we need the crowds. The more the merrier. And speaking of the dart... we're gonna need some help on that one. I sent a message to Doc Tranter. He's calling me tomorrow night."

"Why? He's a doctor, not a vet," Crank remarked.

"Sure, but he's also a shifter, remember?"

Crank shook his head. "Yeah, I keep forgetting that part. The doc... whoa."

"And he'll be able to tell us what we need to know," Hashtag announced. "I've already given him a heads-up as to why we need him. I figured that way he'd have the information at his fingertips." Hashtag met Horvan's gaze. "What's your estimate on the mission time?"

"We'd better signal Crank when we have Dellan ready to go. If it takes us more than ten minutes, we could be screwed. Because someone will spot the chopper."

Hashtag nodded in agreement. "That sounds about right." He looked Rael up and down. "First thing tomorrow morning, you'll need to go shopping."

Rael frowned. "For what, exactly?"

Hashtag's eyes twinkled. "Well, unless you came here prepared with clothing suitable for a military operation...."

Rael blinked, then glanced at Horvan. "Looks like I'm going shopping."

"I'll come with you," Horvan told him. Rael gave him a grateful smile, and Horvan knew all was well between them.

"Yeah, good idea. We don't want you coming back with something that makes you stand out in a crowd," Crank said with a grin. "You know, like a little black sequined number?"

"Gee, I didn't even think about *that*." Rael rolled his eyes. "What do you take me for?"

Roadkill guffawed. "Watch out, Crank. The kitty has claws too."

Crank widened his eyes. "Hey, remember that op we did where Horvan drew the short straw and had to put on that miniskirt?" He cackled.

Hashtag broke out laughing. "Remember his legs?"

"Legs nothing," Horvan growled. "The head and at least two inches of dick fell out when the tape job went tits-up."

"Oh my God." Rael's jaw dropped. "Tell me there are pictures."

Hashtag opened his mouth to say something, but Horvan cut him off. "Remember, I'm a meat eater."

That earned him a tilt of Hashtag's head. "Yeah, so?"

Horvan speared him with a look. "You're meat."

There was a moment of silence before everyone burst into laughter. Hashtag gave a shiver. "Teddy bear my ass." He reached over and squeezed Rael's shoulder. "You know we're all praying that you can get through to Dellan, right? Because if we can get him to come with us, climb the stairs to the roof, and get onto the chopper, it'll make things simpler. But that all balances on one thing—your rapport with him."

Rael nodded slowly.

Horvan was aware of the waves of stress coming from him. He needed some alone time with his mate. "Is that it?" he asked Hashtag.

"For now. Once we've talked to the doc, we'll know what to get for the tranquilizer gun and hopefully where to get it. Later we'll make a start on the placards. Roadkill can do the printing," Hashtag said firmly.

"Hey, I can do that too," Crank protested.

"Roadkill can do the printing," Hashtag repeated, his tone even firmer.

Crank stuck out his chin and grumbled, muttering.

"I have a question," Rael said suddenly. "How do you intend to get us into the office? There are no locks that I could see. That secretary opened a panel with a remote."

"If cleaners can get in, so can we. I'll bet the security guards have a remote." Hashtag smiled confidently. "With the mayhem *we're* going to create, it should be easy to get hold of one."

Horvan glanced around. "Any more questions?" Everyone shook their heads. "In that case, I'm going to bed." He got up off the arm of the couch and held out his hand to Rael. "Correction—*we're* going to bed." Rael nodded, took his hand, and Horvan hauled him to his feet. "See you in the morning, guys."

They left the room to a chorus of good-nights. As he closed the bedroom door behind him, Horvan chuckled.

"They're improving. We didn't get a series of catcalls about keeping the noise down or not doing anything they wouldn't do."

Rael bit his lip. "Ah. Yes. That's my fault." When Horvan gave him an inquiring glance, Rael sighed. "I… sort of told them we're not having sex."

Horvan stilled. "O-*kay*. I'm assuming you had your reasons."

"They asked," Rael said with a shrug.

When nothing else was forthcoming, Horvan sighed. "I'm never gonna hear the end of this." He pulled Rael into his arms. "It's okay. All I want to do right now is climb into bed with you and snuggle until we fall asleep."

Rael's face lit up. "That sounds perfect."

They got undressed in silence, slipped beneath the sheets, and Horvan curled around Rael's body, inhaling his scent.

"Horvan?"

"Hmm?"

"Can I ask you something?"

"Sure. Just don't blame me if I fall asleep midanswer." Now that he was in bed, fatigue had really set in.

"It's about what you said in there... about Hashtag having skills... with his tongue?"

Shit. Horvan should have known Rael wasn't going to brush it aside that easily. "Okay," he said after a moment. "We've exchanged a couple blow jobs in the past—and I'm gonna repeat that part—in the *past*. He's not into guys, I'm not into him. It was...."

"Just sex?"

"Yeah." Before he could say another word, Rael placed his hand over Horvan's heart.

"It's okay, honest. Hell, I'm no saint. I have a past too. Just... making sure it's not going to happen again."

Rael might have made those last words sound like a statement, but Horvan didn't miss the catch in his voice. He rolled on top of Rael, pinning him to the mattress. Rael's breathing quickened.

"No one but you, sweetheart. You and Dellan, from now on." Fuck, Rael felt good. Horvan undulated his body, his own heartbeat speeding up when Rael responded, his hands on Horvan's back, his dick hardening against Horvan's belly.

"Fuck... we said we...." Rael moaned softly, and Horvan nuzzled into his neck, losing himself in Rael's scent, the feel of warm skin, a lean body, and the hard heat that Horvan longed to take into his mouth.

Fuck, Horvan, I want that too, but we can't....

Then Horvan stilled when an image flitted through his mind. Dellan in his cage, pacing.

Waiting.

With a supreme effort, he rolled off Rael, curled around his back, and wrapped his arms around Rael's waist. "I'm sorry," he whispered.

"Nothing to apologize for," Rael replied instantly. He covered Horvan's hands with his own. "In fact... it gives me something to look forward to."

Horvan kissed his shoulder. *You and me both.* His thoughts returned to Dellan.

It is going to work, isn't it? We can pull this off?

99

If Horvan believed in anything, it was his friends. *Yeah. We can do this.*

They had to. Three lives were depending on it.

THEY WALKED slowly along Nineteenth Street, heading for home, carrying their purchases. Rael had been quiet for the last fifteen minutes, and Horvan had caught quick flashes of thought, nothing more.

"You're trying to shield your mind from me, aren't you?"

Rael jerked his head in Horvan's direction. "How do you know?"

He chuckled. "Because it's the only explanation for why I haven't been able to read your thoughts." Horvan couldn't deny feeling a little hurt that Rael would want to do that, but he could understand it. Although the mind link had been a shock initially, Horvan had quickly adjusted to this proof that he and Rael were mates.

"It's not easy," Rael admitted. "In fact, it feels… wrong." He put his hand on Horvan's arm. "And yes, I can feel your hurt. I'm sorry."

He didn't need to apologize out loud. Horvan could almost feel the knots in Rael's belly, the heaviness in his chest. "Want to tell me what you were trying so hard not to share?" Horvan already had a theory about that. When Rael didn't reply, he pressed ahead. "Have you had any more dreams?"

Rael's sharp intake of breath was answer enough to tell him he'd nailed it. "No. And that scares me."

"Have you tried reaching out to Dellan?" Horvan asked gently.

"Yeah. I can't reach him. That's what is haunting me—what if we rescue him and it's too late? What do we do if he's forgotten what it means to be human, or worse, if he's forgotten how to shift back?"

Horvan had been plagued by the same fear. "We'll get him out, and then we'll get help for him. Shifter help. Plus we'll have space so he can go outside, within reason. We don't really want too many people to see him. I don't think they'd buy the explanation that he's a pet."

"So we just… wait?"

Horvan shook his head. "We work with him to remind him what being human is."

Rael said nothing for a moment. Then he announced, "We'll need a car. We can't drive around Salmon in an RV. It'll be too conspicuous."

Horvan agreed. "When we pick up the motor home in Gary, Roadkill will transfer to a car. He'll be right behind us."

Rael stared at him. "You're not planning on driving the whole way on your own, are you?"

Horvan laughed. "No, sweetheart. We'll take it in turns so some can grab a few hours' sleep. Like I said, it'll take at least a day to reach Salmon."

Rael's breathing became more even. "Okay. I spoke to the owner of the cabin this morning. He wants to meet me there Thursday to explain things. Not that there'll be a lot to explain, I imagine. 'Here's the kitchen, here are the beds, don't block the toilets, put out the trash.'" Rael grinned. "Or not, depending on whether there are any bears around."

"Funny." Horvan liked that Rael had relaxed a little. "We'll be waiting to move in as soon as you give the word." A thought occurred to him. "This latest assignment of yours… the article you're writing… who is it for, and when do they expect to see it?"

"It's for *The Economist*, and the deadline is in three months' time. So no need to panic yet." Rael drew in a long breath. "Hopefully by then my life will be looking a little more normal."

Horvan leaned in and said in a low voice, "I hate to break this to you, but with two mates—and not forgetting the people I work with—your life will never be normal."

Rael gave a shaky laugh. "Yeah, you're right."

They reached the steps down to Horvan's apartment. Before he opened the door, he turned to Rael. "Try not to be scared, okay?" Rael nodded. Horvan pulled him into a hug. "I can't wait to hold him, you know?" he whispered. "Even as a tiger."

Rael turned his face up to look at him, his eyes shining. "In my dream, his fur was so soft." His gaze flickered to the keys in Horvan's hand. "Let's get inside. It's cold out here."

"And besides, Roadkill is cooking lunch for us."

Rael frowned. "*Can* he cook?"

Horvan grinned. "You're about to find out why we *really* call him Roadkill."

"Okay, who am I talking to?" Doc Tranter's voice came through the speaker.

"Hey, Doc. Horvan Kojik here. I'm with Crank, Roadkill, and Hashtag. Plus another." That explanation could wait.

"And you want to talk about sedating a tiger that you're going to rescue." The doc's tone was dry. "This doesn't sound like one of your usual exploits. Okay. What do you need to know?"

Horvan gave Hashtag a nod.

"Doc? Hashtag here. First thing… how long would it take to sedate a tiger enough for it to be handled?"

"If the purpose is to do it with as little risk to the tiger as possible, then you'll need to use the least amount of sedative possible. With a tiger, that could take up to a half hour."

"And how much would that be?"

"The sedative is like general anesthetic. It's a mix, and it works the same way as heroin. Too much, and the animal overdoses. Too little, and it may get just sleepy enough for you to get within biting range. You have to get the balance right. What does the tiger weigh?"

Hashtag peered at Rael's notes. "We estimate about four hundred fifty pounds, maybe less."

"Doc?" Horvan interrupted. "I should say at this point that the tranquilizer dart is a last resort. We're hoping to get the tiger out without it."

Silence.

"Doc?"

"May I ask how you plan on doing that? What are you going to do—ask it nicely?" The doctor chuckled.

"Well, that's kinda the plan." Hashtag cleared his throat. "We're hoping the tiger's… mate can communicate with him."

More silence.

"It's okay, Doc. You're among friends," Horvan told him.

Doc Tranter coughed. "When you say mate... you're not talking about the British variety, are you?"

Horvan laughed softly. "No, Doc. In fact, this tiger has two mates. And you're talking to one of them." His heartbeat sped up.

"Dear Lord." A pause. "Where are you planning on taking it— him? Once you've got him out?"

Horvan chuckled. "Relax, Doc. You'll get to meet him. Roadkill will fetch you once he's safe. Be ready to move after Thursday."

"Oh, I most certainly will. I'll email Hashtag with the dart requirements and where to procure them. And then I'll pray you won't need them. Men? I wish you every success with your mission. You'll be in my prayers." The call disconnected.

"I think we gave Doc Tranter a slight heart attack," Roadkill murmured.

"There we have it," Hashtag said at last. "If we have to sedate Dellan, we could be talking half an hour before we can call for the chopper."

"Not a good situation to be in," Horvan had to admit. "Your idea of crowds looks like the best bet."

Anything to cause pandemonium and buy them more time. Because they were going to need every minute.

CHAPTER TWELVE

"CHRIST, CRANK, put some clothes on," Horvan muttered as he entered the living room the following morning. "You're making the place look untidy."

"Fuck you," Crank replied good-naturedly before helping himself to more coffee. "You said, 'Make yourselves comfortable.' Well, this is me, comfortable." He swung his dick from side to side, slapping it against his upper thighs.

Horvan had more important things on his mind. "Where's Hashtag? Has he gone someplace?" Hashtag had made no mention the previous night of not being around, which was kind of surprising the day before a mission. He was usually up with the birds, checking equipment over and over.

"Beats me," Roadkill replied with a shrug, his eyes focused on his phone. "He was gone when I woke up, and that was at six." He peeked at Horvan. "Speaking of which… what time do you call this? It's eight o'clock already. I was beginning to think you two were planning on staying in bed all day." He smirked. "Some of us have already had breakfast."

"Wherever Hashtag is, he apparently doesn't need his laptop." Crank pointed to it on the coffee table.

One look at Rael's face was enough to tell Horvan his mate was concerned by Hashtag's absence. Horvan stroked down his back. "Don't stress. He'll be back. And in the meantime, we have plenty of jobs to be getting on with. You can help Roadkill assemble the headgear."

Roadkill smiled. "Yeah, that'd be great. Me and my fat fingers can use all the help we can get." He put down his phone.

"Have we run out of coffee?" Crank ran one hand over his buzz cut while scratching his ball sac with the other. "'Cause it's flowing like mud around here."

Horvan rolled his eyes. "I'll make some more, Your Majesty, while you put some clothes on. Some of us have delicate stomachs, and the sight of your dick swinging around first thing in the morning is more than we can take."

Crank grinned, grabbed his cock, and waved it at Horvan before reaching into his bag for a pair of sweats and a hoodie.

Horvan went into the kitchen area, Rael close behind.

"Where do you think he's gone? I thought we had all the equipment."

Horvan cupped Rael's face. "Whatever he's doing, you can bet it's for the mission. And probably important. We'll find out when he gets back, okay?" He noted the dark smudges under Rael's eyes. "You're not sleeping well."

"How can I? I close my eyes, and all I can see is Dellan." Even Rael's voice sounded exhausted.

Horvan pulled him closer until Rael's face was buried in his neck. Horvan stroked his unruly hair. "Tomorrow morning, sweetheart. Twenty-four hours from now, we'll have him out of there." Barring any unforeseen circumstances, and Horvan was praying there were none. He gently lifted Rael's chin with his fingers and looked into those tired blue eyes. "Next time you can't sleep, wake me."

"Why, so we can be insomniacs together?" The flicker of a smile lifted Horvan's spirits a little.

He chuckled. "No, so I can hold you, rub your back, do anything to help you get back to sleep." He inclined his head toward the living room. "Now go grab the mugs, and we'll see if we can top up Crank's caffeine levels."

Rael nodded and disengaged himself from Horvan's embrace. Horvan waited until he was out of sight before leaning against the countertop.

Where are you, Hashtag?

Too late, he remembered his and Rael's link.

105

So I'm not the only one worrying, huh?

Horvan had to smile. *Christmas is gonna be a bitch. I can see it now. How the hell am I supposed to surprise you when you can see every damn thing in my mind?*

Rael's response was swift. He laughed.

"That doesn't help!" Horvan yelled. It didn't stop him smiling, though.

By MIDDAY, the living room floor was a picture of ordered chaos. The tranquilizer gun and the small box containing the sedatives sat there, along with the assembled headgear, each with an earpiece and tiny camera. The poles for carrying the sling—if required—were made up of small sections that could be screwed together, enabling them to fit inside a bag. The sling was folded up neatly and stuffed into the bag, along with the poles. Horvan had no idea where Roadkill had found it, but it was perfect for the job. Now all he had to do was hope they didn't need it.

Roadkill was on his laptop, checking the details for picking up the motor home in Gary. Their friend Danno knew where to collect it and have it waiting for them. The plan was to land the chopper in Wheeler, just off the 130. There was a flying club in the vicinity, so a helicopter wouldn't be an uncommon sight. Roadkill had picked a spot away from buildings, isolated enough not to attract attention. He'd arranged for another buddy, Wes, to have a car ready for them at the rendezvous point. Roadkill would drive that.

Horvan knew he could rely on his team. The guys worked well together, and he'd trust them with his life.

Now he was trusting them with his mates' lives too.

"You got the route all worked out?" Horvan asked Roadkill.

He laughed. "Ever the overachiever, I've worked out two. The longer, more circuitous route takes about twenty-seven hours and the shortest, twenty-four hours, door to door. I'm thinking the longer route, simply because we have the time and we're not in any hurry. But seeing as there'll be five guys to share the driving, we can pretty much travel nonstop. I'll schedule breaks along the way so we can swap between the motor home and the car. We can take turns to grab some shut-eye." He smiled. "Of course, I've never traveled this far with a tiger before."

"I'm going to spend as much time as possible at his side," Rael said quietly. "Hopefully that will keep him calm."

Roadkill sighed. "So we're not expecting him to shift back anytime soon?"

Horvan had no clue. "That's why we're sending you to pick up the doc as soon as we're settled in the cabin. Hopefully he might have an idea." He'd been thinking about the motor home. "We'll need fishing rods, rifles, anything that makes it look like we're just a group of guys going on vacation together."

Roadkill chuckled. "Then you'd better hope no one wants to take a peek inside. Because unless we cover him up, Dellan will have to do a great impression of a tiger-skin rug."

The doorbell rang, and Horvan went to answer it. Hashtag stood there in a pair of gray overalls, complete with name tag. He grinned. "Lord, I need a coffee." He pushed inside past Horvan, who followed him into the apartment.

"Where have you been?" Horvan demanded. "And why didn't you tell us you were going someplace?"

"Didn't you get my text?" Hashtag scowled. "Stupid fucking phone. That's it, into the trash it goes."

"When you've finished planning your phone's demise," Roadkill said, handing him a mug of coffee, "maybe you can tell us why you're dressed like a janitor." He peered at the name tag. "Well, I'll be...." Roadkill laughed. "Have you been moonlighting as a *cleaner*?"

"Hey, this was a great plan. No one looks twice at a cleaner. And I got to stick my nose in a lotta places." Hashtag's eyes glinted. "Plus I got hold of one of these." He fished in his breast pocket and removed a plastic card. "That'll get us into most places." He shook his head. "These fuckers are so arrogant. It's like they assume no one would even think of breaking in. I mean it. The security is lousy."

"What do you mean?" Rael asked.

K.C. WELLS

"You know that glass door you went through on the top floor? There's a remote for it hanging on the wall at the end of the hallway."

"But someone might have seen you there," Crank remarked.

Hashtag snorted. "I was the only one around at that time, trust me. That's why I went there early. I figured I'd be able to see what I wanted without fear of being disturbed." He sank onto the couch and took a long drink from his mug. "Mind you, I had to actually clean shit, in case I got spotted by a camera." He met Horvan's gaze and rolled his eyes. "Honestly. Whoever does their security is begging to be taken out and shot." His stomach growled, and Hashtag glared at Horvan. "What does a guy have to do to get fed around here? I just worked a shift. Feed me."

Horvan laughed. "You got it." He went into the kitchen, opened the refrigerator, and scanned its contents for something he could prepare quickly.

Rael appeared at his side. "Why does Hashtag sound so disappointed?"

"Because he thinks this setup is beneath his skills. The jobs we do? They're usually a lot more… interesting."

Rael snorted. "So rescuing a 440-pound tiger doesn't count as exciting?"

"Meh." Hashtag stood in the archway, waggling his hand. "Try getting someone out who has a hundred armed guards and being told you can't kill anyone because it would spark an international incident. *That* job was fun."

Rael's lips twitched. "I suppose that would depend on your definition of fun."

Horvan thrust a packet of cheese, another of ham, and a stick of butter at Hashtag. "There's bread in the cabinet. Feed yourself." He smiled broadly. "You could make sandwiches for all of us if you feel so inclined. It's almost lunchtime, after all."

Hashtag's scowl was response enough.

Roadkill came into the kitchen. "After lunch, Crank and I will go shopping for groceries for the trip. That way, our stops can be

108

as brief as possible. Besides, we don't want Crank running out of munchies, right? He's gotta have his chips."

"You forgot to mention your sodas," Crank yelled from the living area. "Heaven forbid we run out of soda. You might have to drink water."

"And meat for Dellan," Rael reminded them. "Don't forget that. Enough to keep him going."

"Enough to keep a full-grown tiger going? And how much is that, exactly?" Crank asked.

"Maybe as many barbecue joints as you can find, okay?" Rael's gaze flickered to Horvan. "Assuming he's eating properly."

Horvan said nothing. Instead he tried to project calmness, concentrating on sending it in a slow wave toward Rael, picturing it in his head. When Rael's shoulders lost a little of their rigidity and he breathed easier, Horvan knew his first attempt had been successful.

That felt really good. Rael regarded him warmly. *Thank you for that. I didn't even know we could do such a thing.*

Horvan smiled. *Neither did I.*

HORVAN HAD no idea what had woken him, but his heart was pounding, and his upper body was covered in a light sweat. His chest was tight and his breathing constricted.

"What is it?" Rael was awake mere seconds later, reaching for Horvan. "You're agitated. What's wrong?"

"Fucked if I know." Horvan didn't think he'd been dreaming. At least he couldn't recall any details, just a feeling of dread that pervaded his whole body.

Rael switched on the lamp. "Is it Dellan?" His eyes were huge.

Horvan frowned, doing his best to force calm into his mind and body. "I don't see how. He doesn't even know about me, does he?"

Not yet.

Rael threw off the covers and climbed out of bed.

Where are you going? Horvan asked as Rael opened the door.

To grab the laptop.

109

Horvan saw little use in preventing him. He knew Rael would only relax once he'd seen Dellan for himself. Rael crept back into the room with the laptop and got into the bed next to him. He opened it up and logged in. After so many days of checking on Dellan, he clearly knew the log-in details by heart.

Maybe I'm just wound up before the mission. Horvan got like that sometimes, especially when the stakes were high. So it was understandable in the circumstances.

The stakes had never been higher.

When he heard Rael's sharp intake of breath, Horvan knew it had been more than before-mission nerves that had awoken him. "Show me."

Rael turned the laptop toward him, and Horvan groaned inwardly. There was a jaguar in Dellan's cage, and the two predators were mating. The two guys from the earlier encounter were there, standing by the cage door. But what drew Horvan's attention was the man standing beside the cage, watching the proceedings and smiling.

It was not a nice smile.

"Who is that?" Horvan asked quietly, except he had a sinking feeling he already knew.

"*That* is Anson Prescott." Rael sounded numb.

Which opened up a whole new can of worms.

"Does he know that's Dellan? Because if he does, it looks like he's in on whatever is going on." Like there'd been much doubt in Horvan's mind.

"That bastard. I want to shift and tear that smile off his face." Rael's voice was grim.

"I promise you, if I ever get my hands on him, I'll do more than that." Horvan's tone was equally grim. Once they'd gotten Dellan out, Horvan was going to pay Anson Prescott a little visit.

"I may not be able to read what you're thinking right now," Rael murmured, "but I sense how you're feeling." He shivered.

On the screen, the men they'd seen previously opened the cage door, and the jaguar strolled out. Seconds later, a tall dark-haired woman stood in its place, showing none of the fear they'd witnessed from the female tiger shifter. Her hair was short, closely cropped. She was calm but clearly exhausted. However, even via the monitor's grainy image, the loathing in the looks she directed at the men was all too obvious. She stepped into the one-piece garment they held out for her and zipped it up before they led her away.

Anson remained by the cage, staring at Dellan. Horvan could see his lips moving, and wondered what the hell he was saying. Finally, Anson walked away, and Dellan was left in peace, licking his fur.

"Why bring him a jaguar?" Rael placed his hand on the screen as if caressing Dellan's image.

"Maybe they're just keeping him sated." This mission was raising too many questions, and Horvan hoped to God they could find the answers. If not, that was yet another reason for paying Anson a visit. By the time Horvan was finished with him, he'd be singing like a canary.

Gently, he closed the laptop. "Well, that's the last time they get to do that," he said firmly. He placed it on the nightstand before lying down and holding his arm wide. "Now come here."

"Shouldn't we tell the others?"

Horvan shook his head. "Let them sleep. We can tell them in the morning." Then he chuckled. "Later in the morning."

Rael nodded, then did as instructed, snuggling up to Horvan's side, his head on Horvan's shoulder, his right leg hooked over Horvan's, Rael's hand on his waist. His distress was obvious. Horvan concentrated once again on sending out pulses of calm, willing his mate to relax. Eventually, Rael's breathing grew more even.

"You sound so confident," he murmured against Horvan's chest.

"That's because I am. We're going to do this. And you need to be confident too." Horvan stretched out his arm to switch off the lamp, then covered Rael's hand with his. "Sleep, sweetheart. We're up in a few hours, remember? We need to be rested and alert."

"How can I sleep? I'm not tired." Then Rael yawned, and Horvan had to smile.

"Yeah, sounds like it." Horvan made his breaths slow and even, knowing Rael's would synchronize with his. Sure enough, it wasn't long before they were in sync.

He closed his eyes and waited for sleep to take him. He needed to rest.

They had a mission to carry out, and despite his earlier words, none had ever been more important to Horvan or, he guessed, to his team.

CHAPTER THIRTEEN

EVEN FROM fifty feet away, the sight of the crowds gathered outside the Global Bio-Tech building as they approached sent Rael's heartbeat racing. "There must be hundreds of people," he said in an awed tone. Hashtag had done them proud.

In his ear, Hashtag chuckled. "More like a thousand. Seven a.m. and I've brought the street to a standstill. Can I cook, or what?"

Already the sidewalk in front of the building was filled to overflowing, with yet more people hurrying to join in. Banners had been placed against the glass frontage, stark white with the words Free the Tiger in bold red letters. There were even hastily made signs with Tony the Tiger's picture, each with the words Tigers are Greeeat! Traffic had come to a halt as drivers stopped to watch the commotion. The noise level was incredible as the protesters shouted and booed, accompanied by frequent blasts from air horns responding to a guy with a megaphone who was doing a fantastic job of stirring up the crowd. When the car horns joined in, the volume climbed.

"That's Jase," Horvan remarked. "He's one of my team. And the tall guy with him is Finn."

"They're about to crash the main door," Hashtag told them. "Get through the crowd and move to the front."

Horvan led Roadkill and Rael to the edge of the burgeoning throng, and they began to weave their way through the mob, who were chanting, "Set it free! Set it free!" Rael's heart was hammering, and adrenaline coursed through his body. Little by little, they inched toward the entrance, and as they reached it, the door gave way under the pressure of so many bodies. On the other side of the glass, Rael saw the two security guards on their walkie-talkies, obviously panicking.

The crowd surged through the gap, spilling into the wide entrance hall, cheering and yelling. Rael was nearly carried away on the wave of bodies until a strong hand gripped him by the wrist. Horvan pulled Rael over to him.

"Stay close. It's easy to get lost in this pack." He got out his phone and tapped the keys. Seconds later the volume exploded as the chanting reached fever pitch, and people began spraying the walls with red paint. A cacophony of air horns filled the hall, bouncing off the walls and echoing around.

"What did you do?" Rael was impressed.

"Told Jase to step it up a bit. Now, which elevator is it?"

Rael led them to the last elevator on the right, pushing through the hordes. The security guards were nowhere in sight, swallowed up in the thronging mass of angry protesters.

"Let's hope they haven't killed the elevators," he said.

The elevator doors slid open, and they dove inside, shutting out the noise.

Roadkill chuckled. "Nice one, Hashtag."

"Hey, at least someone here was thinking. They tried to shut them down, but we couldn't have that, could we? We're standing by, H. Good luck, guys. As fast as you can, okay? The police will be on their way by now."

Rael's heart was pounding as they sped to the top floor, and his hands were clammy. The doors slid open and there was the glass wall of the office. Roadkill scanned the hallway and grabbed the remote.

"Just like he said. Fucking arrogant. They deserve to be broken into." He aimed it at the wall, and the panel slid open.

Rael raced along the hallway to the next door. "This opens with a card."

Roadkill fished out the key card Hashtag had procured and slid it through. He scowled. "Fuck. It doesn't open this one. Okay, gimme a sec." He knelt in front of it, pulled a screwdriver from his bag, and began removing the panel.

"The video loop is in play?" Horvan asked Hashtag.

"Affirmative. And I've taken out the camera that would have picked up you guys. Roadkill, you got this?"

"I got it." Roadkill threw the panel aside and connected a device to it. "Any… second… now!" Four beeps sounded, and the door opened. "Bingo."

Rael was through it in a heartbeat, Horvan and Roadkill close behind. He ran over to the cage, where Dellan lay on his branch, apparently asleep.

"Whoa. He's even more impressive in the flesh."

Rael barely heard Roadkill's comment. He knelt by the cage and tapped on it gently. Dellan jerked his head up, instantly awake, and got down from his branch. He strolled over to Rael, his eyes focused on Rael's face.

Dellan. Can you hear me?

Dellan gave no indication, and inside Rael's head there was silence. "I was afraid of this." Rael murmured. He got up and went to the cage door.

"What are you doing?" Horvan demanded.

Rael paused, his fingers curled around the handle as he slid back the catch, swallowing hard. "Acting on faith." He was dimly aware of Roadkill removing the tranquilizer gun from the capacious bag at his feet before moving in his direction. Ignoring him, Rael opened the cage and stepped inside, his heart beating like a drum.

Dellan's menacing roar sent ice down his back, but he didn't falter, walking slowly toward Dellan, head bowed, peering at the tiger from under his mop of hair. When he was almost within touching distance, he knelt down, his heart pounding like it was about to burst.

Dellan stilled, and Rael held his breath. Seconds later, Dellan pounced, knocking Rael to the floor on his back. Dellan landed on top of him, and Rael felt the tiger's hot breath on his face. Those teeth were sharp.

"Fuck, get out of there!" Horvan yelled, his hands on the glass.

Dellan. Dellan. It's Rael. Your mate. Remember? Rael kept repeating the words over and over inside his mind, willing Dellan to hear him. He could feel Horvan's fear and knew Roadkill had to be mere seconds away from shooting Dellan.

Suddenly Dellan licked Rael's face, and Rael laughed. "Good God, it's far worse than a house kitty's tongue." Relief flooded through him as Dellan nuzzled Rael's neck and chest. When one word filled Rael's mind, he burst into tears of sheer joy and utter relief.

Mate.

Rael reached up and stroked the thick fur around Dellan's neck. *That's right. I'm your mate.* The tears kept coming, but he didn't give a fuck. Horvan's relief was equally acute.

Dellan settled, half on top of him, licking any skin he could find. Rael twisted his head and sought Horvan. "Get in here before I drown in tiger drool." When Horvan didn't move, Rael glared. "We don't have time for hesitation. Get your butt in here."

Horvan entered the cage, and Dellan lifted his head from Rael's chest and growled, his body stiffening.

"Kneel down here. Talk to him like you talk to me through the link." Rael ignored the weight bearing down on him and concentrated on sending waves of calm over the three of them. He stroked Dellan's neck, hoping it soothed him.

Horvan knelt beside them. *Dellan? Do you know who I am?*

Dellan got to his feet, his snout inches from Horvan's face, and Rael didn't dare draw a breath. Dellan sniffed the air, then tilted his head to one side.

Mate? Then he flopped onto his back before Horvan, paws in the air.

Tears trickled down Horvan's cheeks, and he ran his fingers over Dellan's furry belly. *That's right, baby. I'm your mate.*

Rael was half laughing, half crying. "Well, I guess we know who's boss in this relationship."

Horvan wiped his eyes and chuckled. "Like there was ever any doubt."

Rael drew closer and looked into the tiger's eyes. *Dellan? We're getting you out of here.*

Dellan rolled over and stood. *Out. Out now.*

"Are we good?" Roadkill asked anxiously. "Because if so, we gotta hustle, guys."

Rael stroked Dellan's head and pointed to Roadkill. *This is a friend, okay? Not food. He's going to help you. Can you follow us out of here?*

Dellan was at the cage door and through it before anyone could utter a word. *Dellan go with mates.*

"I guess that answers *that* question." Roadkill stilled as Dellan approached him. "Hey, beautiful kitty." He kept his hands to himself, however. Dellan sniffed the tranquilizer gun and his lips curled, revealing his teeth. Roadkill hastily put it in his bag, and Dellan stopped growling.

"Crank, you copy this?" Horvan said. "It's a go. On our way to the roof."

"Affirmative. Be quick. The streets below are filled with cops."

Roadkill was on his phone, peering at the floor layout. "Okay, the stairs to the roof are through that door."

"That's Anson's office," Rael told him.

Roadkill tried the handle, then growled. "We ain't got time to be subtle." He took a few steps back, then ran at the door, hitting it with his shoulder. The door went flying, and he dashed into the room, Rael behind him with Dellan, Horvan bringing up the rear. Roadkill glanced around the room. "That door. That's it." He peered at it, then kicked it in, splintering it off its hinges. "Okay, there's two flights of stairs. Can Dellan manage that?"

Before Rael could convey that to Dellan, the tiger made a sound that was unmistakably a snort, then headed through the doorway and climbed the stairs.

"Apparently so." Rael followed, trying to keep up, Roadkill and Horvan behind him. At the top was a metal door and no sign of a lock. "Roadkill? Hashtag, you seeing this?"

"Affirmative. Roadkill, blow the door."

"Isn't that more *your* skill set?" Roadkill asked with a grin before reaching into his bag and pulling out a pale brown putty-like substance. He pressed a thin thread of it around the rim of the door, then set a fuse. "Okay, stand back."

Rael protected Dellan with his body, Horvan doing the same, both of them jolted by the explosion. Through the gaping hole, he heard the chopper, and his heart sang. *We made it.*

"We're not there yet," Horvan told him. "Let's get airborne. *Then* we can relax a little." He led them out onto the roof, where a dark olive-green helicopter was touching down, its door slid back. From the front next to Crank, Hashtag was waving them on energetically.

Heads down, they sprinted across the landing pad, Dellan in the midst of them. Roadkill clambered aboard, followed by Horvan. Dellan appeared reluctant, backing away.

Please, Dellan. You have to get on, Rael pleaded with him.

When that didn't work, Horvan gave the tiger a hard stare. *Now, Dellan. Get your furry ass up here.*

Dellan leaped into the seating area, Rael behind him. Rael and Horvan strapped themselves in. "What about Dellan?" Rael shouted.

"We hold on to him, okay? I'll take the butt end, you take the head."

Rael did as instructed, leaning forward, his arms around Dellan's neck. He had no idea if Dellan had flown before in human form, let alone as a tiger. Judging by his agitation and the low growls that escaped him, Dellan wasn't happy. Thank God it was a short flight. Rael did his best to soothe him, stroking him and keeping up a litany of calming thoughts.

"Get us out of here, Crank," Horvan shouted.

"You got it." Seconds later, the chopper lurched into the air. "Flight time is gonna be under thirty minutes. I'll radio ahead to Pickle."

Horvan got on his phone. "Jase? We're up. You and Finn get out of there—once you've shared the good news, of course." He disconnected, then ran his hand along Dellan's flank. *You're safe, Dellan. Safe.*

"Jesus! You should hear what I'm hearing," Crank yelled above the noise of the chopper. "Sounds like the end of a Beyoncé concert, all the cheering and clapping going on down there. Mind you, with the flashing lights, it looks like one too."

"When we land, send the signal to the others to post on social media," Roadkill hollered to Hashtag, who gave him the thumbs-up.

Rael wasn't even looking at the world beneath them. His only concern was Dellan. He held on tight, aware of Horvan doing his best to keep Dellan calm.

He must be so confused. First one mate, now two.

Horvan stroked Dellan's back. "He's coping better than I thought he would."

Roadkill leaned forward. "Can I touch him?"

Rael brought his mouth to Dellan's round ear. "Not food, remember?" When Dellan chuffed, Rael sighed inwardly with relief. *At least he seems to have a sense of humor.*

Roadkill blinked. "Gee. I'm glad you reminded him of that." Tentatively, he stretched out his hand and stroked Dellan's side. His eyes widened and his lips parted, but he said nothing.

It didn't seem long before the chopper touched down in the middle of a field. Rael spied the motor home and car awaiting them. *Are you hungry? We have food for you.* Dellan gave him a long lick, and Rael laughed. "That tickles."

"Everybody out," Crank yelled. "This is a quick stop. We don't want to attract attention, remember?"

They were off the chopper and sprinting toward the vehicles in a matter of minutes, the blades still turning. A short guy dressed in black greeted Crank with a firm handshake.

"You got your heading?" Crank shouted.

The guy nodded. "Now get outta here." His jaw dropped at the sight of Dellan. "Holy fuck."

"You saw nothing, all right?"

The guy held up both hands. "Hey, I wasn't even here." He climbed aboard the chopper.

Roadkill was speaking with another man beside the car, who then ran to join the chopper pilot. Roadkill got into the car after dumping his bag in the trunk. "First stop is half an hour from here, guys. You know the route. Let's haul ass."

Crank climbed into the driver's side of the motor home, and Horvan, Rael, and Hashtag got on board, once Dellan had stepped almost delicately inside. Rael led him through to the rear, where there was a queen-size bed. He covered it with a heap of blankets. Dellan jumped up, pawed at the covers for a moment, then curled up on them while Rael went looking for a bowl to fill with water.

Hashtag strapped himself into a seat, then got on his phone, his fingers flying over the keys. After a minute or so, he looked up with a grin. "That's it. Eight simultaneous posts, all claiming responsibility for snatching Dellan. Wagons roll, boys. We've got a long way to go."

Dellan raised his head from his task of lapping up water. *Where we go?*

Rael stroked his ears. *Somewhere safe.*

"Hey, Hashtag. This is some swanky RV Roadkill got us. I know I should probably have asked this before now, but where'd he get it?" Horvan asked. Rael had barely glanced at the interior; he'd been too concerned about getting Dellan settled. But now that he looked, he was impressed. It seemed well equipped, perfect for their needs.

"Found it online," Hashtag replied. "We offered cash to the seller, who was more than happy to pass it on to us. Then we wired the money to Danno, who collected it and took it into the shop. They made sure everything was in running order, then stripped off the license plates and replaced them with... borrowed ones."

Rael narrowed his gaze. "Borrowed? Why?"

Horvan joined him. "Misdirection and obfuscation. If somehow we have a picture taken, the plates will lead them back to a different vehicle. We usually have two other sets so we can change them out."

"But borrowed from where?" Rael wanted to know.

"Danno keeps up the registration on a few junkers back at the shop. That's where the plates come from. The police are less likely to keep looking if the plates don't show up in a stolen vehicle database." Horvan cupped Rael's cheek. "I know it seems like overkill, but—"

"Can't take chances. I get it." And he did. This was Dellan's life they were talking about. Even if everything around him was like living in some kind of TV show, he had absolute trust in Horvan.

Horvan gazed at Dellan in obvious wonder, and Rael smiled. "Well, now you know he doesn't bite—he just licks you to death—why don't the two of you get acquainted?" He got onto the bed beside Dellan, then beckoned Horvan closer. "Crank is driving, and we've got half an hour before the first stop, so let's spend some time with him."

Horvan returned his smile. "That sounds good." He lay on Dellan's other side, and both of them snuggled closer to Dellan, who relaxed visibly beneath their touch.

Mates.

A sigh shuddered through Rael. *That's right. Mates.* Now all they had to do was pray Dellan remembered how to shift back.

CHAPTER FOURTEEN

"UH, HORVAN?" Crank regarded him with a quizzical look. "Why are you growling?"

"What are you talking about?" Horvan brought his attention back to the road ahead. They were in southern Minnesota and making good time. Behind them, Hashtag was driving the car, and Roadkill was keeping him company. Rael had taken a nap, curled up on the bed next to Dellan. Horvan had been sorely tempted to join them, until he considered their continued combined weight might be more than the bed could stand. Besides, it was his turn to relieve Crank with the driving.

Crank chuckled. "You don't even know you're doing it, do ya? You've been making the same noise for the last hour. Is this a bear thing? You need to go find a tree to get rid of your back itch, is that it?" He snorted. "Why am I suddenly thinking of *The Jungle Book?*"

"Call me Baloo and you're dead." He focused on his driving. Crank was talking out of his ass.

"Horvan?" Rael stood beside Crank, holding on to the back of the seat. "What's wrong?"

"I thought you were sleeping."

"Yeah, well, I was until you started growling."

What the fuck? Horvan snorted. "You guys are hearing things."

Except I heard you in my head. Explain that.

Why the fuck would I be growling? The mission so far was a success, and his mates were with him.

His mates. *Fuck.* Horvan breathed in the scent pervading the RV and scowled.

"I can smell it too. My lion isn't happy, but what can we do?" Rael squeezed Horvan's shoulder.

Yeah, Rael had nailed it.

"Smell what? What the fuck are you two talking about?"

Horvan gave Crank a weary glance. "The other shifters Dellan has been with. We can smell them on him, and it's angering our beasts."

"Why? It's not like either of you is a virgin." Crank's breathing hitched. "Jesus. You're not, are you?"

Rael sighed. "No, but now the three of us know what we are to one another, it's a struggle. My lion wants to find those women and... do bad things to them."

"And by bad things, we're not talking naughty, I take it?"

Horvan admired Rael's understated rage. Horvan wanted to tear them to shreds.

Before he could respond to Crank's question, Dellan intruded. *Dellan out now. Now.*

"I'll go see what's wrong." Rael left them and headed toward the rear.

"What's up?" Crank asked.

"Dellan wants to get out of the RV." Had he awoken and panicked?

Crank snickered. "Well, sure he does. When a tiger's gotta go, he's gotta go. And he sure isn't gonna use the bathroom, right?"

Shit.

Yeah, shit. Exactly. Get Roadkill to find us someplace to stop. And how come neither of us thought of this?

Rael had a point.

"Get Roadkill on the phone," he instructed Crank. "Tell him we need to get off the road someplace isolated enough to let Dellan out of the RV. And soon, otherwise it's going to get messy in here." He snuck a glance at Crank. "And then get some sleep. Which is what you're supposed to be doing right now."

"Pfft. I'm rested enough. I'll be ready to swap with Hashtag at the next stop."

"What about me?" Rael called from the back. "When do I get to drive?"

"You don't," Crank retorted. "And before you start griping about it, you have an important job to do. Your task is to take care of Dellan, to keep him calm. There are four of us to share the driving. That's plenty."

I get what he's saying, but I'm not happy about it.

Horvan was about to remind Rael that Dellan's well-being was the focus of their mission, when Crank's phone buzzed.

"Okay, he's found us a stop, but it'll be another twenty minutes or so. Think Dellan can hold on that long?" When a low roar came from the rear of the RV, Horvan glanced at Crank, who shivered. "Christ. I'll tell Roadkill to step on it."

"Be thankful Dellan can communicate with us. If it was only a tiger, we'd probably be up to our pits in tiger poop," Horvan remarked, picking up speed, aware of the car behind them keeping up.

Crank snorted. "If it was only a tiger, you wouldn't catch me within two feet of this RV." He hollered toward the back. "Cross your legs or something, Dellan."

When another growl emanated, Horvan chuckled. "Care to translate that, Crank?" Not for the first time, he wondered what Dellan was like as a human. From their brief internal conversations, Horvan couldn't get a real handle on his personality, which was only to be expected in the circumstances.

When was the last time Dellan had been human?

By the time Roadkill indicated they should come to a stop at the edge of a forest, Dellan was pacing up and down inside the RV. Given there wasn't all that much space to pace in the first place, Crank and Rael were keeping out of his path. Horvan switched off the engine, and Rael opened the door.

Apparently, that was all the signal Dellan needed. He took a leap from the door as soon as Rael opened it and landed on the ground with a dull thud.

I'll go with him, make sure we're not spotted, Rael told Horvan.

Keep your distance, okay? Give him some private time?

There was a pause. *Yeah. Of course. Just thinking how I'd feel if you were watching me take a dump.*

Horvan chuckled. *Yeah, but we've already established you're a dainty thing, right?* He glanced at the clock on the dash. At the rate they were going, they'd be at the cabin by midday the following day.

Horvan was fine with that. As long as Roadkill was already working on future stops for Dellan. He had to smile.

A tiger's gotta go when a tiger's gotta go. Cute.

It wasn't long before Dellan was back on board the RV, and Crank was in the car's driver's seat, insisting he wanted to be on his own for a while. Horvan wasn't going to argue, but he was definitely intrigued. When Roadkill took the wheel of the RV, Horvan commented on it.

Roadkill laughed. "I know why he wants to be alone, but I ain't tellin'. He'd kill me." He flashed the indicators to tell Crank they were ready to leave. Roadkill looked over his shoulder. "Everything okay back there now?"

Rael laughed. "*Someone* is purring."

"Wait a minute." Roadkill frowned. "Okay, I'm not claiming to be an expert in these things, but I've never heard of a tiger purring. I didn't think any big cats could purr."

"They can't," Rael said simply. "House cats can purr because they have this rigid bone, the hyoid, that allows them to purr continuously. In big cats, the hyoid is flexible, meaning they can roar but not purr."

"Then how can—"

"Dellan isn't a tiger. He's a shifter. And in big-cat shifters, that bone is different. It allows them to purr, making them sound like overgrown kitties."

Roadkill smiled. "A happy kitty. This is what we want."

What Horvan wanted was Dellan whole again.

HORVAN HANDED around the sandwiches he'd made, then took a seat. Dellan was off the bed and lapping water from his bowl. Rael watched him from the bed.

Normal eating times didn't exist on this mission. They were about eighteen hours into the trip, and it was two in the morning. Horvan had gotten the munchies and had assumed the same was true of the others. Roadkill was in the car, and Crank was driving the RV.

Hashtag glanced up from his phone. "Where are we?"

"Just crossed from South Dakota into Wyoming."

Hashtag nodded before returning his attention to his phone. "Do you know how many posts there have been claiming responsibility for releasing him? Fifteen. There are groups we didn't even contact who are claiming responsibility. They have no idea how much this helps us." He grinned. "Well, it's official. No one has a fucking clue where Dellan is."

"And we'd better hope it stays that way," Horvan added.

"You said it. Especially now the FBI will be involved."

What the fuck?

Horvan glanced in Rael's direction. "Did we not mention that part? Sure, Chicago PD will be all over this, but when someone steals an endangered exotic animal, it becomes a federal investigation."

Rael gaped. "We're going to have the FBI on our tail?"

Hashtag shrugged. "Maybe. We've run interference as much as we can, but if they do decide to investigate, there's little else we can do." He gave Rael a confident smile. "Don't be worried. I'll be setting up cameras around the perimeter of the property. We'll know if someone starts taking too much interest."

"What did you mean—you've run interference?" Rael demanded.

"We have a source in the FBI," Hashtag told him. He gave Horvan a sideways glance. "What I *didn't* know until three days ago was that he's also a shifter." He chuckled. "Horvan felt it was safe to reveal that particular piece of information."

"Hey, it was a need-to-know thing," Horvan remonstrated. "Not that he can help us all that much. He can't control all aspects of an investigation." He looked past Rael to where Dellan was settling down once more on his blankets. "I bet he can't wait to get out of the RV. It must feel like exchanging one cage for another."

Rael shook his head. "At least he knows he's out of there." His gaze met Horvan's, and the anxiety in his eyes was all too obvious. "No sign yet that he can shift."

Horvan beckoned Rael, holding his arms wide. Rael gave a glance in Dellan's direction, then came over to where Horvan sat. Horvan pulled Rael into his lap, his arms enfolding him. "I know it's difficult, sweetheart. Once we're in the cabin, we'll work real hard at reminding him there's a human being in there somewhere."

Rael put his head on Horvan's shoulder. *I know. I hate this... waiting.*

"Can I ask you guys something?" Hashtag leaned forward. "You *do* know that Dellan is gay, right?"

Horvan blinked, and Rael sat up. "Well... now you mention it—" Horvan began.

"We don't know that for sure," Rael interjected.

Hashtag frowned. "Yeah, but... I mean, I don't know who decides these things—hell, I know nothing about shifters, and from the sound of it, you two only know slightly more than that—but... would they mate you with a straight guy? Is that a possibility?"

Rael seemed perplexed. "I never thought about that. I assumed he'd be gay or bi, seeing as he has two guys for mates."

"But you're gay, right?" When Rael nodded, Hashtag smirked at Horvan. "And we all know *you're* gay."

Horvan stared at him. "Actually, I'm bi."

Hashtag's mouth fell open. "You... but... have you ever slept with a woman?"

Horvan gave a shrug. "Sure, a couple times. I don't have hang-ups about who shares my bed. Sex is sex, right?" Then he became aware of Rael's hard stare and mentally gave himself a kick up the backside. "Or it was. Before I found out I had mates." Talk about backpedaling.

Judging by Rael's narrowed gaze, Horvan wasn't out of the woods yet.

"Oh." Hashtag gave a knowing smile. "I get it. So shifters are basically sluts?" His eyes glittered.

"Hey!" Rael's eyes flashed. "I haven't had sex in, like, a year."

Aww, sweetheart. I had no idea. Then it hit him. *And yet you told me to wait? Christ, you have fucking strong willpower.* As soon as Dellan was himself again, Horvan aimed to make up for the dry times.

Over and over again.

Horvan? You do know I can feel you getting hard, right?

He stroked Rael's back. *You're sitting in my lap, and I'm thinking about fucking you. Duh.*

Well, stop *thinking, because all I wanna do is grind on it, and I think Hashtag might object to that.*

Horvan chuckled inwardly. *Wouldn't be the first time he's seen me fuck someone. There was that time in—*

Shut. Up. I do not want to hear it, okay? There was a pause. *There is something I was meaning to ask. Have you... have you had many... three-ways?*

Horvan cupped Rael's cheek and gently turned his head toward him. *You haven't, have you?*

Rael shook his head. *But I've been thinking about our first time.*

Horvan grinned. *So have I.*

Rael glared at him. *Stop that. Just listen, will you? I think the first time we're... together should be different. What if we just... touch? To remind Dellan what it feels like to be held and caressed and... loved?*

Horvan's chest tightened. *I think that's a wonderful idea.*

But so we're clear... you are *gonna fuck my brains out at some point, right?*

He laughed and pulled Rael into a hug. *You know it.*

"I'm getting that feeling again." Hashtag's voice broke into their communication. "Like there's this whole other conversation taking place." When both Horvan and Rael smiled, he held up his hands. "Forget I mentioned it. I don't wanna know."

At the front of the RV, Crank was muttering, and Horvan couldn't quite catch the words. "What's up with him?"

Hashtag snickered. "Oh, he's grousing because he can't listen to his favorite music like he can in the car."

"Oh really? And what is that?"

Hashtag's eyes gleamed. "*That* is something that is gonna stay in the closet."

Rael laughed. "I may not have known Horvan all that long, but even *I* know he's not going to stop until he finds out Crank's guilty pleasures. You've set him a challenge." He stilled, glancing toward the rear. "Do you feel that?"

Cold spread through Horvan's body. "He's afraid." Only that was putting it mildly. The waves crawling off Dellan were terror, bordering on panic. Like Dellan was caught up in a nightmare.

Hashtag's eyes were compassionate. "Go be with Dellan. It sounds like he needs you. We'll sort out the driving between us at the next stop. Only ten more hours or so and we'll be there."

Horvan thanked him and got up from his seat, taking Rael with him. Dellan was lying in the nest of blankets, his paws jerking as though he was trying to run in his sleep. Horvan climbed onto the bed and stretched out at Dellan's back, stroking the soft fur. *Easy now. You're dreaming. We've got you.*

Rael was in front of him, his hands buried in Dellan's ruff. *Dellan. It's just a dream.*

Both of them stiffened at the fleeting image in their minds. An unknown man, standing above Dellan, who was clearly on the ground. Anson stood beside the stranger. It was obvious from Dellan's reaction that he feared this man.

Who is that?

Dellan's hackles rose and he growled. The hairs on Horvan's arms stood to attention, and Rael shivered.

Dellan might not have answered them, but the implication was clear.

This man was an enemy.

CHAPTER FIFTEEN

DELLAN OPENED his mouth to growl for the second time in as many minutes, and Horvan laid a gentle hand on his snout. *You have to keep quiet, baby. Just a little while longer, okay?* Rael and Hashtag had gone inside the cabin with the owner. Roadkill and Crank were unloading the fishing rods and anything else to keep up the pretense of being guys on vacation.

Dellan out.

Horvan rubbed along Dellan's back, keeping the motion soothing. *Soon. But we have to wait until that man has gone.* He lowered his face, until he was looking right into Dellan's eyes. *No one can know you're here, okay? It wouldn't be safe.*

Beneath his gentle touch, Dellan stilled, and Horvan knew he'd gotten through. Slowly he removed his hand from Dellan's snout.

Not baby. Dellan's voice was almost sullen.

Okay, that made him want to laugh out loud. *I promise, one day you won't mind me calling you that.* Dellan made that snorting sound again.

Horvan couldn't wait to meet him as a human.

Crank poked his head around the RV's door. "He's leaving," he said quietly. Then he shivered violently. "And for the record, it's fucking cold here."

"Could have something to do with all that white stuff lying around," Horvan commented dryly. "How does the place look on the inside?"

"Looks good. There's a wood stove in the corner of the living area, and it's already lit. I'll make sure we have plenty of wood inside, because I sure as shit am not going outside for it." He disappeared from view.

Horvan glanced at Dellan. "You'll have to forgive Crank. He comes from southern Florida."

Rael climbed into the RV. "Okay, he's gone."

No sooner had the words left his lips than Dellan was off the bed and heading for the door. Horvan followed. "I guess he needs to go again."

Except Dellan wasn't stopping. He was running away from the RV at speed.

"Where's he going?" Roadkill shouted from the cabin porch.

"Fucked if I know." Horvan and Rael ran after him, through snow that lay about five inches deep. The landscape was white but for a few splashes of green where snow had fallen from tree branches. Dellan was a flash of orange-and-black stripes against the stark white.

"He's heading for the river," Crank yelled.

"There's a river?" Horvan could see no sign of it.

Crank caught up with them. "Hashtag says it's on the map."

Seconds later, the sound of ice breaking reached Horvan's ears. "He's found it." He ran to where Rael was standing on the bank, watching Dellan in the water. The tiger disappeared below the surface of the ice, then reappeared again, shaking his fur.

Horvan stared at him in disbelief. "What is he doing?"

Rael shrugged. "Not sure. Tigers love the water, but not when it's so cold. Let me try asking him."

Inside Horvan's head, Rael pleaded with Dellan to get out of the water.

Not mate. Not mate.

Rael turned to Horvan. "What does he mean, not mate? It doesn't make sense."

"Ya think?" Crank rolled his eyes. "Jesus, are you that dumb? You were bitching because you could smell those women on him. You think he can't smell them himself? Or maybe feel the disgust through your link? He's probably trying to wash the scent off."

Fuck. Now that Crank said it....

Horvan stomped through the snow to the edge of the water. "Get the fuck out of there before you freeze your fur off, Dellan."

Not mate.

Horvan took a deep breath. "No, they weren't your mates, but we are."

Not mate. Dellan sounded on the verge of panic.

Rael knelt in the snow, shivering. "No, they weren't your mates," he said softly, "but you know we are. Come into the cabin and let us help you. We can give you a... bath." He looked to Horvan, an obvious plea for backup.

Horvan nodded, silently praying the tub would accommodate a full-grown tiger. "That's right. We'll wash it all off, Dellan."

Dellan stood in the river, the icy water reaching his belly. *Bath.* He made for the bank and clambered out.

"Take cover!" Rael called out to Crank, hastily retreating several feet, Horvan doing the same.

"What the fuck?" Then Crank yelled when a spray of ice-cold water showered him as Dellan shook himself violently. "Christ!"

"We did warn you." Horvan followed Dellan as he headed for the cabin. Roadkill watched their approach from the porch. "Roadkill, run a bath."

"You want a bath now? Can't it wait? We've got to unload the RV."

"For Dellan. And it's kinda urgent."

That was all it took to have Roadkill duck into the cabin.

Crank chuckled. "I don't think we have enough bubble bath for Dellan."

Horvan hoped soap would be enough to rid Dellan's fur of the scent so that he felt comfortable again. He was still kicking himself that he hadn't thought about Dellan's reaction to the shifters they'd brought to his cage. At least Horvan now understood why Dellan had immediately taken to cleaning himself once the intruders had gone.

Rael laid a gentle hand on his back. "Stop that. I didn't think of it either. What matters now is that we help him feel better, okay?"

Horvan nodded. "Once we've got supplies in from that store we passed, I'm sending Roadkill to fetch the doc."

Horvan prayed the doc would be able to help.

"YOU'RE ENJOYING this, aren't you?" Horvan rubbed a soapy hand over Dellan's back before reaching under to clean the fur around his cock. "This is what you wanted, isn't it?"

A GROWL, A ROAR, AND A PURR

Dellan stood patiently in the tub, warm water around his legs, while Horvan and Rael washed every inch of fur they could lay their hands on. The water clung to Dellan, and Horvan knew it was going to take a shitload of towels to dry him, but that was preferable to Dellan spraying the bathroom.

"I think we're done," Rael announced from Dellan's head as he poured a jug full of water over him, rinsing away any last remnants of soap. He looked into their mate's eyes. *Is that enough?*

Enough.

Roadkill stood in the bathroom doorway, his arms full of folded towels. "I think we might need to buy more, guys, if this is gonna be a regular thing."

"It's not," Rael assured him. "Not now that we've gotten rid of... them."

"Is that what Dellan's nightmare was about? Crank told me."

"No, that was something else entirely." Horvan took the towels from Roadkill and spread them over the floor. "Okay, Dellan, out you get."

Dellan stepped carefully out of the rub and onto the towels, and Rael immediately began rubbing him vigorously. As soon as a towel was saturated, he swapped it for another.

"Can I ask you a question?" Roadkill crouched low, watching the proceedings.

"Sure." Not that Horvan could stop him. Once Roadkill got something in his head, there were only two choices—help him work through it or deal with the fallout.

"Dellan's nightmare got me wondering. How much of you is in there when you shift? I mean, obviously there's some of you in there, or Dellan would've killed us all, right?"

Now *there* was a question....

Horvan thought about how best to answer. "The animal is mostly in control. Our thoughts aren't ordered and logical, most of the time." Although he *had* communicated fine with Rael the first occasion they'd both shifted in his apartment. "We act on instinct, but it's... tempered somewhat. Like, when I'm in the forest and I'm hungry,

133

I have to find something to eat. My bear wants fish, so I lumber on down to the river and snatch me some dinner. Now, in *this* form," he said, gesturing to his body, "I wouldn't eat it without deep frying it first in some batter and spices and then washing it down with a six-pack of beer, but all the bear wants is a full stomach. He doesn't care about anything beyond that."

"Our needs are simple," Rael added. "It's why when we're stressed, we head off to the woods to shift and decompress for a while."

Roadkill cocked his head to one side. "Okay… but you said it's tempered."

Horvan nodded. "A lion might see someone walking their poodle and have no qualms about snagging little Fifi off her leash, but the human part keeps that in check."

Rael was nodding too. "We know not to draw attention to ourselves, and do what we need to in order to keep our secret."

Roadkill glanced at Dellan, who was lying on the towels, licking his paws. "And when you mind-talk, or whatever you call it, with Dellan, how does he communicate? It's obviously not all that complex."

"With Dellan, no," Horvan affirmed. "See, we know we run the risk of losing ourselves if we don't shift back to human, and Dellan hasn't been human for a long time. His vocabulary is a little limited, like he's forgotten how to talk. And as for that nightmare, it wasn't so much the words he used to convey his fear, it was more his emotions that we sensed." Right then, all he was sensing from Dellan was profound relief. *You smell of you again, don't you?*

Horvan's throat tightened when Dellan rolled lazily onto his back, presenting his slightly damp belly. Horvan grabbed a towel and gently dried his fur, conscious of Dellan's submission. *My baby.*

Dellan's gaze met his, but this time the tiger made no response.

"And whatever Dellan saw, whatever it is that dream means, it scared him." Rael jerked his head to stare at Horvan. "Maybe it scared him enough that staying a tiger is preferable to facing it again."

Like Horvan hadn't already considered that possibility too.

Hashtag appeared at the door. "I've called the doc. He says he's ready to come here as soon as we need him." He looked at Dellan and smiled. "Hey, a clean kitty."

"Where's the doc now?" Horvan demanded, rubbing behind Dellan's ears and loving the low, rumbling purr that resulted.

"Casper, Wyoming. I've booked him on an early flight tomorrow. He should get into Missoula about 1:00 p.m." Hashtag smiled. "He wouldn't hear of Roadkill driving eight or more hours to pick him up, even though I said Roadkill would have no problem with that."

Roadkill sighed. "Like eight hours is anything to stress about. Still, I can be at the airport when his flight gets in."

"The airport is a couple hours from here," Rael told him. "Maybe three if the snow is bad."

"And it's not like we haven't got space to put him up. There's plenty of room. Which reminds me...." Roadkill inclined his head toward Dellan. "Where's he gonna sleep? On this floor, we've got two loft bedrooms. Plus there are three beds on the floor below this one, along with a couple of couches." His eyes twinkled. "We do *not* have a bed big enough to fit you two and a tiger. Just saying."

Rael glanced at Horvan. "I think we make him comfortable out there in the living room area. We can take one of the loft bedrooms. That way we're close if he needs us. There's space enough for him."

Horvan agreed.

"Then me, Crank, and Hashtag will sleep downstairs. Two of us can share when the doc gets here. Not like we haven't done *that* before, right?"

Hashtag chuckled. "Dibs on not sharing a bed with Crank. He has wandering hands when he sleeps." He winked. "Although between us, I'm not one hundred percent convinced it's subconscious behavior."

"I heard that!" Crank hollered from the kitchen. Rael and Hashtag laughed.

Roadkill got to his feet. "Then let's get a list together, and I'll go to the store for supplies. I'll take Crank." He peered at Hashtag. "You'll wanna set up the perimeter cameras, right?"

Hashtag nodded. "I'll get onto that now. And by the way, boys—we made the national news." He grinned. "Of course, the animal rights groups are taking all the credit, but I think we'll allow them that, right? And speaking of them…." He disappeared for a moment, then returned, carrying a folder he handed to Horvan. "In case we get any visitors who spot Dellan."

"What's in there?" Rael asked.

"Forged papers that say Dellan is a legally acquired animal," Horvan told him, peering inside the folder. "I got Hashtag to procure them for us."

"Forged?" Rael appeared appalled.

Hashtag snorted. "You don't think those papers Anson's secretary referred to are real, do you? We *know* they're not, because we know Dellan was not found in some drug dealer's basement. Well, if he can have forged papers, so can we." He walked over and patted Rael's shoulder kindly. "But we're the good guys."

Hashtag left the room, Roadkill behind him.

"Don't forget to take plenty of cash!" Horvan called out after Hashtag.

"Oh, gee, why didn't I think of that?" His voice was heavy with sarcasm.

"Why cash?" Rael asked. "Put it all on a card."

"We never use credit cards on a mission. Too easily traced. And we want to stay under the radar. That goes for you too." When Rael frowned, Horvan shook his head. "Think about it. You went to see Anson, and you paid a lot of attention to the tiger, didn't you? Stands to reason Anson is gonna check you out, or at least check out your whereabouts. And he's not gonna be able to find you. Which reminds me. I'll give you a cell to use. You can't use yours."

Rael sighed. "And this is how you live all the time? How do you cope?" He put his arms around Dellan's neck and rubbed his face in the thick fur there.

Horvan moved until he was kneeling beside them both. "It's how I've lived up till now. But things change. Now I have two mates to think of. I guess that means taking a look at how I want my future to be."

The loud growl that shattered the peaceful moment came from Dellan's stomach.

Horvan got to his feet. "I think it's time we all ate something, don't you?" He scritched behind Dellan's ears again. "And I know where there's a big juicy steak or two with your name on them."

Dellan was out of the small bathroom in a heartbeat.

"There's nothing wrong with his hearing," Rael commented.

What raised Horvan's spirits was the fact that Dellan was clearly understanding speech better than before.

Maybe whatever they gave him is wearing off. Even through their link, Horvan caught the hopeful note in Rael's voice.

God, I hope so.

HORVAN HAD to admit, Rael had done them proud. The cabin was perfect for their needs. The beds up in the loft rooms were a good size, and the ladders going up to them were a charming feature. A thick wooden beam ran across the ceiling from one side of the cabin to the other. The stove belted out a good deal of heat into the space that was both a living and dining room. Three couches filled up one end of the room, sitting on thick rugs. And the floor below was perfect for the boys, with lots of room.

"They're back," Hashtag told them, looking up from his laptop screen.

Horvan gazed at the image from the camera nearest to the property's boundaries with the road and smiled. Hashtag's defensive system included an alarm that would tell them if someone approached the cabin.

They weren't taking any chances.

Dellan was investigating the cabin's nooks and crannies, strolling around the floor and peering into every corner.

Hashtag chuckled. "Looks like Dellan is checking out his defenses too."

Dellan paused at the foot of the ladder, staring up at the mezzanine where the bed was located. He crouched low, then sprang into the air, landing on the upper level with a thud. The floorboards beneath him creaked.

Hashtag gasped. "That was some jump." Dellan stared down at them from his new lofty height.

Rael laughed. "When it comes to high jumps, tigers are the undisputed kings. They can easily jump over ten feet high. And you should see them spring vertically up a twenty-foot pole."

"Seriously?"

Rael nodded. "In fact, no one knows how high a tiger can jump, because every time one sets a record, another tiger breaks it."

The door opened, and Roadkill and Crank entered the cabin, both carrying heavy-looking boxes. Hashtag went to help them. Crank put his burden on the countertop and glanced at Horvan.

"I got something for Dellan from the store." He walked out of the cabin.

Horvan snickered. "Unless it's a crate full of meat, I can't see much impressing Dellan."

Crank came back into the room, carrying a large box.

"What's in there?" Horvan inquired.

"Nothing. It's empty." Crank set it down on the floor and took a step back. "Cats love playing with empty boxes, right?"

Horvan snorted. "Maybe house kitties do shit like that, but—"

Dellan landed nimbly and ran over to the box. He jumped into it and sat there, staring at Crank.

Horvan turned to Rael. "Did you know he'd like…?" His words died at the sight of Rael's frown. "What's wrong?"

Rael glared at him. "I'm pissed, that's what's wrong. I was two seconds from shifting so I could play in it. Dellan beat me to it."

For a moment, no one said a word. Then all five men were laughing while Dellan got on with the serious business of playing in his box.

Horvan had to hand it to Crank. He knew his kitties.

HORVAN WOKE to an insistent nudging. He cracked his eye open and came face-to-face with Dellan's large round striped head, visible in the light that filtered up from the floor below.

"Hey, you need to go out?" he asked, then yawned. He had no idea of the time. They'd all headed for bed around nine.

Then he realized Dellan had jumped up to the loft again.

Sleep.

"Okay, go to sleep, then."

It seemed all Dellan wanted was permission. Before Horvan could say anything, 440 pounds of tiger plopped on top of him. *What the fuck?*

"Rael?" Horvan gave the sleeping Rael a nudge. "Goddamn it, Rael. Wake your ass up." Dellan weighed a ton.

"Whaaaat?" Rael was lying on his side facing the wall. "Do you know how long it's been since I had a good sleep?" he whined. He rolled over, and even in the dim light, Horvan saw his eyes widen. "Holy shit," he whispered.

"And heavy shit at that," Horvan agreed.

Rael reached out and stroked Dellan's paw. "Dellan? What's going on?"

No sleep without Dellan.

The words were firm, insistent, and to Horvan's mind, they showed the first signs of possessiveness. They also sent a pang of guilt through him.

"You're right. We shouldn't be sleeping without you. How about if we all go into the living room and sleep together? Now that we're a… family, it makes sense to be together, right?"

Dellan got up, climbed off the bed, walked over to the top of the ladder, and leaped into the air, landing on his front paws with a soft thud. Rael rubbed his eyes and followed, climbing down the wooden ladder, Horvan behind him. When they reached the spot where they'd heaped blankets for Dellan, Rael sighed.

"You know what? Let's make him really comfortable." He stepped out of his shorts, pulled his tee over his head, and shifted.

Instantly, Dellan approached him, sniffing, and Rael flopped onto his back. Dellan studied him, brushing his head against Rael's mane. *Mate. My mate. Lion. Lion and human.*

Horvan watched them, his heart lighter than it had felt for days. When Dellan nuzzled Rael's belly, moving lower toward his groin, Horvan had to smile.

Yeah, you're gonna have a lot of fun with that when you finally shift back.

Then Rael rolled over and stood, facing Horvan. Dellan took a step toward Horvan, his head raised as he sniffed the air again. As if synchronized, they walked toward him.

Horvan grinned. "Now I know why I'm a cat person." He stripped off and shifted, standing still as Dellan approached him, his nose in the air as he drew Horvan's scent into his nostrils.

Bear. Beautiful bear. Dellan lowered himself to the floor, and Horvan buried his snout in that glorious striped fur, inhaling his mate's aroma. He lay down on the blanket, and immediately Dellan moved to his side, rubbing against him. Rael went to Horvan's other side, and suddenly Horvan was sandwiched between two purring big cats. They snuggled against his flanks, their three heads almost touching.

Horvan smiled to himself. *Big cats don't purr. Yeah, right.*

He was asleep within seconds.

HE KNEW exactly what had awoken him—Dellan was whimpering, as though in pain. His tail thrashed, hitting the floor. Horvan was instantly alert, checking the space around them for any threats. When he saw they were alone, Horvan shifted, reaching for Dellan, laying gentle hands on him, sending out a flow of calm.

What stopped him dead was the image in his head.

It had to be the same memory as in Dellan's previous nightmare, because there was the stranger again, standing beside Anson. Only this time, there was more than one image. It was as if Horvan was seeing the event through Dellan's eyes.

The stranger pointed something at Dellan, something Horvan couldn't make out, and then pain seared through his neck.

With a cry, Rael shifted before moving closer to Dellan, as though to protect him, and Horvan knew he'd shared the experience. Rael's chest heaved, and his breathing was erratic. He drew in a deep breath before speaking.

"He shot Dellan. Horvan, he shot him."

CHAPTER SIXTEEN

RAEL WAS still shaking. Whatever had struck Dellan, he'd felt it as though it had lanced through his own body. Dellan had come out of the nightmare, and Horvan was curled around him as if he were shielding Dellan with his body. The physical connection seemed to do the trick. Dellan's breathing grew less labored, and he lay quieter, Horvan's hands moving over his flanks in a gentle, soothing motion.

"It wasn't a bullet," Rael insisted. The pain had felt sharp, almost needlelike, and in the immediate aftermath, a burning sensation spread out from the point of entry. Rael shivered. "I think it was some kind of dart, or something very like it."

Horvan nodded. Rael was conscious of Horvan's constant flow of calm thoughts directed toward Dellan.

"Is everything okay up here?" Crank appeared in the doorway that led down to the lower floor. He wore a red flannel onesie.

Despite the shock still jolting through him, Rael smiled. "Oh, that look is definitely you, Crank."

"Fuck off." Crank came over and knelt beside them. "Is Dellan okay? It didn't sound so good from downstairs." He stretched out his hand to stroke Dellan, but hesitated. When Dellan raised his head, pushing against Crank's palm, Rael sighed with relief. Crank let out a shuddering breath and slowly stroked Dellan's sleek fur and velvet nose. "There now. It's okay. Your mates are here." He kept his voice low and calming.

Rael was impressed, both by Crank's gentle approach and Dellan's reaction. "He likes you."

"That's a relief. He's obviously not thinking of me as dinner." Crank met Horvan's gaze. "Another nightmare?"

Horvan nodded. "Only this time, we shared part of it."

Rael quickly told Crank what they'd seen and felt, and Crank's face darkened. "That bastard. I don't know who I hate more right now—the fucker who shot him or the fucker who let him. Because it's obvious Anson was in on this. He was there, wasn't he?"

"What is this, a pajama party?" Roadkill emerged through the door, looking sleepy. He blinked when he caught sight of Rael and Horvan. "Oh. Apparently not. Is it one of *those* kinda parties? And if so, why wasn't I invited?"

Horvan rolled his eyes. "We shifted, doof." He reached over for his clothing, shivering.

Rael wasn't sure that reaction was entirely to do with the temperature. He pulled on his own shorts and tee.

Crank rose to his feet. "Well, seeing as we're all awake, I'm gonna make hot chocolate. I'm freezing my ass off here."

Roadkill came over and crouched beside Dellan. "Yeah, good idea," he said absently, stroking Dellan's back. "You okay, Dellan?"

Tears pricked Rael's eyes when Dellan responded. "He said 'good friend.'"

Roadkill's smile was huge. "I'll take that." He leaned in until his nose was inches from Dellan's. "I'm gonna be your friend as long as you need me." When Dellan's nose touched his, Roadkill chuckled. "That tickles." He straightened before rubbing his hand over Dellan's ruff.

"We think that guy shot him with a dart or something. Maybe that was the first time he was drugged," Rael mused.

Roadkill nodded. "And when Dellan finally shifts back, hopefully he can tell us what happened. *If* he remembers."

"What do you mean?" Horvan demanded.

"I *mean*, this has obviously been a traumatic experience. I wouldn't be surprised if he wasn't able to remember part of it. The brain does that. It's like a safety mechanism to suppress things that might hurt us." Roadkill's eyes were focused on Dellan. "We need to be careful not to press him too much. Let him remember what he can."

Stay. Mates stay.

Rael leaned over and rubbed his face in Dellan's fur. *We're not going anywhere. And from now on, we sleep with you. Okay?*

Okay. There was a pause. *No dreams.*

Rael's throat tightened. He would give anything to make sure Dellan had no more nightmares, but unfortunately that was beyond him. He prayed that when Dellan was human once more, the dreams would end.

He didn't hold out much hope of that, however.

Hashtag came into the room, rubbing his hand over his scalp and yawning. "Does that delicious aroma mean someone's making hot chocolate?"

Horvan laughed. "Looks like none of us are getting back to sleep anytime soon. What say we find a movie and get comfortable?"

Rael thought that sounded like a great plan. He intended watching it from a pile of pillows on the floor next to Dellan.

Horvan gave him a warm smile. *That makes two of us.*

RAEL STARED out the window, watching for the car. "How old is the doc?"

"In his late fifties maybe? He's retired from the military now." Horvan joined him on the couch. "He's a good guy."

"What is he?" So far, Horvan hadn't mentioned what kind of shifter the doc was.

"I don't know because I didn't ask. I just knew he was a shifter." Horvan chuckled. "A very *big* shifter. I don't know about you, but it always struck me as kinda rude, demanding to know what someone shifted into. If they want to tell you, fine. Supposing they shift into something tiny, like a mouse? They might not wanna share that."

Rael totally got that. He glanced across to where Dellan was sitting on the floor, front paws crossed almost daintily, head erect, looking very regal. "I've told him we're expecting a visitor, so it won't be a shock." He yawned.

"I told you to grab some shut-eye before the doc arrives. You look tired."

Rael narrowed his gaze. "Gee, you think that's maybe because we were all watching movies in the early hours when we should have been sleeping? And yes, I blame you. It was your idea." Before Horvan could come back with a response, Rael sighed. "I'm sorry. I get cranky when I don't get enough sleep."

Horvan bit his lip. "I'd never have guessed."

"We've got company," Hashtag announced, walking into the room. "Roadkill's back. I'll tell Crank to get his ass in here."

"Crank's outside?"

"Sure. He's bringing in wood for the stove. Of course, he's bitching about it too."

The door banged open, and Crank staggered into the room, his arms full of logs. "Take these, one of you, before I drop them on my toes. Not that my toes would feel a thing because they're fucking frostbitten."

Horvan and Hashtag relieved him of his burden and piled the logs in the basket next to the stove. Crank stamped his feet on the floorboards, the snow falling off his heavy boots. Moments later, the car pulled up outside and doors slammed.

The doc knocked on the doorframe before entering. "Anyone home?" he said with a smile. In one hand he carried a black leather bag.

Rael liked the look of him instantly. He had a kind face and blue eyes that held a twinkle. His hair was mostly gray, and there were lines around his eyes. Laughter lines.

Crank helped the doc out of his thick coat before clasping hands with him. "Glad you're here, Doc."

The doc peered at him. "You've put on weight. It suits you." Crank raised his eyes heavenward. Roadkill and Hashtag took their turns greeting him, and Rael liked the way the doc shook their hands warmly.

Horvan went over to him and gave him a hug. "Hey, Doc. Good to see you."

The doc patted his arm. "I swear you're bigger than the last time I saw you."

"Sure, *he's* bigger, but *I've* put on weight," Crank flung out.

The doc arched his eyebrows. "Have I touched a nerve?" His gaze flickered to Rael, and his smile intensified. "You must be Horvan's partner. Hashtag didn't tell me much, except that you existed." He walked over, his hand extended, still smiling. "That was a shock in itself. Horvan Kojik settling down."

"Hey, why does everyone act like it's such a surprise?" Horvan retorted.

There was a moment's pause before the doc, Hashtag, Roadkill, and Crank burst into laughter. Horvan muttered something about "so-called friends," but no one was paying him any attention.

Rael shook the proffered hand. "I'm Rael Parton, Dr. Tranter."

He waved his hand. "Please, call me Doc." His gaze alighted on Dellan. "Oh my." The room fell silent as he crossed the floor to where Dellan sat.

Doc Tranter knelt gingerly beside him. "Hello, my friend," he said quietly. "I am so very happy to see you here." He held out a hand, and Dellan sniffed it before nudging it with his head. The doc stroked him, inhaling deeply.

Horvan came over and joined them. "I know you're more used to dealing with humans, but anything you can tell us would help."

Doc smiled. "I can tell you one thing. He smells healthy. That's important." He opened his bag and withdrew a stethoscope. "I'm not going to assume he knows what this is, so please communicate it to him."

Rael knelt beside Dellan, his hand resting on Dellan's back. *The doc is going to listen to your heart and lungs, to make sure you're okay. He won't hurt you.*

Dellan gave a little snort. *Good man.*

"Yes, he *is* a good man," Horvan agreed.

The doc listened carefully to Dellan's heart, his expression neutral. Then he listened to his lungs. He looked at Dellan's eyes. "Beautiful," he murmured. Finally he sat back on his haunches and put away the stethoscope.

"Well? What can you tell us?" Rael asked.

"Other than he appears to be healthy? Very little." He glanced at Horvan. "What's his appetite like?"

"From what I've gleaned, normal for a tiger. He's eating more now than he was on the way here." Horvan helped the doc to his feet. "Let's sit somewhere more comfortable."

"That would be much appreciated." Doc went to the nearest couch and sat, leaving his bag at his feet. He sniffed the air. "Is that coffee I can smell? I'd love some. Anything would be preferable to that muck they gave me on the plane."

"I'm on it." Hashtag headed for the coffee machine.

Horvan sat at the other end of the couch, while Rael stayed with Dellan. "We think he was drugged." Quickly, Horvan told him about the female tiger shifter and the way the men had injected her with something.

Doc frowned. "You think they gave her something to force a shift?" He shivered. "That's diabolical. Who would create such a drug, and for what purpose?"

"So we thought that's how they kept Dellan in his present form." Rael gazed earnestly at the doc. "And if that's the case, how long will it be before the drugs are out of his system and he can shift back?"

Doc gave Roadkill, Hashtag, and Crank a wry smile. "I imagine you three have had quite an education this last week."

Crank snorted. "Not so much as you'd think." He pointed to Horvan and Rael. "These two know diddly squat about shifters. But yeah, as for finding out shifters even exist? That was… unexpected."

"Not to mention totally cool," Hashtag added, his eyes gleaming as he handed the doc a mug.

"Can we get back to Dellan, please?" Rael asked anxiously.

Doc gave him a compassionate glance. "Okay. In a human, we're talking two to four days, max, for drugs to leave the body. I don't know much about tiger physiology, but let's assume there's little difference. How long has he been out of their clutches now?"

"Fifty-six hours, give or take," Horvan told him.

The doc nodded. "Then all you can do is wait. He could shift today, tomorrow, or any day after that. But it's not just the drugs.

From what you've told me, there's a possibility that Dellan might be keeping himself in tiger form."

"Is there nothing we can do?" Rael's heart sank.

Doc sighed. "All you can do is what you're already doing—make him feel safe and loved. Because he'll only shift if he feels that."

"He knows we're his mates," Rael said softly, stroking Dellan.

"And that is wonderful." Doc shook his head. "You three are the first mates I've ever encountered."

"Seriously?" Horvan's mouth fell open. "I felt sure you'd have come across others."

Crank huffed. "It sounds like you don't know much more than we do, Doc."

"And we have so many questions," Roadkill added. "Like, where do shifters come from?"

Doc chuckled. "You may not believe this, but if I'm honest? I don't have a clue."

Hashtag stared at him. "But... you're one of them. How can you know nothing about your own origins?"

Doc scrubbed a hand over his lined cheek. "There are a lot of rumors, of course. Some say we came about because of something the government did that got out of control, but that's nonsense. I get the feeling shifters existed before there was such a thing as government. Others believe we're an evolutionary offshoot, and there are even those who think shifters are the children of a moon goddess." He shook his head. "For every shifter, there are a dozen different stories and ideas. Sadly, we aren't immune to conspiracy theories any more than humans are."

Crank chuckled. "That part right there... you saying 'humans' like that...." He shuddered. "Welcome to the world of the paranormal."

Roadkill sagged into the couch. "So you don't know anything?"

The doc shrugged. "Nothing concrete. When I was little, I used to wonder all the time where we came from. As I grew up and saw man's inhumanity to man and animals alike, I felt that shifters were the better species, but after some of the things you've told me...." He sighed heavily. "It would seem shifters are just as susceptible to greed and lust for power as any human."

"We don't know shifters had anything to do with this," Horvan insisted, even though Rael's gut told him otherwise. The doc said nothing but gazed steadily at Horvan.

"So you can't help us." Rael had hoped for more information.

Doc held up a single finger. "Now, I didn't say *that* exactly, did I? I do know *some* people you could probably talk with. Just... keep in mind you'll need to take everything they say with a grain—or maybe a saltshaker—of doubt."

"That sounds more promising." Hashtag sat upright. "How do we find these people?"

Doc laughed. "Patience, my boy. I'll get in touch with them initially. After that, *they* will approach *you*, not the other way around. Remember what I said about conspiracy theories, that's all."

Crank chuckled. "This gets more and more interesting by the day."

"You have no idea. The first time I met one of them, I got the distinct feeling he already knew everything about me." Doc gave another shiver. "Very unnerving."

"Now you've got me intrigued." Horvan cocked his head to one side. "Do you trust these people?"

"That's the strange part. Yes. However—" He speared Horvan with an intense look. "—if you do get to meet with them, be careful."

"Why?" Rael blurted out. "What does your gut tell you?"

The doc locked gazes with him. "That they're dangerous."

CHAPTER SEVENTEEN

RAEL STARED at the doc. "You're kidding, right?" His heartbeat sped up a little. "If they're dangerous, then we shouldn't even be thinking of meeting them."

Doc smiled. "Rael, did you ever stop to think that you're sharing a cabin with four dangerous men?"

He laughed. "They're not danger—" The word died in his throat. *What do I know about them?* They'd been in the military together, hadn't they? That didn't exactly suggest they were members of a sewing circle.

Horvan nodded knowingly. "Fifty-seven ways, remember?" His eyes twinkled.

Rael took a deep breath. "Then if these guys do come calling, I'm in the right company."

"You know it," Roadkill said, his voice brimming with confidence.

"Can I ask you something?" The doc's gaze alighted on Dellan. "Have you tried to get him to shift?"

Rael cleared his throat. "Not exactly." When the doc gave him a quizzical glance, he sighed. "Okay, it was… in a dream. Only perhaps it was more than that." He looked the doc in the eye. "Dellan came to me in a dream. I know that sounds strange, but—"

"I wouldn't even think of presuming such a thing," Doc declared. "You three can hear one another in your minds. If that isn't evidence that there are things we know nothing about, then I don't know what is." He smiled kindly. "Tell me about the dream."

Rael tried to remember Dellan's exact words. "I asked if he could switch back to human, and he said he wasn't human like me. He was a tiger."

"Which you might expect if he's been locked in this form for so long," the doc said, nodding.

"We were waiting for the drugs to wear off before we asked him to try," Horvan added.

"But maybe things have changed," Doc declared. "Those nightmares of his... was he a tiger in his memories? Or a human? Because if he can recall that, maybe it's a step in the right direction." He indicated Dellan with a nod. "Why not give it a try?"

His heart racing, Rael lowered his head until he was eye-to-eye with Dellan. *Remember your bad dream? When that man shot you?*

Dellan curled back his lips, baring his teeth, and a low roar filled the air. Rael cupped his head. *You're safe here. With your mates and friends. He can't hurt you.* He glanced over at Horvan, who was off the couch and beside Dellan before Rael had time to blink. He laid his hands on Dellan, gently rubbing him.

Rael looked into those beautiful green eyes. *In the dream, were you a tiger?*

Dellan stilled, and Rael felt the waves of confusion that rippled through him. The room was silent, so silent that Rael couldn't hear anyone breathing. *Please, Dellan*, he begged. *Try to remember.*

Suddenly, Dellan was on his feet, pulling away from them and pacing the room, his tail thrashing from side to side. Rael didn't dare move or breathe, sensing Dellan's extreme agitation. Horvan was staring at Dellan, following his every move. The others appeared to have frozen in place, all eyes on the agitated tiger.

And there it was again in Rael's head, that fragment of a memory. Anson and the stranger, standing in that office. "That's it, Dellan," he called out excitedly. "Remember."

Then his heart stuttered when he saw in his mind a hand, stretched out toward the two men as if to stop them.

Dellan's human hand.

Dellan was human. Like mates. Dellan stopped pacing, and Rael scrambled over to him and put his arms around him. He pushed his face into Dellan's ruff.

"Yes. Dellan is human too." Rael wanted to weep.

Horvan crawled over to them and stroked Dellan's nose. *Dellan, you've seen me and Rael shift from human to bear and lion. Can you do that? Can you shift to human?*

How?

Even inside Rael's head, that one word carried so much frustration.

Think. Concentrate. See yourself as human. Let it happen.

Rael was caught up in the elation that coursed through Horvan. His excitement was addictive. *You can do it, Dellan.* Tremors spiked through Dellan's body, and Rael held him, willing his mate to be calm.

When Dellan let out a roar, his body stiffening, Rael knew it wasn't going to happen. Horvan was there instantly in his head, sending out thoughts of calm to Dellan, and Rael thanked God for him when Dellan responded, leaning into Horvan.

Doc crossed the room to them and knelt before Dellan. "Even I could feel his frustration. Don't push him any more today. I think one breakthrough was enough."

When Dellan was calm again, Rael expelled a long breath. For the first time since they'd freed Dellan from the cage, he was awash with relief.

I feel it too. Horvan met Rael's gaze. *He's going to shift back. Not right this second, but soon.*

Rael nodded. Dellan would shift when the time was right, but it would be his timing, not theirs.

"Now… what does a man have to do around here to get fed?" Doc's lips twitched.

"Leave that to me." Roadkill got up off the couch and went into the kitchen area, Hashtag following.

"You're gonna stay tonight, right, Doc?" Crank inquired. "We've got plenty of beds downstairs, plus some real comfy couches."

Doc didn't take his eyes off Dellan. "I'd love to," he said quietly. He glanced at Horvan. "What do you know about Dellan? His family, I mean." Then he returned his gaze to Dellan.

"His parents are dead. Dellan's father, Jake, died when Dellan was seven. Well, we assume he died. He was declared dead when

Dellan was fourteen, after he'd been missing for seven years. His mother married Dellan's stepdad, but she passed a year or so ago."

Doc froze. "Jake? As in Jake Carson?"

"Yeah. Why do you ask?"

"I knew him," Doc said simply. "Way before Dellan was born. Jake was a tiger shifter too. Immensely strong and fast." He stroked Dellan's flank. "He's exhausted. All this agitation has worn him out. Let him sleep a while." He made as if to stand, and Rael helped him to his feet. "Thank you. I seem to be aching more than usual today."

"One thing's for sure, Doc," Crank told him. "You won't go hungry around here. Not the way Roadkill cooks. Of course, it might not *look* that appetizing...."

"Fuck you, Crank." Roadkill gave him the finger from across the room.

Doc sat on the couch, his focus still on Dellan, who was lying on his side, eyes closed, paws crossed, his flank gently rising and falling as he slept. "I don't suppose you know his mother's first name."

Horvan chuckled. "Rael will. His memory is amazing."

Rael laughed. "Thanks for the accolade. And yes, her name was Miranda."

Doc's face lit up. "Oh. Oh, that is wonderful. They were childhood sweethearts. I'm so happy they stayed together. She was a tiger shifter too."

"I wonder what happened to him," Rael mused. "It must have broken her heart when he disappeared." Not to mention Dellan's. Losing a father at so tender an age had to be hard.

"How and when did she die?"

Even Rael had to consult his notes for that. He got out his phone and scrolled through. "About a month before Dellan was declared missing. As to how, I don't know. It wasn't in the records."

Doc's brow furrowed. "I don't like it. I don't like it at all."

"What do you mean?" Horvan asked.

"Too many coincidences." Doc pursed his lips. "Think about it. His father goes missing. No one knows what happened to him. His mother dies a month before Dellan, too, is declared missing. Only we know exactly where *he* was. But her dying like that? Very convenient."

Cold spread over Rael's skin. "Why convenient?"

"Because if Dellan was drugged and unable to shift back, it's very likely she would have known about it. The bond between shifter parents and their offspring can be incredibly strong. And I don't think for one second that she would sit back and do nothing. Miranda was a fighter."

Horvan's eyes widened. "You think Anson had something to do with her death? But... she was his mother too. He may be a bastard with designs on his half brother's company, but to resort to matricide?"

Doc blinked. "You're right, of course. And it may be that I'm reading too much into these events. Ignore my paranoia."

Except it was too late for that. Rael couldn't get his mind off the doc's propositions.

What if he's right?

DELLAN LAY snuggled against the bear, sharing his warmth. The lion slept there too, and the thought gave him comfort. *Safe. I am safe.* He couldn't see the other men, but he knew they were close by. The place was quiet, and the only sounds came from outside, the hoot of owls looking for mates and the scurrying of other night creatures. The nest of mice beneath the floorboards was active, and he could hear the patter of their tiny feet as they went on their nocturnal maneuvers.

Dellan should have been sleeping as well, but there was too much going on inside his head for that to happen. He had never wanted anything like he wanted to shift right that second.

Time was kind of a fuzzy concept and had been for a while. He had no idea how long he'd been in that cage, but since his mates had freed him, things seemed to have moved fast. His thinking seemed sharper, his reactions quicker. The arrival of the Good Man—*Doc. His name is Doc*—had set something in motion. It was nothing short of a revelation.

I am human too.

The key had been that remembered fragment from his dream. He remembered shouting at—the name eluded him for a moment, and then he had it—Anson. He'd shouted at Anson, something about the man Anson had brought to see him. He recalled the fear that raced through him when the man raised the odd-looking pistol and pointed it at him. Then there had been the sharp pain in his neck, followed by a burning sensation that had spread from the point of entry, and he knew no more. The next time he was conscious, Dellan had awoken to find himself in the cage, somehow locked into his tiger form.

I need to tell them. He had to warn his mates, but to do that required a conversation that wouldn't be possible in his present state.

I need to shift.

He recalled what Horvan had said, something about concentrating, seeing himself as human. Dellan focused on the memory of that hand, imagining the body that it belonged to, and for one moment, he felt something ripple through him, a surge of energy. Then it was gone.

The energy had dissipated, but what remained was a sharply focused mind.

Anson. Dellan was certain Anson was the key. He scoured his memories for more clues, more information.

"No one is coming."

Those words. Anson had said those words. And the look on his face. How could Dellan have forgotten that? His lips twisted into a cruel smile. His eyes dark and dangerous as he stood over Dellan, who was clearly on the ground. That gloating voice.

"And you can forget about shifting, brother dear. You're going to stay as you are for a long time to come."

Rage surged through Dellan, and he let out a roar that made his own ears ache, reverberating inside his head.

I will not let him win. I will not let him win!

There was that ripple of energy again, and his whole body tingled. A primal scream filled the air, and Dellan wanted to know what could cause so much anguish. The cry came from neither of his mates, who were suddenly awake, shifting back into their human forms. They instantly reached for him, and Dellan was dismayed to see tears spilling down their cheeks.

What's wrong? he asked them.

Horvan pulled Dellan into his arms, his tears dripping onto Dellan's bare shoulder as he held Dellan to his chest. "Oh thank God." His voice quaked.

"Mates," Dellan croaked.

Wait. What?

"You did it. You did it," Rael whispered before leaning in to kiss Dellan on the lips, his hand curved around Dellan's stubbled cheek.

I have lips. Shoulders. Stubble. The scream had been his. And the tears coursing down his face were his too.

Holy fucking God, he was human again.

CHAPTER EIGHTEEN

BEFORE DELLAN could rasp out another word, there was the sound of feet thudding on stairs, and men piled into the room, all in varying states of dress. They came to a halt when they saw him.

"Oh my fucking God." One of them gaped, his eyes wide.

Dellan gave him a watery smile. "Hey… Crank." He shivered.

Rael noticed immediately. "Let me go find you something to wear." He got up, heedless of his own naked state, and crossed the floor to the ladder. Horvan still held on to Dellan, and he leaned into him, sharing Horvan's warmth, relishing his strength.

Dellan waved to the men, the action instinctive. "Hi, guys." The words came out more firmly that time and were apparently all the invitation the men needed to surge around him, patting his back and arms and staring at him in obvious wonder, tears sparkling in the eyes of both Roadkill and the doc.

"Welcome back," Doc said, his voice quavering. Dellan clasped his hand.

"This is the second time in twenty-four hours you've woken us all up, and I couldn't be happier about it." Hashtag patted Dellan's shoulder. "You make a nice human, Dellan."

He laughed. "Thanks." His stomach rumbled, and he glanced at Horvan. "Is there… anything to eat? I'm… starving."

Roadkill grinned. "Stay where you are, H. I'll see to this." He headed for the refrigerator.

Rael came down the ladder wearing a pair of sweats and a T-shirt. In his hands he held another pair and a sweater. "These should fit. We're about the same size." Dellan took them, his breath catching when their fingertips brushed.

Thank you… mate. Dellan squirmed into the pants.

157

"Do you know who we are?" Hashtag asked. "How much were you able to pick up?"

Dellan smiled. "I know... your names." Speech wasn't as easy as he'd hoped, but with every passing minute, his mind sharpened.

"Baby steps," Horvan whispered, stroking his back. "Eat first, then get some sleep. Talking can wait until the morning."

Crank snorted. "Hate to break it to ya, but it *is* morning."

A wave of fatigue rolled over him, and Dellan realized Horvan was right.

"Do you want a shower before bed?" Rael asked him.

Dellan was about to say no, when the thought of hot water on his skin changed his mind. "That sounds good," he admitted. Only thing was, he hadn't tried standing on only two feet yet, and part of him wondered if he remembered how to keep his balance.

"Want me to take a shower with you?" Rael asked.

The snickers and chuckles that erupted left Dellan in no doubt where his new friends' minds were located. He laughed, shaking his head. "You guys."

Rael rolled his eyes. "He's been human for *how* long?"

"Take your shower now," Roadkill called out. "Food will be another five minutes or so. Just soup and a grilled cheese sandwich."

Okay, that sounded fucking amazing. "Fastest shower... in history," Dellan joked. "Time me." Horvan helped him to his feet, and he stumbled a little. "After I've learned... to walk again," he added, chuckling.

"I think we should leave them to it," Doc commented. "As Horvan said, there'll be plenty of time for questions when Dellan has had some sleep. Back to bed, boys."

Crank grumbled as he headed for the stairs. "Christ, it's like Christmas when I was a kid and I got up in the middle of the night to see if Santa had paid a visit. My parents told me if I didn't get my ass back in bed that second, there'd be no Christmas."

Hashtag laughed. "Well, we've already got our present," he said, pointing to Dellan. "So I suppose this counts as Christmas." He smiled. "Good to have you with us, Dellan." And with that, he tugged Crank down the stairs.

"I need my sleep too," Doc added. His gaze met Dellan's. "We have so much to talk about." He followed Hashtag and Crank.

"You wanna try walking to the bathroom?" Horvan looked him up and down. "You seem to be a little steadier on your feet."

"That's because… I'm standing still," Dellan said with another wry chuckle. He held on to Horvan's arm as they walked slowly across the floor, Rael behind them. "Same place where… you gave me a bath?" Words were coming more easily to mind, as though he was shrugging off the tiger with every step. Except he could still feel his tiger within him, at peace.

Dellan sat on the side of the tub, removing his clothing. Horvan seemed unruffled by the fact that he was naked, and even in a flaccid state, Dellan could tell his mate was on the large side. Not to mention ripped as fuck.

Not now. That pleasure would have to wait.

Rael stripped off and climbed into the tub, helping Dellan into it while Horvan flipped on the shower. Dellan groaned aloud at the first feel of hot water cascading down his body. "That feels so good," he moaned.

Then it got even better as Rael wiped soapy hands all over him, getting into every crevice. Dexterous fingers rubbed shampoo into his hair, massaging his scalp and sending waves of sensual pleasure through his body. Dellan raised his hands, staring at them. *When was the last time I saw hands instead of paws? Skin instead of fur?*

Questions that badly needed answers.

We'll talk about that, I promise. Rael rinsed away the last of the lather. *But right now let's get you dry and fed.*

And asleep in a bed, Horvan added.

Oh my God. A bed. Sheets. Pillows. Dellan was in heaven just thinking about it.

He stepped carefully out of the tub, his legs trembling slightly, and Horvan instantly enfolded him in a soft towel that smelled of lavender.

Too many sensations.

He clung to Horvan, his heart racing. "Too much," he murmured.

Horvan enveloped him in his strong arms. "Bed. Now." Then he lifted Dellan and carried him out of the bathroom. "Bring the food," he told Rael. "He can eat it in bed." Dellan buried his face in Horvan's broad chest, his arms looped around Horvan's neck as Horvan headed for their loft bed.

"If I find toast crumbs," Rael warned, but Dellan heard the laughter in his voice. Horvan aided him in climbing the ladder, and Dellan couldn't help but remember leaping that distance like it was nothing. Right then instead of a powerful tiger, he felt like a newborn lamb.

It wasn't long before his belly was full and sleep was tugging at him. The bed needed to be a little wider, but Dellan wasn't complaining, not when he was sandwiched between his mates, their arms around him protectively, their bodies warming his. His thoughts grew fuzzier, and yet through the fog that was creeping into his mind, one thing remained sharp.

Will they come after me?

"There are things I need to tell you," he said, striving to stay awake, but the combination of shower, food, and bed was having a soporific effect.

"And they can wait for a few hours," Horvan told him firmly. "Sleep now." He kissed Dellan softly on the lips, and the tender embrace brought on a bout of fresh tears, as though his emotions were in complete disarray.

Rael's hand was gentle on Dellan's face. "Please. Get some sleep. You're safe now."

Dellan couldn't keep his fatigue at bay any longer. He closed his eyes and sank like a stone into the waiting arms of sleep.

WHEN HE opened his eyes, it was daylight. The sunlight reflected on the floorboards below, casting a warm glow in the room. The curtain that separated them from the living space beneath them was drawn back, and Dellan caught the sound of voices.

Horvan was missing, but Rael was lying on his side, his head cupped in his hand, staring at Dellan. "Hey, sleepyhead."

"Were you watching me sleep?" The idea filled Dellan with warmth.

Rael grinned. "I was about to tickle your nose with a feather to wake you up. Breakfast is ready."

Dellan sniffed the air, and his stomach responded with a loud grumble. "This is getting to be a habit," he said apologetically.

Rael laughed. "I'm always ravenous when I shift back. You definitely have an excuse." He handed Dellan the pants and sweater he'd briefly worn a few hours previously. "There's a new toothbrush in the bathroom, and a razor if you want to shave."

Dellan scrubbed his hand over his rough cheek. "I think I was trying to grow a beard. Should I remove this?"

Rael's eyes gleamed. "Not on my account. Beards are sexy as fuck."

That did it. Dellan was never going clean-shaven again. He recalled his brief glance in the mirror. "Even with the bits of gray?"

Rael chuckled. "*Especially* with the bits of gray. Now get dressed before I change my mind."

"Change your mind about what?"

Rael's blue eyes seemed to darken. *Staying in bed and spending all day just touching you. Kissing you.*

Heat barreled through him. *Do you hear me complaining about that prospect?*

I can hear you two. And if you stay up there any longer, two things will happen. I won't be held responsible for the consequences, and we'll shock the fuck out of all these guys. Not that I care.

Rael laughed. "I think that's our cue to get dressed." With obvious reluctance, he threw back the sheets and began putting on his clothes. "We're coming," he called out to Horvan.

Down below, Crank guffawed. "Oh, is that what the noise is?"

161

Dellan stared unashamedly at Rael. He was slighter in build than Horvan, his chest covered with a soft-looking down of pale brown hair that was almost blond. His thighs were toned, his belly flat, with very little body fat. Dellan liked the fact that Rael wasn't rippling with muscles.

That's my job. Even in Dellan's head, Horvan's voice resounded with pride.

Dellan laughed softly. "Hearing you two in my head… already feels like it's normal." He pulled on his pants and sweater, then smiled when Rael handed him a pair of thick socks. "To keep my back paws warm?"

Rael bit his lip. "We usually call them feet, remember?"

Which only served to remind Dellan of his most pressing question—how long had he been a tiger?

"But on the plus side?" Rael kissed him, a lingering kiss that stirred his senses. When they parted, Rael smiled. "You sound much better. Your speech is almost back to normal."

"Really?" That filled him with pride. He was making a concerted effort to speak accurately.

Dellan climbed carefully down the ladder, to be greeted warmly by the others. Social niceties would have to wait, however. "What's today's date?"

"Saturday, March fourteenth," Roadkill told him.

That explained it. "Then I've been locked into my tiger form… for about ten weeks," he calculated. "I knew it had been a while." When silence fell abruptly, he frowned. "What have I said?"

"Dellan," Horvan said softly. "It's March 2020."

Breathing became difficult. A sudden coldness hit him at his core. His head was spinning. "2020," he repeated, struggling to draw air into his lungs.

"Sit down," Rael urged him, guiding him to a chair at the table. Dellan sank onto it, putting his head in his hands.

More than a year. I was a tiger for more than a year.

Horvan's hand was at his back, gently rubbing him. Dellan detected the familiar aroma of coffee under his nose.

"We did wonder if you were aware of the passage of time." That was the doc's quiet voice.

"The answer to that would be a big fat no." Dellan picked up the mug and sipped the hot brew. He sighed. "Wow. Talking about not knowing what you have till it's gone. I missed this."

"Apparently, your brain responds well to caffeine," Hashtag commented. "You're sounding better by the minute."

"How much do you remember about what happened?" Doc asked him.

Before Dellan could reply, Horvan was in there. "How about we give him a chance to get used to walking on two feet again before we grill him?"

Dellan stretched out his hand and took Horvan's. "Hey, it's fine. And believe me, I want to know what I've been missing." He straightened. "Okay. The last thing I remember was going to my office right after New Year's—that would be New Year's, 2019." He closed his eyes, visualizing the room, his desk. It was harder than he'd imagined.

"You okay?" That came from Hashtag.

Dellan opened his eyes. "Yeah. It's just that everything's still a bit hazy in here." He tapped his temple. "Speech is coming back, but the memories?"

"Lemme help you," Crank said suddenly. "Your fuckwit half brother came to see you, and he wasn't alone."

Dellan blinked. "How did you…?" Then it came to him. He met Rael's gaze. "You saw it inside my head." Rael nodded, and Dellan took a sip of coffee before continuing. "Anson had asked for a meeting. Said it was important."

"Do you know why your stepdad left the company to you rather than Anson?" Roadkill asked, his expression thoughtful. "Was it his age, or was there something else?"

Dellan smiled, then turned to Horvan, who'd taken the chair next to his. "I like him. Astute man." He returned his attention to Roadkill. "Tom always told me the company would be Anson's one day. That was fine by me. I was only Tom's stepson, right?"

"But something changed his mind," Rael concluded.

Dellan nodded. "Anson was twenty when Tom showed the first signs of cancer. He'd been working for Tom for two years at that point. I'd been with the company since I was eighteen, and by then I was a manager. Anyhow, one day Tom said he'd been making plans. That was when he sprang it on me. He wanted me to run the company. I assumed it was because of Anson's age, and I said as much." Dellan paused, his throat tightening.

"That was a long speech. You don't have to talk about this now, you know?" Horvan said in a low voice.

"Yeah, I do. Because I think this lies at the heart of what happened to me." Dellan took a deep breath, framing his thoughts before uttering them. "Tom said it wasn't Anson's age and inexperience that bothered him—it was his attitude toward people. His… overbearing stance. His inflexibility. The fact that he could be very… opinionated. Tom said I was quite the opposite. He said I made up my mind based on facts, not emotion. That though I was firm, my mind could be changed by a decent argument. He liked the fact that I was logical." He drank a little more, then shrugged. "He felt the company would do better with me at the helm, rather than Anson." Dellan smiled at Hashtag and held up his coffee. "I think you're right about my brain and caffeine."

"What happened when Anson discovered his father's plans?" Horvan asked.

"Tom had left him with a more than generous allowance, as well as what he earned with the company, and a position on the board. I think it's fair to say Anson resented me from then on. And he wasn't quiet about it or his dislike for the situation." Dellan sagged into his chair. "I never dreamed he'd go to these lengths to gain control of the company."

"Did you tell him you were a shifter?" Doc inquired.

And there it was, the question that had been nagging Dellan ever since he'd been freed.

"No, I did not," he said slowly. "I told no one at the company."

"Well, *someone* did. How else could he turn up with that guy who drugged you, forcing you into a shift?" Rael demanded. "He had to know."

"He did know." Quickly, Dellan shared with them the fragment of memory from his dreams the previous night. "He was planning on keeping me as a tiger."

"And what about the rest of it?" Crank coughed. "Are you aware of times when you weren't… alone in your cage?" He glared at Horvan. "And in case you missed it, that was me being tactful."

Horvan snickered. "I'm amazed. I didn't know you possessed any."

"Okay, what is Crank hinting at so delicately?" Dellan said, puzzled.

Rael covered Dellan's hand with his. "We saw men putting female shifters into your cage. In one case, they forced a shift by drugging her."

"Shifters… in the cage with me?" Dellan was completely baffled. "Why would they do…?" He stilled. "Oh."

"Do you remember any of those times?" Rael asked.

Dellan closed his eyes, suddenly weary. "Apart from that one memory of Anson, I can't remember a whole lot in any great detail." He tried to work out how far back his memories went. "Do you think I find it easier to remember your names because once you got me out of there, I wasn't being drugged anymore?" It had to be a possibility.

"I think part of you remembered the shifters," Rael commented. "Your dive into the river as soon as we got here?"

Okay, *that* part he remembered. But he was drawn back to that cage. Why the hell would they put shifters in there with him? To calm him when he got stressed out?

"Do you remember me coming to the office that first time?"

Dellan opened his eyes and stared at Rael. "No."

Rael swallowed. "You spoke to me, inside my head. You asked me to help you."

Dellan had reached his breaking point. Tears trickled down his cheeks, and he couldn't stop them. "Oh, thank God you came. I could still be there if not for you. For all of you."

Horvan's arms were around him, and Rael knelt beside his chair. Dellan clung to his mates, his sobs gradually dying away.

Dellan was aware of Horvan's voice, gentle yet firm. "I think that's all for now. He's had enough."

"There is one last question I think we all want to ask." Doc's voice was quiet. "Did you know the man who shot you?"

"I'd never seen him before." Dellan couldn't suppress the shudder that rippled through him. "And I never want to see him again." Every instinct he possessed told him that the man was not only cruel, but dangerous.

"Then let's hope he doesn't want to see you either," Roadkill remarked. All heads turned his way, and he nodded. "That's what we're all thinking, isn't it? That someone is going to come looking for Dellan?" He shivered. "This isn't over."

CHAPTER NINETEEN

DELLAN WATCHED as across the room, Rael and Horvan were making dinner. Their preparations involved a good deal of laughter, and the sound lightened Dellan's spirits.

My mates.

Rael glanced at him and smiled. *Yours.* Then he returned to his task of slicing eggplants, and Dellan had to smile at how… *normal* it felt. Two men had walked into his life and turned it upside down. Two men he was destined to be with.

It should have been awkward, but it wasn't. It felt right.

He should have fought the notion that someone was directing his life, but he hadn't. Because it felt…

Right.

"You seem to have taken that part of this whole business in your stride."

It took Dellan a moment to realize Doc was talking to him. He blinked. "Sorry. I must've zoned out for a second. You mean, discovering I had two mates?" He chuckled. "After everything I've been through, suddenly finding out that some higher power or other had decreed I should have two soul mates is somehow easier to swallow."

"Interesting choice of words." Doc's eyes twinkled. "Soul mates."

Dellan couldn't think of another word that was more apt. "I've known them for less than a day." He gestured to his body. "In this form, at any rate. But it feels like I've known them for much longer." It seemed like every few minutes, one or both of them would connect with him: a light touch of their hand on his, a gentle caress of his cheek, or the soft stroking of his hair. It served as a constant reminder of two things—he was indeed human again, and there were two men who clearly cared for him. Dellan wondered if all mates felt this… connection, this overpowering need to be close to one another.

He peered at Doc. "Was it like that when you met your mate?"

Doc stilled. "Ah. Then you don't know *that* part." When Dellan gazed at him, perplexed, Doc sighed. "The fact that someone has… decreed, as you put it, that you should have two mates isn't what intrigues us. It's the fact that you have mates *at all*, when finding one is as rare as hen's teeth."

Dellan laughed. "I've never understood that saying."

"It's simple, really. Hens don't possess teeth. So something as rare as that would be rare to the point of nonexistence." Doc gave him an intense look. "Does that adequately convey why the three of you finding one another is so special?"

Holy fuck, it truly did.

Dellan reached for his mug of coffee and wrapped his hands around it. "It's peaceful here. I like that." This time of quiet seemed exactly what he needed.

The doc chuckled. "It's only peaceful now because the boys have gone to the store. Once they return, it'll be back to business as usual." He met Dellan's gaze. "I knew your parents, by the way."

Dellan stilled. "Really?"

Doc nodded. "Before they got married. We were all in our early twenties."

Dellan was aware of the ache in his chest. "What was my dad like?" When Doc regarded him quizzically, Dellan shrugged. "I can barely remember him, beyond flashes of playing with a ball in our yard, him helping me to fly my kite. I was seven when he disappeared."

Doc stared at his hands clasped in his lap. "Your father was remarkable, even at that age. A highly intelligent young man with a great capacity for empathy and tolerance. He adored your mother and apparently had done so since they were both fifteen." He smiled. "But Lord, he was fast when he shifted. A streak of fur, racing across the prairie. Mind you, your mother had no trouble keeping up with him."

Dellan laughed. "The prairie? Where were you?"

"The three of us vacationed in Kansas one summer. Well, I tagged along at your parents' insistence, trying hard not to feel like the proverbial third wheel. The spot they chose was perfect for them. I think I was there mainly as a lookout, to keep an eye out for anyone who happened on them."

"You didn't shift with them?"

Doc coughed. "That would have been inadvisable. Two tigers in the tall grasses could avoid detection. Me? As Crank is fond of saying, 'Hell, no.'"

Dellan had to ask. "If it's not a rude question… what are you?"

Doc regarded him without blinking. "An elephant."

He had to admit that, based on what he knew of the doc so far, an elephant was perfect. "I've always thought of elephants as wise gentle giants."

"I'll take that as a compliment." Doc tilted his head to one side. "Your mother had no idea what happened to him?"

"None whatsoever. She said he went away on a business trip and never came back. The last time she heard from him was in a phone call from whichever hotel he was staying at. But she didn't give up hope. She hired private detectives once the police had explored all possible avenues and come up empty. Nothing. It was like he'd vanished from the face of the earth."

"And then she died at too early an age."

Dellan closed his eyes. The memory of her death was too raw, considering the lapse of time. Then he reasoned that she'd died in December, and Anson had initiated his plan the following month. Dellan hadn't had sufficient time to grieve before he was locked into his tiger form.

"Hey." Horvan's voice was soft.

Dellan opened his eyes to find both his mates close by. Rael took hold of Dellan's hand, and Horvan sat on the arm of the couch, his hand on Dellan's shoulder.

"I don't need to say a word, do I?" Dellan opened up his mind to them, letting them in. He leaned into Horvan, aware of his strength, his scent.

"We've got you," Horvan said quietly, pulling Dellan to him while Rael joined him on the couch, the pair of them the sturdiest, most reliable brackets Dellan had ever encountered. Little by little, he got his emotions under control, but still they held on to him until he was breathing normally again.

"I share your grief," Doc said softly. "They were dear friends, and I'm sorry we lost touch."

Dellan held out a hand to him. "I'm glad I got to meet you. Thank you for coming all this way on nothing more than a phone call."

Doc smiled as they shook. "When Horvan said you were his mate, I knew I had to meet you. But please remember. If you ever need my help, just ask." He paused. "I mean that, Dellan. I think your father would want that."

"Thank you." Tears pricked Dellan's eyes. He felt like he'd been adopted.

Rael lifted his chin, his head inclined toward the window. "The guys are back."

Dellan cleared his throat. "Then I'm going to paste on a smile. I don't want them thinking I'm a basket case." He wiped his eyes with the back of his hand.

Horvan gave him a hard stare. "You're hardly that. And no one expects you to be firing on all eight, not after the year you've had."

Dellan gave a sad grin. "I know that's something to do with cars, but no idea what. I have a mechanic for that."

The door burst open, and the three men spilled into the room, weighed down by boxes of groceries. Roadkill's gaze went straight to Dellan.

"I've had an idea," he blurted out.

Crank laughed. "Can it wait until we've unpacked the groceries?" He sniffed the air. "Something smells good. When's dinner?" Hashtag shook his head and followed Crank into the kitchen area.

"*You* unpack—*I'm* talking to Dellan." Roadkill placed his box on the countertop, then came over to the couch where they were gathered. He perched on the coffee table, his fingers laced, elbows on his knees. "I've been thinking about the drug they gave you."

It had been on Dellan's mind too. "Did you come to any conclusions?"

Roadkill nodded. "Whatever it was, someone had to have developed it, right?"

"Obviously." Horvan frowned. "And?"

"And?" Roadkill rolled his eyes. "What was the name of that company we raided a few days ago?"

"You've forgotten already?" Hashtag called out. "Global Bio-Tech."

"It was a rhetorical question," Roadkill fired back. "And what kind of company is Global Bio-Tech?"

Rael became very still. "Pharmaceutical."

Roadkill folded his arms and smiled smugly. "Exactly. So how does someone who didn't even know shifters existed—we assume—suddenly start developing a drug that not only forces a shift but keeps them locked into it? Because I don't think Anson woke up one morning, after a particularly vivid dream, suddenly aware that the world contained shifters and Dellan was one of them." He cocked his head to one side. "Unless… your mom told him?"

Dellan shook his head. "No chance of that. In fact, she warned me never to tell him." He shivered. "When Anson found out he wasn't being handed the keys to the kingdom, he was incensed. I got that. After all, his dad had chosen me over him. When he'd calmed down, he acted all sorry and swore it wasn't going to be a problem. But…."

Horvan gazed at him thoughtfully. "But?"

Dellan sighed heavily. "You can't hide that kind of loathing for long. He smiled to my face, but there was something else there, you know? Something… hidden. I thought it was because I'd gotten the job he wanted, but surely that doesn't explain why he did what he did. I mean, did he hate me so much that forcing me to shift and be locked in a cage was what it took to satisfy him?"

"Then I go back to my previous question," Roadkill said emphatically. "If he didn't know you were a shifter, then how did he cook up this whole drug scheme?"

Horvan expelled a long breath. "You think there's someone else involved?"

"I think it's a distinct possibility."

Dellan had been thinking the same thing. Anson was only twenty-two for God's sake. What twenty-two-year-old could devise a plan like that?

"And speaking of Anson…." Roadkill's eyes glittered. "When are we going to pay the son of a bitch a little visit?"

Horvan cleared his throat. "I get that you want to exact your own particular form of revenge for what he did to Dellan, but that's not your decision—it's Dellan's."

Dellan gave him a thankful glance. "I don't intend letting him get away with it, but he can wait." Right then, other things were more important.

"Why?" Crank scowled. "He needs pounding."

Hashtag scowled. "That sounds way too kinky." Then his eyes twinkled. "What am I saying? You *are* kinky." He got a glare for that.

"Okay, Anson needs… pounding, but only when I feel ready to confront him. Yes, I will take my company back, but not right this minute. When I feel one hundred percent again. *Then*. And hopefully, you'll still be in a pounding mood." Dellan shook his head. "Hashtag is right. That sounds way too kinky." When Rael's hand tightened around his, Dellan knew his mates were with him.

His physical state raised a question. Dellan turned to the doc. "That bag of tricks you brought with you—do you have what you need to take some of my blood?"

Doc blinked. "Why, yes, but—"

"I know you said I seem healthy," Dellan explained, "but I need to be sure. We have no idea what they did to me during the time they had me in that cage. There could be traces left in my body of whatever they were drugging me with. Plus… I need to know everything is as it should be. That I haven't… picked up anything, if you get my drift."

It seemed as though everyone in the room caught the significance of his remarks. Hashtag and Roadkill exploded into a fit of coughing, and Crank merely grinned. The doc's face was flushed.

You're forgetting something. Horvan smiled. *You're a shifter. You're immune to… such things.*

And who knows what other diabolical shit they came up with in that lab? I want to be safe, okay? I want us to be safe. Dellan wasn't going to be moved on that point.

Then we'll make sure, Rael affirmed.

"Ugh, Doc?" Crank was frowning. "Is it safe to send Dellan's blood off to some lab? I mean, could they tell from testing it that he isn't quite… normal?"

Hashtag snorted. "I wonder what your blood test would reveal about you."

"Actually, Crank has made a valid point." Doc gave him a nod of approval, and Crank preened. "I wouldn't send it to just any lab." He reached into his black bag and pulled out a laptop.

"Don't tell me—you have a secret network of shifters spread out all over the country," Roadkill said with a twinkle in his eye.

Doc glanced at Dellan. "Your analysis of Roadkill was correct— he is very astute."

Roadkill stilled, his lips parted. "You mean I'm right? Well, fuck me."

Doc laughed. "There are shifters in every walk of life, but when it comes to medical personnel, it pays to know who you can rely on when you need help. So yes, there is a network of shifters who are medical staff, lab technicians, et cetera. We have to hope there's one within traveling distance."

"Hey, wherever you need to go, I'll get you there," Roadkill announced.

"I had no doubt," Doc replied confidently. He peered at the screen and then broke into a wide smile. "Shifter network strikes again. We have a lab technician at the Steele Memorial Medical Center in Salmon. Drake McIntyre." Doc pulled his phone from his pocket and tapped the keys. "I'll see if he'll be at work during the next few days."

Hashtag laughed. "This is amazing. And you know what? It's really got me thinking. Remember that LGBT meme they put around ages ago, saying be careful who you hate, 'cause it might be someone you love? Well, how many shifters are there in my life I don't know about?"

Horvan waggled his eyebrows. "We are ev-ery-where," he whispered dramatically.

"I believe you." Hashtag shook his head. "We need some kind of a badge or a code sign or something. You know? Like, something to show any shifter you might come across that you're an ally."

Rael laughed, but the doc shook his head. "You three were told because you had to know. The fewer humans who know of our existence, the better."

"But it shouldn't *be* like that," Roadkill stressed. "Humans and shifters should be able to live together, right?"

"In an ideal world, perhaps." Doc's face tightened. "But we don't live in such a world. I think what happened to Dellan proves that."

"You said you were gonna contact someone who could tell us more about shifters. Are you still gonna do that?" Crank demanded. "Because I really wanna know more." There were nods from Hashtag and Roadkill.

"Hell, so do I." Dellan was tired of knowing so little about his origins.

"To be honest, after what I've learned about Dellan's experiences, I was going to contact him anyway. This drug they've developed...." Doc shivered. "There are unpleasant implications."

Dellan's stomach clenched, and his heartbeat sped up. "Call them, Doc. We have to spread the word." And just like that, the peace he'd been enjoying was shattered.

You know whatever happens, I'll protect you, don't you?

Dellan met Horvan's gaze. *I know. But I'm not thinking about me.*

He was more concerned for the world of shifters out there who had no idea something so evil existed.

Rael gave a start. "Holy shit. I completely forgot." He fished his phone out of his pocket.

"What's wrong?" Horvan's expression was suddenly watchful.

Rael stared at him. "My parents are going to kill me. I promised to let them know when Dellan was safe."

Dellan laughed. "Well, you *have* had a few busy days. I'm sure they'll forgive you."

Rael's eyes twinkled. "In case this hasn't occurred to you yet? These are your future parents-in-law."

Oh my God. I'm as good as married.

Horvan chuckled. *Yeah. That was kinda my reaction too. Brave new world, huh?*

Should I be worried here?

Horvan shrugged. *No idea. I've yet to meet them. How scary can they be?*

Rael glared at them. *I can hear you, you know.*

Dellan's stomach clenched. "Maybe we should wait a while before you introduce me."

Rael's brows knitted. "Why?"

"Because the world we live in just got really complicated, and probably dangerous." He shivered. "The last thing I want to do is put them in danger."

"There's nothing to connect them to any of this," Rael protested.

"Yet," Horvan reminded him. "And let's pray it doesn't come to that." He gave Rael a nod. "Call them, but don't tell them anything vital, okay?"

"Gotcha." Rael's shiver matched Dellan's. "Fuck. Now you've got *me* scared too."

"Good." When Rael gave Horvan a perplexed glance, Horvan stared back at him. "Fear gives you an edge. It keeps you alert. Better scared than complacent."

Dellan's chest tightened. *Brave new world indeed.*

CHAPTER TWENTY

DELLAN CLIMBED the ladder to their bed, his legs feeling heavy and his body aching. "I feel like I've aged twenty years," he complained. The cabin was quiet except for the faint sound of laughter coming from the lower level. Dellan hoped Doc wasn't in any hurry to get to sleep; it sounded like the boys weren't ready for bed yet.

Horvan was waiting for him at the top, holding out his hand. "And that might be a result of the overly long shift. Your brain has gotten back in gear, but it sounds like your body is taking its time. Let's face it, none of us have ever dealt with anything like this before."

"And it's like you said," Rael added, sitting on the edge of the bed. "You're not going to dash off right this second and go see Anson. Let him stew a while. You have better things to do with your time." His eyes gleamed in the soft light of the lamp beside the bed. Behind Dellan, Horvan carefully drew the curtain that cut them off from the rest of the cabin.

"Oh, I do, do I?" Dellan said with a smile. His heartbeat raced as Rael got to his feet and approached him slowly. Dellan shuddered out a long breath as Rael leaned in to kiss his neck, then move down to his collarbone. Next he grew aware of Horvan's solid body behind him, Horvan's hands on his waist. "Feels like a trap," he joked. "I've got nowhere to go." His pulse quickened. *Guys, it's been a while, okay?*

Relax. Horvan slipped his hands under Dellan's sweater and stroked his belly, making Dellan shiver with anticipation. *Tonight is for getting acquainted.*

Tonight is for touching. Rael moved higher until he was looking Dellan in the eye. *And especially kissing.* Before Dellan could react, Rael took his mouth in the sweetest kiss Dellan had ever known. He gave himself up to the waves of pleasure that ran through him, losing himself in the kiss.

When they parted, he caught his breath. "How can a simple kiss blow my mind?"

Because we're your mates. Rael smiled. *And if that was mind-blowing, you're not going to survive what comes next.*

"Enough talk. Bed," Horvan whispered, maneuvering them toward it. Dellan allowed himself to be pulled onto the bed, placing himself between Rael and Horvan.

"Isn't this where *you* should be?" he asked Rael teasingly.

Rael rolled his eyes. "Okay, okay. So we all know my lion submits to both of you. Well, tonight, you let *us* do all the work." And before Dellan could utter another word, Rael leaned over and kissed him again, taking his time. Dellan couldn't lie still. He put his arms around Rael, pulling him closer, investing himself fully in the lingering kiss.

Feeling a little left out here, boys. Horvan pushed up Dellan's sweater, and Dellan gasped into Rael's kiss as a warm, wet mouth enclosed his nipple while Horvan stroked and caressed his chest and belly.

Dellan was in heaven.

He had no idea how long they lay like that, still clothed, enjoying one another's touch. Little by little, clothing was discarded, but they were in no hurry. Exchanges were a mix of whispered words and shared thoughts, Dellan carried along on a wave of exquisite sensual bliss. When at last they were naked, he explored them, stroking and caressing, kissing, licking, and sucking until soft moans that apparently none of them could contain filled the air. He enjoyed the feel of Horvan's strong, firm body beneath his fingertips, the feel of Rael's soft lips as they kissed every inch of him, and the sensations that filled him with delight as both Horvan and Rael teased his body with inquisitive fingers.

"This feels amazing, and we haven't even gotten to the best part yet." Dellan arched his back as Rael kissed his belly, his lips softly grazing the root of his dick. He shuddered, then found the presence of mind to place his hand on Rael's head. "Stop."

Rael turned to look at him. "What's wrong?"

Dellan laughed quietly. "Nothing is wrong. On the contrary, I really want your mouth on me. But...."

"You want to wait until the blood test results are in, don't you?" Horvan wrapped his hand around Dellan's cock and gently tugged it, making Dellan groan. "That's okay. We can wait a few days more. After all, we've waited *this* long."

Dellan stilled. "Hold on. What do you mean?" He looked from Horvan to Rael. "You guys haven't...?"

"No, we haven't." Rael crawled up Dellan's body and kissed him lightly on the lips. "We were waiting for you." Horvan joined him, and Dellan was locked into a three-way kiss, something he'd never experienced.

When they parted, he gazed at them in awe. "You waited," he said simply. He looped his arms around their necks. "I know it's probably me being overly cautious, seeing as we're immune to human infections, but—"

"But you don't want to put us at risk, because we're dealing with unknowns here," Horvan interjected. "It's okay, honest."

Rael stroked Dellan's chest. "I'd rather wait until you get the all clear too. Well, it's either that or condoms." He brushed his lips over Dellan's ear, making him shiver. *And I don't want anything between us when you both come inside me.*

Oh fuck. Dellan closed his eyes and enjoyed the image in Rael's head, the three of them locked together in a chain, Dellan rocking between them, all of them covered in a light sheen of sweat.

Okay, you need to stop that right now. I've only got so much willpower, you know? Horvan kissed Dellan on the mouth. *So we're all going to curl up and go to sleep. Got it?*

Rael was shaking with laughter. *Yes, Mama Bear.*

Dellan bit his lip. *Mama Bear?* He had to fight hard not to react.

Horvan let out a low growl. *I am gonna fucking kill Crank for that.*

Not right now you're not. Dellan pulled the sheets over them and snuggled down between his mates. They hooked their legs over

178

his, joining hands on his belly. Their breath stirred his hair and their bodies warmed his.

It was the perfect way to sleep.

"I COULD eat a mountain of bacon and a ton of home fries this morning," Dellan announced as they sat down to eat breakfast.

Crank snorted. "Gee, I wonder why?"

"Crank." Roadkill's voice held a note of warning.

He arched his eyebrows. "Don't give me that, not when you're thinking exactly the same thing." Crank gave a gleeful grin. "I'm surprised the whole cabin wasn't rocking." Beside him, Hashtag snickered.

Ignore him. Don't give him any ammunition, Rael advised.

Dellan had no intention of responding. He helped himself to more eggs and dug in. That had been the best sleep of his life. He'd awoken early, feeling rested and buzzing with energy.

Enough energy that for the first time since his release, he wanted to play.

"Being serious for a minute?" Crank took a slurp of his coffee. "Maybe we should, you know, leave."

Horvan frowned. "Who's 'we'?"

"Me and these two." Crank gestured to Roadkill and Hashtag.

"Why? Is there someplace you have to be?" Horvan inquired.

"Well, no, but—"

"Besides, I thought you wanted to be there when we confront Anson," Rael observed. He peered intently at Crank. "You *do* want to be part of that, right?"

"Sure, but...." Crank pushed his plate away. "Look, it occurred to me we might be... in the way, y'know?" He coughed.

Horvan smiled. "Oh, I see." Rael chuckled.

"Okay, you can stop that right now. You're not in the way," Dellan assured him.

Crank's eyes gleamed. "Oh, cool. Are we talking an orgy, then?" He glared when a chorus of "Crank!" filled the air. "What? Like you wouldn't wanna piece of that?"

"I swear, you are the gayest straight guy I ever met," Roadkill declared, rolling his eyes.

"Doc, do you want to leave too?" Dellan didn't want to be an imposition.

The doc smiled. "Believe it or not, I'm enjoying being here. It's been a while since I got to spend time with these guys, and it's great to catch up. Not to mention, it's peaceful here. At my age, you need all the restful moments you can get."

Something the doc said struck a chord. "How did you all meet?" Dellan inquired.

"When I was on active service. I met Horvan first. He was still green, bless him, but he learned fast. Then as we met in various combat zones, I was introduced to these three." Doc smiled. "Once met, never forgotten."

Crank preened until Hashtag hit him upside the head. Crank glared at him. "Hey, what the fuck was that for?"

"Because you needed a wallop, that's why."

"By the way, Rael, I looked you up," Doc said quietly. When Rael gave him an inquiring glance, he smiled again. "I've seen your pictures. Excellent stuff. I particularly liked the article on the mating habits of the condor. How on earth did you get those photos?"

"Would you believe hanging upside down from a cliff for two hours?"

Dellan gaped. "Seriously?"

Doc laughed. "Now I *know* there's something in this mates business. You and Horvan are a perfect match. He's an adrenaline junkie."

"But I'm not," Dellan commented. *Where do I fit in?*

Before either of his mates could react, Doc spoke up. "You're their anchor. *You* are what grounds them. Their work takes them away from home, but you are what will draw them back."

"How can you know that?" Dellan demanded. "You've only just met me."

"But you told me everything I needed to know when you shared why Tom Prescott had left the company to you and not Anson."

Dellan shook his head. "You can't know I'm perfect for them based on only that."

Crank and Roadkill got up from the table, and Hashtag cleared away the dishes. Doc refilled Dellan's coffee mug, then leaned back in his chair, regarding him with a speculative gaze.

"Tell me something. One of the biggest debates going on now concerns the price of medicines. Your company could have been making billions more, yet when you took on the company, you kept your prices low. Tell me why."

Dellan didn't have to think about it. "Tom told me we were there to help people. To do what we could to make their lives better. We weren't going to profit from illness."

"So when you took over the company…."

"I believe the same as he did. I won't gouge people who are trying to survive."

Don nodded slowly. "And you still think you're not the one who can care for two men like Rael and Horvan here? They go out and have to deal with dangerous assignments, but with you to come home to, I guarantee neither of them will be taking nearly as many risks."

Horvan huffed. "You got that right." Rael nodded.

"Now wait a minute." Dellan stared at them. "You make people's lives better too. I don't want you to give that up. None of us should change who we are at the core."

"I agree," Doc said at once. "But that's why you three will have to be open and honest with one another."

Rael chuckled. "We can all read the others' thoughts, Doc. I don't think we can get much more open than that."

Doc's chuckle echoed his. "After all my years dealing with people who aren't going to make it, let me tell you one thing. Those with the biggest fears find ways to hide things from those they love." He shook his head. "Don't do that. Be there for each other. Be open and honest. So what if you're mates, bound together by fate? That's the easy part." His eyes twinkled. "Not screwing it up? That's all on the three of you."

Dellan regarded Doc with interest. "You seem to know a lot about my company."

"When I did a search on Rael last night?" Doc grinned. "I looked you up too."

Dellan folded his arms. "I'm sure that as soon as I was out of the picture, my beloved half brother raised prices."

"Actually, he didn't," Rael said quickly. "He believes, like Tom did, that meds shouldn't cost the earth. He told me that much himself."

"Being ethical hasn't done him any harm," Doc added. "The company has gone from strength to strength during the last year."

Dellan growled. "Don't give me a reason to like the little bastard, not when I'm ready to kick his ass out of the building."

Horvan snorted. "Trust me, you can still do that. He had you locked up in a cage. That warrants *major* ass kicking."

"Don't forget pounding," Crank called out from across the room.

Horvan guffawed. "Crank, if you wanna pound his ass, we won't stop you." He grinned. "I may even bring popcorn."

"And I'll record it on my phone, then put it online," Hashtag added, his eyes gleaming.

Crank paled. "Hell, no. My mom might see that shit."

"Your mom checks out porn sites?"

Crank shuddered. "You wouldn't believe half the stuff she gets up to. Makes my hair curl."

"What hair?" Horvan teased.

"Fuck you." Crank grabbed his cigarettes. "Smoke time." He pulled on his boots and headed for the door.

"Whereas for me, it's playtime." Dellan needed to get out into the fresh air. He pushed back his chair and stood. A familiar tingle trickled over his skin, and he welcomed it. He knew exactly what it meant.

Dellan needed to shift.

CHAPTER TWENTY-ONE

RAEL GRINNED. "Playtime. I like the sound of that."

Dellan's eyes sparkled. "Good. Because I want to play out there."

"In the snow."

Dellan nodded slowly.

Rael narrowed his gaze. "You're not talking about dressing warmly and throwing snowballs, are you?"

Dellan shook his head, his gaze locked on Rael's. "I'm talking lions and tigers and bears." He grinned.

"Oh m—" That was as far as Crank got before Roadkill slapped a hand over his mouth.

Horvan laughed. "Thank you, Roadkill. And as for playtime, I like it. What's wrong with a little snow?"

"Ugh, lions aren't big fans of snow?" Rael shivered. He didn't know if this was true of all lions, but it was for him, so that was good enough as far as Rael was concerned.

"Is it safe to go out there?" Doc inquired.

Hashtag grabbed his laptop and opened it up. "Time I checked the perimeter cameras anyway. Not that I'm concerned—we'd have heard an alarm if anyone crossed the property boundaries." He grinned. "And if you *really* wanna play, I have an idea that might make it fun."

Rael glared at him. "No. No ideas." Nothing that meant they stayed out in the snow longer than necessary.

Doc cleared his throat. "Something to be aware of. I made a phone call last night to that contact I was telling you about."

"The dangerous guy?" Horvan frowned.

"I wouldn't have asked him to come here if I thought he was a threat," Doc commented.

"Then he is coming?" Hashtag asked.

Doc nodded. "I only gave him the bare bones of the situation. But as soon as I mentioned taking Dellan from his cage, he became very interested. Of course he knew about it—the op was national news—but finding out it wasn't perpetrated by an animal activist group was a surprise. He wants to meet Dellan."

"And you're certain his coming here presents no danger?" Horvan didn't appear convinced, judging by his narrowed gaze and pursed lips. "I'm not happy about you inviting someone here who I haven't vetted."

"Did I mention the fact that he is also a shifter?" Doc met Horvan's stare head-on. "I would never do anything that might endanger you."

Hey. I trust the doc. I thought you did too. Rael's stomach clenched.

Horvan drew in a deep breath. "I know that, Doc. Sorry. It's just that—"

Doc got up from his chair and walked around to where Horvan sat. He patted Horvan's shoulder. "I do understand. You have mates to protect now," he said softly.

"Guys?" Hashtag coughed. "All clear, so if you wanna shift and go play, I'll keep an eye out." He smiled. "A little exercise will do you good. That's if you didn't get enough exercise last night." He waggled his eyebrows.

Horvan rolled his eyes. "You couldn't resist, could ya?"

"I want to know about Hashtag's idea of fun," Dellan declared.

"That will be a surprise." Hashtag's eyes lit up. "Trust me, you'll love it."

Rael sighed. "Okay. If we're going to do this, let's do it." He shrugged off his clothes and shifted.

That is so fast! Dellan gaped.

Rael shifted from lion to human to lion and back to human again, loving the sound of Dellan's delighted laughter.

Horvan let out a low whistle. "You are amazing. I can change that fast now and again, but you do it like your body flows from one form to another. What's your secret?"

Rael grinned. "Most teens masturbate. I practiced shifting."

Horvan snorted. "Well, if that's what it took to learn to shift so fast, I'm glad I stuck with jacking off." He undressed, and a short while later, there was his beautiful bear.

Out. Now.

Rael crossed the floor to the cabin door and opened it, laughing. "Can you get through this gap?"

Seconds later, Horvan was back in human form. "Smartass." He stepped outside and shifted again, then lumbered over the snow.

"Looks like our mate wants to play too," Rael said, smiling.

Dellan squirmed out of his sweats and top, leaving them in a pile on the floor, and Rael's heart soared to see him shimmer into a healthy-looking tiger, his fur sleek, his eyes bright. Dellan leaped from the door to land on the snow with a soft thud.

"If you can't beat them," Rael said with a smile. He shifted and followed his mates.

Dellan pounced on him as soon as his paws touched the snow. Soon they were both rolling around in the cold powdery substance, Dellan batting at it with his heavy paws. Horvan was on them in a heartbeat, and there began a playful chase as they padded over the ground, leaving their prints in it.

Dellan gave Rael a nip on his rear, then ran off, clearly wanting Rael to retaliate. Horvan wrestled Dellan to the ground, and Dellan was on his back, twisting and turning, batting Horvan as the bear nuzzled his belly.

A strange low-frequency buzz attracted Rael's attention, and he sought the source. Dellan rolled onto his front and froze, his attention riveted on the object that flew toward them. Then he gave chase, running at it. *Catch it.*

Horvan followed suit. *Drone. Catch drone.*

Rael caught sight of Hashtag in the doorway, grinning, his hands occupied. The drone led Dellan and Horvan a merry dance, both of them running in circles and sprinting across the snow, Dellan executing huge leaps to try to catch it.

Rael was not playing. Rael was freezing his furry ass off.

Dellan leaped into the air, trying to clamp the drone between his paws, but the device rose higher, evading him. Then it dropped, and Dellan went for it again, only this time he caught it, pulling it to the ground, where it lay, steam rising from it. Dellan and Horvan approached it with obvious caution, Dellan pawing at it. Both reared back when it rose into the air again, and the chase was on once more.

Watching them made Rael tired. Not to mention the fact that his paws felt frozen.

He ran back to the cabin, and Hashtag hastily stepped aside as he leaped through the doorway into blessed warmth. Rael shifted, then hurried over to the wood stove in the corner.

"Fuck, it's cold out there." He stood in front of it, letting the radiating heat warm his body.

"Did you like my little toy?" Hashtag called from the door. "I figured cats like to chase things."

Rael had to admit it was a brilliant idea. "I think Dellan got more out of it than I did."

"They're having fun out there," Doc observed, watching through the window. "They seem well suited to these conditions."

"You want to know what *I'm* well suited to?" Rael grinned. "Staying indoors and drinking hot chocolate."

Crank moaned. "Oh yeah. Now you're talking." He went to the cabinet.

Mate. It was Dellan's voice, soft and coaxing. *Maaaaate.*

Uh-uh. Lions and snow don't mix. Rael was staying put. He'd had enough exercise for one day.

Get your ass out here, Rael. Now. Horvan's order sent a pleasurable shudder through him. *Ever been fucked in the snow?*

Rael laughed. *If you're trying to persuade me, you just lost.*

Danger.

He stiffened instantly, his heart hammering. *What danger, Dellan?* Rael raced to the door.

Man coming.

"Hashtag, we've got company." Rael scanned the landscape and spotted the figure in the distance. *Get inside now, both of you.* He grabbed his clothing and dressed quickly.

Hashtag dropped the drone's control module onto a nearby chair and dashed over to his laptop. "Okay, he's crossed the boundaries."

"Who is he?" Roadkill demanded, striding across the cabin floor, a rifle in his hand. "Can you see him yet?"

Crank had grabbed a gun and was peering through the window. "Okay, I see him." He opened it and took aim through the gap. "Got him in my sights." He held the gun rock steady.

Dellan shifted as he crossed the threshold. "It could be Doc's contact. He's too far away for me to tell if he's a shifter." He stepped into his sweats and pulled his top over his head.

Horvan stepped into the cabin, shivering, and closed the door behind him. "Tell me what you see, Crank." Rael threw Horvan his clothing.

"Male, Caucasian. Dressed in black." Crank smirked. "Nice of him to make himself such an easy target. He's armed. And definitely coming this way."

"What's he carrying?" Horvan demanded.

"Rifle. Looks like he could pass for a hunter, but…." Crank paused.

"What is it?" Rael's heartbeat was still climbing.

"This guy is military, or ex-military at the very least."

"I'm with Crank." Roadkill was aiming his rifle through another window.

Doc peered through the glass before inhaling deeply. "Relax, boys. He's okay."

"Stand down," Horvan instructed them.

Pouting, Crank lowered his gun. "I guess that's one more for hot chocolate, then." He went back to his task.

Doc opened the front door. "Vic? I didn't think you'd be here so fast."

Vic stomped his feet outside, then stomped his boots on the mat inside the cabin. "I got on the first flight I could." He glanced around the interior, arching his eyebrows at the sight of Roadkill's rifle. "I guess I should have told you I was coming."

"It might have been advisable," Doc commented dryly. "Come sit at the table and I'll do the introductions."

Vic nodded, then sniffed the air. He stiffened. "Are they staying?" he asked, pointing to Crank, Roadkill, and Hashtag.

Horvan set his jaw. "You're free to talk in front of them."

Vic scowled. "You trust them?"

"Hey, *buddy*." Crank snarled. "We've probably been fighting together since before you were an itch in your daddy's pants. How old are you anyway? Twelve?"

Rael had to admit Vic looked very young. He was clean-shaven, with dark brown eyes framed by long black lashes.

He's pretty, isn't he?

Rael flashed Horvan a glance. *Stop that.*

Well, he is.

Vic frowned. "Am I missing something?" He looked from Rael to Horvan.

"You'll have to forgive my three friends here," Doc said pleasantly. "They have a gift the rest of us can only dream of."

Rael moved to stand with Dellan, and Horvan joined them. "Right now, I'm not convinced you're a friend," Rael declared. Horvan held himself stiffly. Dellan was trembling, so Rael inched closer to him. "And if I think you're a threat to me or my mates, you won't leave here alive." It was an empty threat on his part, but instinct told him the others would have no qualms about wasting the guy.

You know it. Horvan's hand was at Rael's back, a comforting touch.

Vic stilled. "Mates?" Instantly his whole demeanor changed. "Oh my God. Seriously?" He dropped into the nearest chair and gaped at Doc. "You didn't tell me that part."

"I didn't want to spoil the surprise," Doc said with a smile. He gestured to Roadkill and Hashtag. "Let's all sit down, okay? Crank, how's that hot chocolate coming along?"

Vic snickered. "I could use something stronger, if you've got it."

"Only if I see some ID first," Crank retorted. "Because no fucking *way* are you twenty-one."

Vic smiled. "I'm thirty-five, actually."

"Get the fuck out of here." Crank guffawed. "Thirty-five, my ass."

"When your animal has as long a lifespan as mine, you tend to age slower. And before you ask?" His eyes glittered. "I'm a Greenland shark."

"Is that supposed to impress us?" Hashtag folded his arms. "Because the only shark I've ever heard of is a great white." He grinned. "*Jaws* scared the shit out of me when I was a kid."

"Then let me educate you. Greenland sharks can live more than five hundred years, so technically speaking, I'm only a baby."

Hashtag held up his hands defensively. "Okay, okay, I'm officially impressed."

"Well, I'm not." Crank looked smug. "What you're telling me is, I was right. In shark years, you're not old enough to drink."

"For fuck's sake, grow up," Roadkill gritted out.

"Me?" Crank appeared offended. "*He's* the one who admitted to being a baby." Everyone stared at him, and he grinned. "Okay, *now* I'm done."

Rael returned his attention to Vic, who was shaking his head. "I've never met a shifter that wasn't a land animal before."

Roadkill got up from the table, then returned with a bottle of whiskey and several glasses. "This is all we've got." He poured Vic a glass.

Vic downed it in one gulp. "Now," he said, setting his empty glass on the table. "Suppose you start at the beginning."

Rael started the tale, with Horvan and Dellan adding in additional details at various points. Vic listened intently, nodding in places and scowling in others. He smiled when they recounted details of the rescue, especially the part where Dellan's release was claimed by several groups. Dellan then took over, sharing what had happened to him, as well as their suspicions about Anson and the part he might have played in the development of the drug.

Vic helped himself to another glass of whiskey. "And you're positive you never told him you're a shifter?"

"Positive." Dellan met Vic's direct gaze.

Vic nodded before taking a drink. "I'm glad you called me," he said to Doc. "This is something we need to be aware of."

"Who's 'we'?" Rael said suddenly. When Vic remained silent, he crossed his arms. "I think we have a right to know. Because this obviously concerns us."

Vic became very still. "This is a need-to-know situation, and—"

"Fuck that," Crank said, his voice harsh. "We know as much about shifters as they do, and that ain't a lot, believe me. So how come no one knows anything? How come they have *no fucking clue* how many shifters are out there?" He banged the table with his fist. "We want *answers*, goddammit!"

"This is nothing to do with you," Vic fired back at him. "You're human, for Christ's sake."

Crank nodded. "And we just risked our lives to save a shifter. I'm thinking you owe us for that." His face tightened.

Vic stared at him for a moment, then sighed. "I guess I can tell you a little of our history."

"You know about it?" Rael asked, his heart racing. Finally some answers to the questions that had plagued him since puberty.

Vic smiled. "I should. I'm an oral historian."

Crank snickered. "He said oral."

Roadkill rolled his eyes, then addressed Vic. "Ignore the infant in our midst and tell us what you know."

Vic leaned back in his chair. "As long as there have been shifters, there have also been oral historians. Our job is to learn by heart, retain, and pass on to future historians."

"Like in *Roots*?" Crank asked. When Roadkill made an impatient noise, Crank scowled at him. "Hey, it's a valid comment."

"And a correct one," Vic told him. "In case you haven't worked it out, as far as mankind is concerned, shifters are a myth. There are writings about us, stories that date back almost a thousand years."

"Does your oral history go back that far?" Hashtag leaned forward, his eyes shining.

Vic smiled. "It does. The general consensus among humans is that if there was a grain of truth to the stories, shifters have long since died out."

"Except we know they haven't," Roadkill announced with a gleam in his eye.

"Exactly. We have survived, but not in great numbers. Only two shifters can produce shifter offspring. If a shifter mates with a human, the children will be human too."

"Survived what, exactly?" Doc asked.

Vic fell silent.

"Vic?" Dellan's voice was quiet. "What can you tell us?"

Vic stared into his glass. "One thing remains unclear—when shifters first emerged. That is too far into the past. It's thought that shifters existed in great numbers until the arrival of man."

"Let me guess." Horvan's brow furrowed. "They tried to wipe us out."

"Yes, and they almost succeeded. Those who survived spread out to all parts of the world. Where the oral history proves less shaky is the story of the two brothers."

Hashtag sighed. "This is fascinating."

Vic took another drink before continuing. "They had very different ideals, and even their names pointed to this. Ansfrid, which means divinity and peace, lived up to his name. He wanted to live in harmony with mankind. His brother, Ansger, did not."

"What does Ansger mean?" Rael inquired.

Vic paused. "Divinity and spear."

"Oh fuck." Crank reached for an empty glass and filled it. "We're not gonna like this part, are we?"

"Ansger wanted to rule over mankind, thinking men weaker than shifters. It is said the brothers couldn't bear to live together, and they split. One bloodline mated with whoever they loved, human or shifter. The other chose to mate only with shifters."

"I don't like the sound of this," Dellan murmured.

"Me neither," Doc added. "Because all this brings one word to mind, and it's not a word I like."

"Doc?" Rael shivered. "What's wrong?"

"This business of shifters only mating with shifters. In other words, they were trying not to water down the gene pool. And the next step would be weeding out the inferior genes, the weaker genes."

"Are we talking… eugenics?" Hashtag gazed at Doc with wide eyes.

"I don't know." Doc turned to Vic. "Are we?"

"We don't know." Vic finished his drink. "Since the split, there's been little information on what the Gerans are doing, beyond snippets and rumors. Nothing that's verifiable, at any rate."

"Gerans?" Horvan frowned.

Vic nodded. "That's what the followers of Ansger became. I'm a Fridan. We follow Ansfrid's example."

"Oh, I *really* don't like this," Crank announced. "Different bloodlines, gene purity, followers, cloak-and-dagger bullshit…."

"Ansger and Anfrid were apparently very charismatic men. They drew followers from all kinds of shifters."

"Yeah, but from the sound of it, there are 'followers' out there who think all shifters are equal, but some are a little more equal than others." Crank shuddered. "And before you know it, you've got a civil war on your hands." He peered at Vic. "What else can you tell us?"

"Believe me, I've said more than I'm allowed to already." Vic shook his head. "Anything else I say would be hearsay, rumor, and innuendo. As an oral historian, I won't sink to that. I'll follow up, sure, to ferret out the truth, but I won't be the one to spread misinformation."

"Is that it? Are you done now?"

It was obvious to Rael that Crank and Vic were never going to be bosom buddies.

"Actually? Could I stay a while? I have so many questions for you." Vic's eyes shone. "We know so little about mates, and for there to be three of you...."

Rael looked to Horvan and Dellan. *What do you think?*

Horvan nodded. *I think he needs all the help we can give him.*

Roadkill sighed. "Well, what's one more mouth to feed?" He winked at Rael. "We can always give Crank a smaller portion."

"You could sure as hell try," Crank said with a growl.

"Then I can stay? It wouldn't be for long because I have places to be, but for a day at least."

Rael liked this new Vic. He'd gone from being a menacing, brooding figure to an eager man, excited to learn more. Despite his actual age, Vic gave the impression of being younger.

Rael smiled. *Well, Crank did say Vic is a baby for his species.*

It was as if Crank read his mind. "Hey, wait a minute, Mr. Oral Historian. All that guff about how it's your shark that keeps you looking so young? That shit don't add up."

Vic arched his eyebrows and folded his arms. "Oh?"

Crank pointed at Horvan. "After he told us about shifters, I got curious. I went online and looked up bears and lions. Bears only live about twenty-five years. Lions don't even live that long. So by your reckoning, they should already be dead."

Vic chuckled. "You're applying human logic and human rules here? Well, I got news for you. Human rules don't apply when you're talking about the paranormal. And no, I can't explain why shark shifters live as long as we do, because every other shifter I know lives a normal human life span. Is it because oral historians have always been sharks? Who knows? We don't know everything about shifters." His face darkened. "I can only say living a long time isn't as hot as you might think. I don't make friends, for one thing."

"Why not?" Rael asked, struck by the sadness he saw in Vic's eyes.

"Because I don't want to be the one watching my friends die hundreds of years before I do. Not that *you'd* care," he added, glaring at Crank. "You don't give a shit about me."

Crank opened and shut his mouth, his eyes wide. Then he sighed. "You're wrong. About me caring." He glanced around the table. "My buddies are The. Fucking. Best. Thing in my life. I wouldn't be without them. And what you just described sounds like an incredibly lonely existence." He locked gazes with Vic. "I apologize."

Vic blinked. His expression softened. "Thanks. I appreciate that."

"And I had a thought...."

Hashtag bit his lip. "Did it hurt?"

Crank fired him a warning look before giving Vic his full attention. "I don't think sharks live long because they're historians. I think they're historians because they—you—live long. You'll know things long after generations have turned to dust."

Everyone around the table stared at him.

"What?"

Roadkill shook his head. "That was pretty damn eloquent. After all these years, you still manage to surprise me."

Vic smiled. "I was thinking the same thing." He shook his head. "The thing you have to remember about shifters is, there are no rules. For every fact we *think* we know, we discover contradictions to that fact. Like my species, for example. But there are other things. Like why a two-hundred-pound human can become a four-hundred-pound bear, and others turn into six-ounce mice." He laughed softly. "It makes my head spin."

"I hear ya on that one," Crank remarked. "My head's been spinning ever since Horvan shifted into a teddy bear." He grinned.

"Or should that be a *Mama Bear*?" Roadkill added, his eyes glinting with mischief.

Rael loved the low growl that rumbled in Horvan's throat.

Vic's gaze alighted on the whiskey bottle. "Is that really all you've got?"

Roadkill chuckled. "I said all we've got is whiskey. What I *didn't* say is how much of it we have." He refilled Vic's glass, then poured one for himself. He raised his glass. "Glad to have you here, Vic."

Vic stilled for a moment, then raised his own, clinking it against Roadkill's. "Glad to be here."

"You might not say that after you've put up with a night of Crank snoring," Hashtag muttered, helping himself to whiskey.

Vic smiled. "I think I can cope."

Rael couldn't dismiss the thought that their little band had just gotten bigger.

RAEL WAS about to call it a night when Vic yawned. "Is it that time?"

Hashtag laughed. "I'm not surprised you're tired. You haven't stopped talking all day."

Vic flushed. "Sorry." He peered at Rael, who was sitting on the couch with Dellan. "Did I ask too many questions?"

"Not at all," Rael assured him. "I hope our answers helped." Not that they'd been able to share all that much. Vic had wanted to hear about the first time Dellan had spoken to Rael, his dreams, and how the three of them communicated in both forms.

"There were a couple of questions I didn't get around to," Vic confessed. "Not because we ran out of time, but because they were, shall we say, a bit… personal." He coughed.

Crank snorted. "Aw. That could've been entertaining." Roadkill gave him a hard stare.

"I think we could all do with some sleep," Doc said suddenly. "It's been a long day." He smiled at Vic. "You'll be downstairs with me and the boys."

Hashtag clicked off the lamp in the corner of the room. "You're sleeping on the couch."

Vic frowned. "Okay, but isn't there another bed up there?" He pointed to the loft bedroom above the kitchen.

Rael opened his mouth to tell him it was available, but Dellan got there first. "There is, but it's… not comfortable."

Rael blinked. No one had even spent a night in that bed.

"Besides, that couch is comfy," Doc told him.

"Yeah, and it's nice and peaceful down there," Roadkill added.

"Quieter than it would be up here, that's for damn sure," Crank muttered.

Warmth filled Rael as he realized what their friends were up to.

"If you say so." Vic got up from the couch, stretched, and yawned again. "Although it sounds like it's going to be crowded down there. Especially when there's only these three up—" He snapped his mouth shut, his face flushing. "Oh. Right." He coughed. "Well, I'll be saying good night, then." He gave Rael, Horvan, and Dellan a cheerful nod. "Sleep well."

There were smothered chuckles and snickers from Crank, Hashtag, and Roadkill as they followed him out of the room. Doc was the last to leave, his lips twitching.

He could have slept up here. Rael gave his mates a reproachful glance.

No, he couldn't. Even in Rael's head, Dellan's voice was firm.

Why not? It's not like we'll be doing anything tonight.

Dellan's eyes sparkled. *Says who?*

Rael stared at him. *How can you be in the mood to fool around? After all that?*

All what? Dellan frowned. *It's not like he came to tell us we're in danger, right? He told us about the two groups of shifters, that's all.*

Although I'm pretty sure there was stuff he didn't tell us, Horvan added.

You think? Rael's stomach clenched.

Horvan snaked his arms around Rael's waist. *Not that you need worry about it now. Personally? I'm all for a little fooling around.*

And I'm damn sure I am. Dellan's eyes gleamed.

Part of Rael's anatomy was already convinced. *But... you haven't gotten your results back yet.*

So? Dellan smiled. *I had something else in mind for tonight.*

Care to let us in on it? Horvan gazed at him mildly.

Dellan went over to the foot of the ladder and grasped a rung. He stared at them, and a wave of heat surged through Rael, leaving him breathless.

Dellan nodded slowly. *I want to watch.*

CHAPTER TWENTY-TWO

HORVAN GRINNED. "Kinky. I like it." He peered at Dellan. "Well, what are you waiting for? Get that cute ass up that ladder." He grabbed hold of Rael's asscheek and squeezed. "Because I'm gonna do exactly what I promised."

"And what's that?"

Dellan gazed down at them, loving the shiver that rippled through Rael as Horvan's lips brushed against his ear.

"Fuck your brains out," Horvan whispered as he reached out to mold his hand around Rael's hard-as-steel dick.

Dellan groaned. "Fuck, guys."

"That was the idea, wasn't it?" Horvan followed them up the ladder, and when they reached the bed, he didn't waste a second, pulling them both into a fervent three-way kiss. They kept their hands in constant motion, slipping under sweaters, sliding under waistbands, as the air filled with the sounds of muted gasps and rapid breathing.

Horvan broke the kiss and undressed Rael hurriedly before he stripped off his own clothing. Then he roughly tugged Rael to the left side of the bed and stuffed pillows under Rael's head. He nodded to Dellan. "Get comfortable."

Dellan was already naked, pulling on his erect cock. He climbed onto the other side, lay back against the pillows there, and spread his legs. "Don't wait on my account." His body tingled, and he realized he was experiencing Rael's anticipation.

Horvan's grin was positively evil. "I was thinking of taking my time." With one arm under Rael, he reached down to cup Rael's stiff dick and stroked it gently. Rael writhed against him, apparently unable to remain still.

"Fuck, he loves that," Dellan whispered.

Horvan glanced at him. "You can feel that?" His eyes gleamed. "Then tell me how this feels." He let go of Rael's cock and took Rael's hand, dragging it to his own heavy, thick dick. Rael wrapped his fingers around the shaft and tugged on it, soft moans spilling from his lips.

Dellan's groans echoed his. "I think you just turned up the heat." He pulled on his cock, keeping time with Rael, his breathing staccato. When Horvan lowered his head to kiss Rael, a pang lanced through Dellan. His mates were beautiful together, but what enhanced the sight was his awareness of their urgency, their spiraling desires, which sent Dellan's heart racing.

Then Horvan broke off, panting. "Move," he instructed Rael. "I wanna sit there."

Rael chuckled. "Bossy." He sat up, allowing Horvan to take his place against the pillows.

"Now kneel astride me, facing me," Horvan instructed. Rael complied, and Dellan caught his breath as Horvan took Rael's hard cock into his mouth, his hands on Rael's ass, spreading his cheeks, fingering his hole.

Dellan tugged harder on his dick. It was as if Horvan's mouth was on his own cock. He could feel every slide into that wet heat, and his own hips matched Rael's as Rael rocked between mouth and fingers. But what made him gasp was the look in Horvan's eyes as he gazed up at Rael.

He's worshipping him. The realization flooded him with warmth, and Dellan ached to touch them. Before he could move, Horvan lifted Rael into his arms and lowered him to the bed. He stretched out his hand to the nightstand and yanked open the drawer.

Horvan smiled at Dellan as he held up a bottle of lube. "At last I get to use it on someone else."

Dellan sensed the longing in him to be inside his mate. "Don't make him wait. Take him. He needs you." Rael's soft moan confirmed Dellan's words.

Horvan spread Rael's legs, slicked up a couple of fingers, and slid them into Rael's body while he hunched over to take Rael's cock into his mouth once more. Rael groaned, arching his back, his eyes closed, and Dellan felt the wave of exquisite pleasure that coursed through him.

Rael raised his head from the bed and stared at Horvan. "Now. He's right. I need you."

Horvan slicked up his own cock, turned Rael onto his side, facing Dellan, and guided his dick into position. Rael shifted his leg higher, and Dellan was afforded the perfect view of Horvan sliding leisurely into Rael's tight hole. Horvan cradled Rael's head in his hand as he gently rocked into him, and Dellan moaned aloud at the sensations that flooded Rael's body.

"I feel that too," he whispered. "Even the burn as you inch your way inside him."

Horvan groaned, lifting Rael's leg and hooking it over his own, spreading him wide before kissing Rael with such tenderness that Dellan wanted to weep. Rael shifted onto his back and flung his arms around Horvan's neck, his breath catching as Horvan kissed and teased his nipples and pulled on his cock, moving gently inside him.

Dellan couldn't remain an observer a moment longer.

He moved closer, leaning over to kiss Rael while he slid his hand down Rael's body, until his fingers met Horvan's warm, silken shaft as it stretched Rael's hole, moving rhythmically. Their lips met in another three-way kiss, feeding each other soft cries and gasps as Horvan picked up speed.

Dellan grabbed the lube and slicked up his fingers.

"Oh yes, please," Rael moaned.

Horvan stilled for a moment as Dellan carefully pressed a single finger into Rael's heat alongside Horvan's dick. Rael's eyes widened, and Dellan groaned at the burst of pleasure that surged through him. "More," Rael demanded.

Dellan added another finger, and Horvan began to move again, slowly at first, only now the two of them were fucking Rael, ramping up the sensations.

"Fuck, he's tight." Dellan stared at Rael's flushed face and chest, the concavity of his belly, the rise and fall of his chest.

"Let us share your pleasure." Horvan met his gaze. "Feed him your cock."

The thought of it was enough to send more heat barreling through him, but common sense tempered his libido. "But I thought… the test results…."

Both Horvan and Rael growled at the same time, and Dellan gave up any idea of protesting. Dellan withdrew his fingers, and Horvan shifted position, moving between Rael's spread thighs. Rael wrapped his legs around Horvan's waist, his hands on Horvan's back as Horvan thrust into him.

Fuck, he feels amazing. Horvan kissed Rael, both of them moving together as Horvan filled him over and over again. *Do you feel this?*

Every inch of him, Dellan assured him. He moved to kneel at Rael's head, holding his dick steady. Rael didn't waste a second. He turned his head toward Dellan, opened wide, and Dellan groaned aloud as Rael took him deep. He rocked back and forth, going further with every thrust, until his cock was slick with Rael's saliva and tears pricked Rael's eyes.

Don't stop, Rael pleaded, his fingers digging into Horvan's back. He rolled his eyes. *Holy fuck, what you're feeling….*

Dellan rocked faster, moaning as Horvan kissed Rael's chest. Every touch, every intimate caress only added to the sensations, and Dellan was lost in a world of sheer sensual bliss. Rael's mind was a blur, his thoughts losing their coherence as Horvan pushed him closer to the edge.

This is… transcendence. Dellan's body was on fire, his senses alight as each sight, smell, and touch propelled him to the mind-blowing orgasm he knew awaited them, their trajectory assured.

Horvan sat upright, his hips in constant motion, his hands gripping Rael's ankles as he spread his legs wide. Dellan leaned back to meet him in a blistering kiss, and the intimate embrace served to deepen the connection. Dellan shuddered as wave upon wave of sensual rapture took Rael higher and higher. Rael cried out, the sound muffled by Dellan's cock, as Horvan snapped his hips, driving his dick into him with almost savage thrusts.

Dellan held on to Horvan as he pistoned into Rael's mouth. *Close. So close.*

Rael gazed up at him. *Come on me. Let me feel it.* Dellan pulled free of his mouth, and Rael cried out as Horvan filled him to the hilt, his hips rocking.

Oh fuck, we're there. Horvan stiffened, and Dellan shot his load onto Rael's chest, the three of them locked into a mutual climax as Rael came with a drawn-out, almost euphoric, cry. Their thoughts collided, merging into a chaotic mess of ecstasy, fulfillment, and joy.

Horvan collapsed on top of Rael, and Dellan laughed at Rael's undignified squeak. "Feels like a bear squashed me," Rael gasped.

Horvan laughed and rolled off him to lie beside him. Then all three kissed, a tender, unhurried embrace accompanied by sated murmurs and gentle caresses, until they were breathing normally again, their bodies warm and sticky.

Dellan stared at them both in wonder. "You sensed what I was feeling too."

Rael laughed softly. "Are you kidding? Why the hell do you think I came so fast?"

"Because I fucked your brains out?" Horvan suggested with a grin.

Rael rolled his eyes. "Duh. But...." He shook his head. "I have no words." He peered at Horvan. "Have you ever had sex with a shifter? Not that I really want to know, but...."

Horvan gave a casual shrug. "A couple of times. Not in shifter form, though. But that was just sex. This? This was off the scale. No comparison." He cupped their faces, his eyes shining. "Imagine how it's gonna feel when the three of us are making love."

In the quiet that followed, as they held one another, Dellan let Horvan's words seep into his mind.

Making love. That was the perfect description.

Rael cleared his throat. "Now, can we get down the ladder and into the bathroom without waking up the others? I need a cleanup."

Dellan chuckled. He met Horvan's gaze. "I love his naivete. He thinks they're asleep. With all the noise we made."

Yeah, right.

Something still nagged at the back of his mind. "I wanted us all to be safe."

Rael sighed. "You wait and see. Those results will come back, and you'll have nothing to worry about."

"You know something I don't?"

Rael smiled. "Just what my senses tell me. I'm learning to pay more attention to them."

Horvan grinned. "What he said. Although I am jealous. He got to taste your dick." His pout was adorable.

Rael rolled his eyes. "Have you seen that cock? Trust me, there's plenty to go around."

Okay, that made Dellan feel like a million bucks.

"GREAT. YOU'RE awake. Get your ass over here."

Dellan laughed as he reached the floor, Rael on the ladder above him. Horvan was finishing getting dressed. "And good morning to you too, Hashtag." He peered at the white sheet hanging from the crossbeam. "What are you doing?"

Hashtag pointed to a spot in front of the sheet. "Stand here, facing me."

Dellan chuckled. "Will that get me an answer?"

"If you do as I say, sure." Hashtag narrowed his gaze. "Here. Now."

Dellan stood where instructed. "Now what?"

Hashtag grabbed his phone. "Now you look at the camera and don't smile." Dellan ran his fingers hastily through his hair, but Hashtag stopped him with an impatient wave. "You look fine." He held up the phone. "Keep still. And remember, no smiling." Seconds later, he clicked a couple of times. "Don't move yet," he warned, holding up a single finger. "I gotta check if these are okay."

"Are you going to let us in on whatever you're doing?" Rael inquired. He glanced around the cabin's interior. "Where is everyone?"

"The doc had to go into Salmon. Roadkill and Crank took him, as they were hunter-gathering groceries. Vic went along for the ride." Hashtag beamed. "Perfect. Okay, Dellan, you can move now." He went to the table where he'd set up his laptop. "There's coffee made." Hashtag gestured absently toward the countertop as he sat down.

Dellan poured two mugs and then joined Hashtag, while Rael went about preparing breakfast. "So why do you need my photo?"

Hashtag held out his empty mug. "I'll have another while you're there." Dellan took it, and Hashtag pointed to the monitor. "I woke up realizing there are things to be done sooner rather than later. My first task of the day is to organize a temporary ID for you."

"ID?"

Hashtag arched his eyebrows. "Well, unless you were carrying ID in a cute little bag around your neck when we got you outta there, you don't have any. Correct?"

For the first time since he'd arrived at the cabin, Dellan realized how much of a bubble he'd been living in. "I didn't even think about ID," he said slowly.

Hashtag gave a knowing nod. "You've had other things on your mind. Well, leave the ID to me."

"You can do that? Get me an ID?"

Hashtag grinned. "You'd be amazed at some of the things I can do. And no, it's not exactly legal, and it could be detected if it's examined too closely, but if you're gonna travel, you'll need it. And seeing as there was no little bag with an ID, that means no credit card either." He peered at Dellan. "I don't suppose you *happen* to remember the number, expiration date, and security code."

It was Dellan's turn to grin. "You'd be amazed at some of the things I can do." Hashtag chuckled at the repetition, but his eyes widened as Dellan rattled off the figures.

"What the fuck?"

Dellan shrugged. "What can I say? I have a head for numbers." Then Hashtag's question sank in. "Why do you need my credit card details?"

"Because you never know when you'll need 'em to lay a false trail."

"Excuse me?" Rael stared at him.

Hashtag sighed. "Okay. Picture this. Dellan goes back to Chicago to kick little half brother's ass and take back his company. But Dellan's been gone for more than a year. People are bound to ask where he's been. Now, he can't exactly say, 'Hey, I was forced to shift into a tiger and then I was kept like that in a glass cage,' can he? So we need to show he's actually been places during his absence."

"How can you do that?" Dellan was officially impressed.

Hashtag tapped the side of his nose. "The trick is not to go overboard. I create digital receipts that show you were someplace. Not too many, just enough. Of course, they wouldn't stand up to too much scrutiny, but why should anyone look too closely? It's not like you're wanted for murder, right?" He pointed to a notepad and pen beside the laptop. "Write down your card details for me, please."

Dellan did as asked. At that moment the cabin door opened and Doc and Vic entered, stomping their boots on the mat and shivering, Roadkill and Crank behind them.

One look at the coffeepot told Dellan he needed to make more.

"So you finally got up?" Crank commented as he dropped his box of groceries onto the table. "Not that I'm surprised. I guess you had a disturbed night." He smirked. Roadkill smacked him on the arm, and he glared. "Just because you're too prissy to say anything."

"*Prissy* has nothing to do with it," Roadkill retorted. "It's called being polite. Considerate. Insert other appropriate adjectives as required."

Horvan snorted. "I could've laid money on Crank being the first to say a word."

Hashtag gave Crank a smug glance. "I managed to have an entire conversation without bringing it up once. *You're* in the place for less than two seconds, and your mouth runneth over."

Doc walked over to Dellan and held out an envelope. "This is for you."

Dellan opened it and slid out the single sheet of paper. Warmth flooded him. "Oh. I see." Rael looked at him with interest, and Dellan smiled. *Guess who got the all clear.*

Horvan snickered. *Guess who forgot to add lube to the shopping list.*

Crank looked from Horvan to Rael to Dellan. He groaned. "I don't need to ask what that was about, do I? That's it. I'm wearing earplugs tonight."

Vic coughed. "Guys? I think it's time I was out of here. I just want to say… if you ever need an extra body, I'm your man." He handed Horvan a card. "Here's my number." Then he handed out cards to all of them. "So any of you can call me." Crank was the last to receive one, and Vic looked him in the eye. "Any of you," he stressed.

Whatever smartass reply Crank was probably about to make was lost when a phone rang. Doc blinked in obvious surprise as he pulled it from his jacket pocket. "Hello?"

They left him to his call. Vic came over to where Hashtag was working and nodded in approval. "I was going to ask if someone was dealing with this." He smiled. "You make a good team."

Hashtag shook his hand. "It was good to meet you. And if we need you, we *will* call."

"Boys?" Doc pocketed his phone. "I need to leave too. I'm needed to deal with an emergency."

Dellan was struck by Doc's grave expression. "Is it bad?"

Doc regarded him sadly. "It's something I can't discuss. I need to be on the first available flight out of here."

Roadkill grabbed his keys. "Okay. Both of you go get your stuff. I'll drive you to the airport." Vic gave a nod and headed downstairs. Roadkill addressed Hashtag. "Can you book a flight for Doc, once he gives you the destination? You can message him the details."

Hashtag nodded. "I'm on it." He tapped on the keyboard.

"I'll make you guys some snacks for the trip," Crank said. "It'll be better than anything you'll get at the airport."

Doc gave them a grateful smile. "Thank you. Sorry to have to leave like this."

Horvan patted his arm. "Hey, no need to apologize. You need to go." He clasped Doc's hand. "Thank you for everything you've done."

Doc pulled him into a hug. "Take care of your mates. I have a feeling your adventures are only beginning."

Dellan didn't contradict him. He had the same feeling.

HORVAN'S PHONE warbled, and he peered at the screen. "The doc's just touched down." He gazed at Dellan. *I wonder what kind of emergency he had to deal with?*

Dellan had been wondering the same thing.

"Have you guys thought about where you're gonna live?" Roadkill inquired. "I mean, once Dellan goes back to Chicago."

To Dellan's mind, it felt like reality was making an unwelcome intrusion. "I haven't given it much thought," he confessed.

"Why would you have?" Rael said quietly. "Think about it. I met you for the first time a mere thirteen days ago. I met Horvan twelve days ago." He smiled. "And we all met—in the flesh, as it were—in the early hours of Saturday. All of two days ago."

Dellan expelled a long breath. "Wow. When you put it like that…." It felt like he'd known them for… well, forever.

Horvan sipped his whiskey. "It's not like we don't have options. Rael has a house in Salmon, and I—"

"A tiny house," Rael added quickly.

Horvan nodded. "And I have my place in Indiana."

"I like the sound of your place," Rael admitted. "With all those forests on your doorstep. I couldn't survive without this forest." He gestured to the landscape beyond the window.

"Whereas I have a large house in Chicago Anson and I inherited from Tom." He shuddered. "Which reminds me. When we go to Chicago, I'm staying in a hotel. I don't even want to share the same air as Anson."

"Don't worry," Horvan told him. "You can stay with me. I have an apartment there."

Rael narrowed his gaze. "That bed will *not* take three."

"Then I'll buy a bigger bed," he replied practically. Rael laughed.

"Trust me, if it wasn't for Anson living there, I'd invite you all to stay at my place."

"Would there be room for all of us?" Roadkill inquired.

It was all Dellan could do to keep a straight face. "Oh, I think so."

Rael gazed at him quizzically. *What's so funny?*

Dellan smiled. *Tell you later.*

Rael shrugged and turned his attention to Crank. "And what's next for you guys?"

Crank laced his fingers behind his head. "We wait for the next call. There's never a shortage of work, right, boys?" He peered at Horvan. "Though Doc was right. You'll obviously be taking fewer of the dangerous ops."

Horvan blinked. "Next thing you'll be saying I should retire." Everyone laughed, except Rael and Dellan.

"Why not?" Dellan asked softly. "We won't want for money. You can start up any business you want. Rael can keep doing what he's doing." His stomach churned at the thought of Horvan going off on some mission and never coming back.

"About that...." Rael coughed. "I've been thinking. Doc was right about a few things. I mean, hanging upside down off a cliff isn't exactly a safe occupation, right? Maybe it's time I considered a different career. One that keeps me home. After all, I have to be there when you come home, right?"

Horvan's hand covered Dellan's. *Let's wait and see, okay? We're not at the stage where we can plan our future yet.*

Dellan knew he was right, but it didn't quiet his fears. *Remember what else Doc said? We have to be open and honest with each other if this is going to work.*

Horvan leaned in kissed him. *No if, baby. This* will *work. We're meant to be together, right?* He looked into Dellan's eyes. *How can it not work when we love each other?* Another gentle kiss, then Horvan took a deep breath. "I love you."

Dellan's heart almost stopped. "How did you know I needed to hear that?" There had never been sweeter words.

Horvan's smile lit up his face. "Mates, remember?"

Rael's lips were soft against Dellan's cheek. "Love you."

Dellan opened his heart and his mind to them. "I love you. Both of you."

They sat together, leaning into one another, bodies and minds connected, those precious words still in Dellan's head. *You love me.* It was one thing to know they were mates, fated to be together—it was another to acknowledge they were joined by love.

Always. Rael kissed him.

Forever. Horvan locked gazes with him.

The magical moment was broken by the hitch in Crank's breathing, and they glanced across at him. Crank was staring at them, his expression so unexpectedly serious that Dellan was concerned.

"You guys are fucking beautiful together. Gives a man hope, y'know? That maybe there's someone out there who's as fucking perfect for me as you three are for one another."

No one said a word, but Roadkill put his arm around Crank's shoulders and squeezed.

By the time they climbed the ladder to their lofty bedroom, however, Dellan's initial bloom of panic had blossomed into deeper anxiety. They undressed in silence, and Horvan got into bed, his arms wide to envelop him and Rael.

"You got the all clear," Horvan reminded him.

Dellan stilled. Sex was the last thing on his mind.

It's okay. Horvan kissed his forehead tenderly. *We don't have to do anything. We have the rest of our lives for that. How about tonight, we just curl up together?*

Rael's lips twitched. *Okay, where is the real Horvan? What have you done with him?*

Dellan said nothing, but rested his head on Horvan's broad chest, his mind easing a little. "About what we said downstairs. The thought of Rael off on some dangerous assignment.... Does it make me nervous? I'd be lying if I said no. But the thing is, I don't want you to change, either of you." He covered Rael's hand with his. "Horvan is the one you called when you needed help. You were the one I called out to when I was in trouble. That tells me what you do—what we all do—is important. It'll take work and patience—and a whole lot of love—but we will figure it all out, like Horvan says." After all, whoever had decided to put the three of them together obviously knew what they were doing.

Horvan sighed. "The problem is that right now all our lives are in upheaval. We all appear to want to change for one another. Why? It seems to me what matters here, what is truly important, is to accept each other for who we are... who we're falling in love with."

Horvan's quiet words were a balm for Dellan's soul. He closed his eyes and drank in his mates' presence. His newfound peace was shattered by a single thought.

Anson. I have to see him at some point.

Despite the love they shared, there were metaphorical gray clouds on the horizon, and the threat of a storm looming. *Let's hope someone is still watching out for us.*

CHAPTER TWENTY-THREE

DELLAN OPENED his eyes. Sunlight had begun to creep into the cabin. At his back, Horvan was asleep, his arm stretched over Dellan, his hand on Rael's hip.

Even when he's asleep, he has to be touching both of us.

Horvan stirred, and Dellan stifled a moan at the feeling of a hard cock rocking against his ass.

No noise. We don't want to wake them up, right? Horvan slid his hand between Dellan's asscheeks, ghosting over his hole.

Anticipation trickled through him. *That will depend on what we're doing.*

Rael stirred and turned over, sleepy blue eyes peering at Dellan from beneath a shaggy mop of hair. *Good morning.* He let out a happy sigh. *I feel great.*

Dellan kissed his forehead. *Last night was amazing. I had no idea simply cuddling could feel so good.*

Me neither. Horvan kissed Dellan's shoulder, then leaned over to kiss Rael. *I could get to like this mates business.* He sighed happily. *And while I have nothing against cuddles, there's no better way to start the day than with a good-morning fuck.* There were Horvan's fingers again, this time gently probing his hole.

Okay, I'm sold. Like he needed much persuasion. He yearned to feel Horvan inside him. Then he heard voices below. Dellan sighed. *Talk about bad timing.*

Possibly. Or maybe they're doing it on purpose. Horvan withdrew his fingers, and Dellan's tiger growled.

Rael glared. *What the hell are they doing awake at this hour?*

Horvan chuckled. *Spoiling our fun, that's what. I told you. They're evil.*

Evil or not, despite his friends' teasing and sexual innuendos, they clearly respected him. Dellan had to admit, they were an awesome bunch.

It was this knowledge that settled him. *I can do this, with their help.* A night of sleep in his mates' arms had worked its magic too.

"Do what?" Rael was instantly more alert.

Dellan sighed. "I think I'm ready." He inhaled deeply. "I want my company back. And I want to make sure Anson pays for what he did to me. *And* those women. If he drugged them, that means they were victims too. I can't let that go unanswered."

Horvan rolled him onto his back and peered into his eyes. "You're sure about this?" he said quietly.

Dellan nodded. "But we do it my way."

"And what does that mean?" Rael narrowed his gaze. "You're not thinking of going there alone, are you?"

Dellan laughed. "Do I look stupid? Why would I do that when I can walk in there with my mates and those three awesome guys downstairs?"

"Then what did you have in mind?" Horvan inquired.

Dellan's stomach growled. "I'll tell you all over breakfast." He sniffed the air. "After I've had a shower."

"Uh-uh. I want to know *now*." Horvan cocked his head. "Why can't I read your thoughts?"

That made Dellan laugh. "Because I'm not ready to—wait. You mean you and Rael can read each other's thoughts *all* the time?"

A slight flush stained Horvan's cheeks. "Yes. It's a little maddening at times. I mean, it's nice, don't get me wrong, but think about Christmas. How can I surprise you two?"

"Oh. Well, um… if you have something you don't want to share, file it away in a lock box in your brain."

"A… what?"

Rael nodded. "What he said."

"When I was a kid, I made little boxes in my head," Dellan explained. "When I was angry or horny or whatever, and those thoughts were overwhelming me, I pushed them into one of my boxes. It allowed me to let them go so I could focus on other things."

Horvan gaped. "That must have taken years to learn."

Dellan shrugged. "Not really. Just a determination to get things done. Try it. Make a mental box."

Horvan frowned. "Easy to say, but how do you do that?"

"Think of it like a safety deposit box. Only you have the key. It can be whatever size you want, but make it strong, able to withstand someone trying to get into it."

"Like a nosy mate?" Horvan asked with a chuckle.

Rael reached over and whacked him on the arm. "Hey! I heard that."

Horvan's eyes twinkled. "Good. Wasn't sure I said it loud enough. Now hush, I'm learning."

Dellan ignored the banter. This was important. "Imagine it in your head, and once you have it, call up the memory you want to stuff in there. Once you've got it where you want it, lock the box and put it away with the others."

Horvan closed his eyes for a moment. "Okay, I've made my box."

"Now pull up something you don't want me to know about, shove it in your box, and lock it away."

Horvan stilled, and Rael peered at him. "I'm curious to know what you come up with."

"Like I'm gonna tell you." Horvan's brows knitted in an expression of intense concentration. After a moment, he relaxed. "Done. What am I thinking?"

Dellan stared at him for several moments, then smiled. "I can only read the things you want me to know. Like you want us to hurry up because you're hungry."

"Seriously?" *It's that simple?*

Dellan laughed. *Yes, it is.*

Horvan narrowed his gaze. "What if I think about it now?"

Dellan focused on Horvan again. "You want bacon."

"So you can't see the thoughts? Really?"

"Nope. You've got a tight lock on the thoughts, so even if they're in your mind, you've still got them put away enough where they're not surface thoughts."

Horvan wiped his forehead dramatically. "That's good, because some of them would make most people blush."

Rael pouted. "No fair. I want to see them."

Horvan's eyes glittered in the filtered light. *You don't need to, sweetheart. You get to live them.*

Heat coiled inside Dellan, and his already stiff dick twitched. Maybe a good-morning fuck was a great idea, and to hell with the fallout.

"Guys? We know you're awake." Crank snickered.

Then again…. Dellan looked at his mates. *Later?*

Horvan's slow smile did nothing to wilt his erection. *Later.*

DELLAN DRAINED the last of his coffee, then peered around the table. "Hashtag, how's that ID coming along?"

"It's done and already on its way. I'm having it couriered to the main post office in Salmon. It'll be there by this afternoon." Hashtag grinned. "You can all call me Mr. Miracle Worker."

"Okay, Mr. Miracle Worker, you need to get working on organizing flights for all of us."

Roadkill frowned. "Are we going somewhere? Not that I'm not having a good time here, you understand. I'm kinda getting used to the peace and quiet. I mean, I'm not a fan of the snow, but I was thinking how amazing this place would look in spring." When Crank stared at him, Roadkill grinned. "Just kidding."

"*We* are going to Chicago," Dellan announced.

Around the table, everyone sat up straight.

"You sure?"

"You feel ready?"

"We're gonna pay Anson a visit?"

Dellan smiled. "Yes, I'm sure. Yes, I feel ready, and as for paying Anson a visit… I want to give him a little shock first."

"What did you have in mind?" Horvan regarded him thoughtfully.

"A Skype video call." Dellan's heartbeat raced. "I want him to know I'm alive and kicking. Oh, and human again."

"Is that such a good idea?" Hashtag's brow furrowed. "Won't that put him on his guard?"

"What's he going to do—have a load of armed heavies waiting for us? He's running a business, for God's sake. My business. He won't want to attract attention." Dellan had put a lot of thought into this. "Remember, when they brought shifters to my cage, it was always at night when no one else was around, right? And he's twenty-two—wait, now he's twenty-three. I repeat, what's he going to do?"

"Okay, two things," Crank said suddenly. "One, what the fuck does his age have to do with anything? He has money, he runs a huge corporation so he has plenty of assets at his disposal to secure the place, *and* he's already managed to drug and keep Dellan shifted in a cage for a year."

"And what's the second thing?" Rael asked.

"Two… maybe it's not him we should be worried about," Crank observed. "We think he's not working alone, remember?"

"It's not like I'll be telling him when we're arriving," Dellan remonstrated. "I just want him panicking a little. He won't have a clue when we're going to walk into that building. Anticipation is everything."

Horvan sighed. "You're not gonna be dissuaded from this, are you?"

Dellan shook his head slowly. "Sorry, but no. I have to do this."

Rael cleared his throat. "Dellan was the one in that cage for all that time. Dellan was the one drugged and locked up. And Anson did it. So I say, whatever Dellan wants, he gets. He's earned it."

From around the table came slow grudging nods.

"You did say 'we,' right?" Crank peered at him. "I mean, we're all gonna march in there, right?"

"We are," Dellan confirmed. "I wouldn't dream of doing this without you guys."

"Do you remember Anson's Skype address?" Hashtag asked. He rolled his eyes before Dellan could reply. "Look who I'm talking to. Mr. I Can Recite My Credit Card Details By Heart." That brought out a ripple of laughter. "Fine, but let me set things up first before you call him. I know Skype calls are encrypted, but I don't want him to trace the call back to here. Let me bounce it around a few satellites first."

"You can do that?" Then Dellan smacked his palm against his forehead. "Why am I even asking that? Of *course* you can. You're Mr. Miracle Worker." That earned him more laughter.

Hashtag got up from the table. "I'll go get the equipment I need and set it up. Oh, and I want nothing in the background that gives away the location either. We'll use that sheet again as a backdrop." He stared pointedly at Dellan. "Work out what you're going to say ahead of time. I don't want you talking for long." With that he left the room, heading for downstairs.

Crank handed Dellan a notepad and pen. "Get composing. Keep it short and sweet. You know, something like 'Hey, asshole. I know what you did, okay? I'm coming to get ya. And if you're real lucky, it'll be *me* you face, and not the fucking tiger you kept locked up for a fucking *year*.'" He preened. "Whaddaya think?"

Dellan bit his lip. "Subtle, Crank. Very subtle." He gave Rael and Horvan a sideways glance. Their lips were twitching too.

DELLAN SAT in front of the laptop, his pulse rapid. He had his notes, only he wasn't sure he'd use them. He had a feeling he'd take one look at Anson's smug face on the screen and lose his train of thought.

Horvan and Rael sat facing him. "You've got this," Horvan stated with quiet confidence. Dellan knew the wave of calm slowly spreading through him was Horvan's doing.

Rael lifted his chin and looked Dellan in the eye. *Love you.*

Dellan's heartbeat was suddenly pounding for a different reason entirely. *I don't think I'll ever tire of hearing those words.*

Rael smiled. *That's okay, because I don't think I'll ever tire of saying them.*

Horvan smiled. *What he said.*

Dellan wanted to dance, he felt that fucking *light. When this call is over, we are going up to our room, we are going to get under the covers, and we are going to—*

Make love, Horvan interjected. *You know it.*

Right then Dellan felt invincible. He inhaled deeply. "Let's do this."

Beside him, Horvan checked the various devices he'd set up on the table. "Okay," he said in a low voice. "Make the call."

Dellan reached out to tap in the address, and his heart hammered. "What's wrong?" Horvan's eyes widened.

"I…." A wave of nausea rolled through him. "I don't think I can…."

Horvan was out of his seat and around to Dellan's side of the table in seconds. He knelt beside Dellan's chair, his hand on Dellan's back. "Let me do this."

Dellan swallowed. He'd felt so powerful, so sure, but….

Horvan squeezed his arm. *Dellan. It's okay to be afraid. After what they did to you? Hell, yeah.*

"Let Horvan do it," Rael entreated, his face anxious.

Dellan looked from Rael to Horvan. "Are you sure?"

Horvan nodded. "Please, baby. Let me."

The sweet endearment was all it took to make up Dellan's mind. He got up from the chair, and Horvan slid into it. Dellan reached over to tap in the details, and the familiar Skype ringtone filled the air. It went on for so long that Dellan was afraid it was going to time out, but then the call connected.

When he saw the face on the screen, he shrank back. It wasn't Anson. *Oh fuck.*

Horvan stilled. *That face….*

Dellan swallowed. *That's the man who shot me.* Then he recalled Horvan had already seen that face in his mind.

The man calmly stared back at Horvan. "Can I help you?" he asked coolly.

"Where's Anson Prescott?" Horvan demanded.

The man gave a thin smile. "Why, he's right here. I'm looking at him as we speak, but I'm afraid you can't talk to him. Now, who are you?"

"I'm the man who took something from Anson's office."

Dellan was blown away by Horvan's cool demeanor. *Doesn't he feel the menace in this guy?* The man's voice sent ice down Dellan's spine.

In his head, Rael snorted. *Horvan doesn't do intimidation.*

The man arched his eyebrows. "Indeed. So *you're* responsible for stealing my property."

Horvan scowled. "He's not *your* property. He's *our* mate. And who the fuck are you?"

That got him a look of mild surprise. "Language, please. Let's be civil. And let's just say I am an *associate* of Mr. Prescott." Then he widened his eyes. "Mate? Well, that is interesting. We've never had true mates before." His smile broadened. "And more than two of you, by the sound of it. How perfectly splendid. I think we'll need to collect the whole set. Don't you agree, Anson?"

"Quicker," Hashtag hissed. Crank and Roadkill appeared horrified by the exchange, their faces pale, their eyes wide.

Horvan glared at the man. "You'll get to my mates over my dead body."

He let out an evil chuckle. "Oh, I don't think that will be necessary. We'll simply drug all of you. The drug we gave Dellan... you *have* worked out what it does, haven't you? It locks a shifter into their animal form for as long as we desire. It subsumes their humanity, their intellect. In essence, they become the animal they are."

In that moment, Dellan wanted to leap through the screen and tear the man apart. Inside him, his tiger issued a menacing roar.

"One of these mates wouldn't be a certain Rael Parton, would it?" The man's eyes gleamed.

Rael gazed at Dellan with panicked eyes.

Despite Horvan's outward calm, Dellan felt the sudden flush of fear that rippled through him. Horvan said nothing, remaining very still.

"Your silence is telling. I was informed of the interest he took in Dellan when he came here. During *both* his visits. Anson's secretary remarked on the apparent affinity between them. And in case you're wondering, we made a point of checking out *all* recent visitors to the office. What made it all the more likely Rael was involved was that we tried to trace him, but failed. He seems to have dropped off the face of the earth." His lips twisted into a cruel smile. "I don't believe in coincidence. Dellan was in that cage for a year, and in that time no one blinked. Rael shows up, and suddenly Dellan is on the news, and we are under the spotlight." He gave Horvan an inquiring glance. "So, is that all of you? Or are there more? I can't wait to meet you all."

"Disconnect," Rael urged Horvan in a whisper.

"Don't bother," the man advised. "We'll find you in due course, but for the moment we have other, more pressing matters to deal with." He smiled. "Your calling now has turned out to be quite fortuitous."

"What do you mean?" Horvan asked quietly.

"I was here for a simple business meeting, but now I know Dellan is alive and well and obviously human again—albeit out of my control for the time being—certain individuals have become surplus to requirements." His gaze shifted to the right.

"What? What do you mean?" a voice cried out.

"That's Anson," Rael whispered. Dellan's throat had seized.

"You told me I could keep him." The genuine note of fear in Anson's voice sent Dellan's pulse rocketing.

The man arched his eyebrows. "That was before I realized how blinded you've become. You've let your… thirst for all this overwhelm you. You told us you could handle any situation that arose, yet here we are."

"It wasn't my fault they broke in here and grabbed him."

"Perhaps not, but your lax security measures certainly aided them. However, that doesn't matter. You're no longer an asset to us—you're a liability. One who has outlived his usefulness." He gave a nod.

Before Horvan could say another word, a bloodcurdling scream rang out, followed by the unmistakable growl of an animal. Dellan couldn't move, frozen to the spot as the room filled with the sound of fabric tearing and something much, much worse. Dellan didn't have to see to know what was happening. And through it all, the man on the screen watched, smiling.

They're tearing him apart. Holy fuck, Horvan, they're tearing him apart!

Then the man froze as a shot rang out and the growling stopped. He frowned. "I knew I should have searched him when I arrived. That was remiss of me. Still, he's tied up a loose end. Pity. Gorillas make such efficient killers." He shook his head. "All he's done is provide himself with a slow death while he bleeds out."

Anson's screams died into a gurgle, and Dellan shuddered.

At last the noises faded away, and the man returned his attention to Horvan. "Now, if you'll excuse me, I'll take my leave before the authorities arrive." He locked gazes with Horvan. "I'll be seeing you soon. *All* of you."

The call disconnected.

The room was silent. Dellan sagged into the empty chair next to Horvan, sick to his stomach. Rael's face was white, as were Crank's and Roadkill's. Horvan simply stared at the screen.

Hashtag was the first to speak. "I think...." The words came out as a croak, and he cleared his throat. "I think we just got the proof we need that this is way bigger than Anson wanting control of the company." He gazed around the table. "Does anyone here think Anson is still alive?"

Silence.

"Is that it?" Dellan demanded. "You're going to leave it there?"

"What do you suggest we do?" Hashtag seemed perplexed.

Dellan gaped at him. "We have to call someone."

Crank stared at him. "Are you fucking kidding me? What the fuck would we say?"

Dellan glared. "We can tell them Anson and I were having a Skype call, he got up from the laptop, and he was attacked. We didn't see who else was there, and the call got disconnected." He folded his arms and gazed steadily at Hashtag. "You said you wanted to establish a pattern for me. Well, here I am in Bumfuck, Idaho, hundreds of miles away from Chicago. It's not likely I could have done this, right? Apart from the fact that they're going to find a… gorilla next to the body." He wanted to throw up.

Hashtag nodded slowly. "He's right. Okay. Then here's what we do. Dellan calls the Chicago PD, ASAP. Any delay would look suspicious. We watch the news, and if this doesn't make the headlines, then we really are in shit."

"What do you mean?" Rael asked.

"I *mean*, if this gets covered up, then someone is pulling some very long strings." He drew in a deep breath. "Next, once I pick up Dellan's ID, I book us all flights. Dellan needs to go back there, but only after I've laid that false credit card trail. Because if the police know he's coming, you'd better believe they'll want to know where he's been."

Rael's skin was the color of milk. "They're not going to suspect him with a dead gorilla next to the body. With Anson's blood on it, no doubt."

Crank frowned. "Wait a sec. If the guy who killed Anson is a shifter, doesn't he change back into a human when he's dead? You know, like in the werewol—"

Hashtag silenced him with a hand over his mouth. "For the last time, shifters are *not* like werewolves, okay? And obviously when you die as a shifter, you stay in shifter form." When Crank mumbled, he removed his hand. "Have you got it now?"

"I've got it, I've got it," Crank groused. "Jesus, I just asked a simple question."

Hashtag's face softened. "I'm sorry. This is such a mindfuck."

Mindfuck? Dellan could still hear Anson's screams. He could still hear the soft ripping that had to be flesh being torn apart.

He couldn't stand still. "How the fuck do you all stay so… so calm? After hearing that?" He paced up and down the space between the table and the wall, his stomach churning.

"Dellan…. This is what we do, remember?" Horvan stopped his pacing with a hand to Dellan's arm, his voice soft.

"What—you deal in *death*? So often it doesn't even register?" He pointed to Hashtag's laptop. "Because *that* was horrific. Revolting. And yet you're standing around like… like it's nothing."

"It's not *nothing*," Roadkill insisted. "It's never that. But Horvan's right. We were in the military. Death was what you faced every time you went on a mission. And yeah, we still face it. But it is *never* something you get used to."

Dellan. Rael swallowed, his face still pale. "I've experienced death. I've seen some awful things. But you… you're a CEO. You've never had to face anything like this. And no one expects you to just take it in stride."

Dellan struggled to breathe. "He was a bastard, I know that. But… he was my half brother too. And no one deserves to end their days like that." He couldn't dwell on it. Such thoughts would drive him mad. At last he forced air into his lungs. "I've been away for over a year, and from what you say, Anson covered his tracks with regards to my sudden disappearance. They'll want some explanation for where I've been." He met Horvan's gaze. "That guy had Anson torn apart by a shifter, didn't he?"

Horvan nodded. "It's the only explanation."

"I'd say it's time for lunch, but I seem to have lost my appetite," Roadkill announced.

"I think that goes for all of us," Dellan commented bitterly. When Horvan's arms enfolded him, and Rael joined them to do the same, Dellan closed his eyes. *I really need you. Christ, how I need you both.*

Why do you think we're here? Horvan kissed the top of his head.

You've got us, Rael assured him.

"You guys go up to your room and snuggle," Crank suggested. When Dellan opened his eyes and gazed at him in surprise, Crank sighed. "You need time together. We've got this. Leave all the arrangements to us."

"That sounds great," Dellan remarked, "but I've got a call to make first, remember?" *I'll tell the police I'm on my way home. I'll be there to answer any questions they might have.* His throat tightened.

Horvan's gaze met his. *Shit suddenly got way more complicated.* Understatement of the fucking century.

"Fine, go make the call, then let Horvan do his thing."

Dellan regarded Crank in puzzlement. "His thing?"

Crank nodded. "He needs to take care of you. That's what he does. *That's* why he's Mama Bear. And I say that with love."

Retreating up to their room sounded like the only way to leave some of the horror behind Dellan. Because he was certain he would never be free of the memories for as long as he lived.

Chapter Twenty-Four

I DON'T *have to ask if you slept, do I?*

Dellan gave Horvan a weary glance. *It shows, huh? So much for a nap.* He hadn't meant to fall asleep, but being in his mates' arms had provided some brief respite from the morning's gruesome incident.

Not enough respite, however. Anson's screams still echoed inside his head.

Rael curled around Dellan's back, his arm draped over him. "I don't know about you two," he murmured, "but every time I closed my eyes, all I could see was his evil smile while Anson was clearly being torn apart." He shivered.

"When do you want to go back there?" Horvan's expression was grave.

Dellan answered without hesitation. "As soon as possible. I told the police I'd be at the office to answer any questions."

Horvan nodded. "Then that's what we'll do. How about we go downstairs and see how far the boys have got?" He grimaced. "I should have been helping."

"You were helping—up here," Rael said firmly. "We needed you."

Dellan attempted a smile. "What he said."

"Guys? There's coffee if you want it. Crank has made sandwiches, too, if you're hungry," Roadkill called up to them.

"Then we can bring you up to date," Hashtag added.

Dellan sighed. "Back to reality." He shuddered. Reality was the last place he wanted to visit.

Horvan kissed him. "Any time you want a break, let me know. There's always time to hold one another, okay?"

Rael leaned over to make it a three-way kiss. *There's always time for love,* he affirmed.

K.C. WELLS

"You know what I like best about this whole 'mates' deal?" Dellan informed them. "You can kiss *and* talk at the same time."

If only their kisses could take away the horror. The screams.

"I won't say you'll forget all of this," Horvan said softly, "because you won't. But I do promise it will fade with time. And if I could kiss away all the heartache and pain, I'd do it."

Dellan knew that with every fiber of his being. He leaned over until his forehead touched Horvan's. "Thank you." He was conscious of Rael's hands on his back, gentle and soothing. "Both of you."

"ARE WE okay to leave before the rental is over?" Roadkill asked Rael. The sandwiches were all gone, and they were on their second pot of coffee.

"I told the owner originally that we'd want the place for a couple of weeks, with an option to renew, seeing as we're out of season," Rael replied. He peered at Dellan. "We had no idea how long it would take for you to shift back." He got out his phone. "I'll give him a call." Rael put on his jacket, then walked to the other end of the cabin and stepped onto the back porch.

Hashtag got up from the table and walked over to where Dellan stood by the window. "This is yours, I believe." He held out a small plastic card.

Dellan took the ID and turned it over. "You are amazing. It looks like the real thing."

Hashtag huffed. "It'll get you on a plane. That's the main thing. If anyone decides to take a really close look, we're screwed." He went back to his laptop. "And now we have that, I'm organizing the flights. I couldn't get us on any today, but how does first thing tomorrow morning sound?"

"Like you're a miracle worker," Horvan said as he placed another mug of coffee in front of Hashtag.

"That does leave us with a couple of loose ends to tidy up," Hashtag informed him.

224

"Like what?"

Hashtag pointed to the window. "Those two loose ends out there, the car and the RV. As in, what do we do with them? I can sell them, but not that fast. We're gonna need to store them someplace for the moment and come back at a later date for them."

Rael came back into the room. "Okay, we're going to have a visitor." He seemed pissed.

"The owner?" Dellan inquired.

Rael nodded. "Because we want to leave after less than a week, he seems convinced we're pulling out early because we've trashed the place. He wants to check on it before we go."

"Okay, boys. Operation Cleanup," Horvan announced. "Let's not give him anything to complain about. We're just six guys enjoying a vacation together. Six very tidy guys."

"I'm on it. I'll break out the cleaning supplies." Crank headed for the cabinet beneath the sink.

"I'll spirit away anything we don't want him to see," Roadkill added. Then he paused. "And you've just given me an idea. Dellan, can you and Rael give the RV a once-over?"

"What are you up to?" Dellan was intrigued.

Roadkill grinned. "Hopefully tying up one of those loose ends." He glanced at Rael. "How long have we got until he gets here?"

"He's in Salmon at the moment, so he said maybe an hour."

Roadkill nodded. "That's plenty of time."

"What do you want me to do?" Hashtag demanded.

"You're booking flights, remember?" Horvan reminded him. His gaze flickered to Dellan. *They're a great team, aren't they?*

The best, Dellan assured him. He was counting on them to have his back.

"Er, guys?" Crank paused, a bottle of cleaning fluid in his hands. "Maybe you need to clean up outside too?"

Horvan frowned. "And what are we cleaning, exactly? The snow?"

Crank stared at him pointedly. "I was thinking more about paw prints. You know, lions and tigers and bears? It hasn't snowed since you all went out to play."

Dellan smiled at Horvan. *Like I said, the best.*

MR. LANE hadn't stopped smiling since he walked into the cabin. "I think you're leaving it in a cleaner state than it was when you arrived."

"That would be his fault," Crank said, indicating Horvan with a flick of his head. "He's very house-proud. You should see him with a feather duster."

Dellan bit his lip, trying his damnedest not to laugh. Rael's shoulders were shaking too.

"I'm glad you enjoyed your stay," Mr. Lane said brightly. "Perhaps we'll see you around here again?" He glanced at the rifles. "How was the hunting? There was some talk of a bear in these parts, not that I've ever seen one." He glanced toward the window.

"A bear? Wow." Roadkill kept a straight face. "I've never seen one outside of a zoo."

Mr. Lane was staring at the RV. "That's a beauty, isn't it? I was after one of these myself. The kids would love it. How many does it sleep?"

"Well, there was room for all of us," Hashtag remarked.

Mr. Lane's eyes lit up. "Yeah, perfect. We've got four kids. That's why I have to drive that bus out there." His expression grew wistful. "When we first got married, I drove the sweetest little Miata. Of course, the first kid came along, and my baby had to go." He coughed. "Listen to me, running on like this."

"Actually, we were going to ask you a favor," Roadkill said suddenly.

Dellan blinked. *Do you know what he's talking about?*

Before Horvan or Rael could respond, Roadkill pressed ahead. "Would it be possible to keep the RV and the car somewhere on your property for us to pick up at a later date? We'd pay you, of course. And you'd be free to use them."

Mr. Lane stilled. "Seriously?"

Roadkill nodded. "We're flying out of Missoula tomorrow morning. It would be a big help if we had a place to store them." He smiled. "And that kinda guarantees we'd be back, doesn't it?"

"Yeah, it does." Mr. Lane smiled broadly. "I think we can come to an arrangement." His brow furrowed. "But if you're leaving the car here, how will you get to the airport?"

Roadkill gave a casual shrug. "Oh, we'll call a taxi."

Dellan had to admire the nonchalant act.

Mr. Lane snorted. "Yeah, no. I know most of the taxi drivers around here. They'll fleece you. Of course, *I* could drive you all."

"Really?" Rael stared at him. "That would be a four- or five-hour round trip."

Mr. Lane waved his hand. "What's four or five hours? Besides, I'll be taking your RV out on the weekend with the family. Everyone gets what they want." He grinned. "And it gets me away from the mother-in-law. She's visiting right now."

Dellan watched as Roadkill, Rael, and Mr. Lane worked out a price for storing the vehicles. Hashtag gave him the time of the flight, and they arranged when Mr. Lane would be at the cabin to pick them up. Then he thanked them again, and Rael walked him outside to his people-carrier.

Horvan's hand was gentle on Dellan's back. "See? Sometimes things have a habit of working out fine," he said quietly.

Dellan glanced around the cabin's interior. "I won't forget this place." His gut felt like it was in knots.

"We have one more night." Horvan slipped his arm around Dellan's waist.

Dellan turned to look at him. "And if all I want is to be held all night long?"

Horvan's smile sent a slow pulse of warmth through his body. "That was precisely what I had in mind."

Rael stepped back into the cabin. "Hashtag, did you finish laying a false credit trail for Dellan?"

"About two hours ago." Hashtag stilled. "Why?"

"Because we might need it. There's a police car coming down the road."

Horvan let go of Dellan and went over to the window. "Yup. It's pulling up here."

Dellan's heartbeat slipped into a higher gear, and Rael was at his side in an instant. "Of course they're here. It was inevitable."

Roadkill nodded. "Just keep calm, okay? And stick to the story you told the Chicago cops."

Dellan nodded, breathing deeply.

"You remember what we discussed?" Hashtag asked him.

"Yeah." Outside, a car door slammed, and Dellan straightened in his chair.

Roadkill went to the door and opened it. "Good afternoon, officer."

"I believe Dellan Carson is staying here?" The cop sounded young.

"Yes, he is. Please, come in." Roadkill stood aside and the cop entered the cabin, glancing around. His gaze alighted on Dellan, and he came over, taking a notebook from his breast pocket.

"Mr. Carson? I'm Officer Logan from the Salmon police department. I'm following up on a call you made this morning to the Chicago PD."

Dellan nodded. He gestured to a chair. "Please, have a seat."

The cop took it and peered at the others. "You're all here on vacation?"

"Since last Thursday," Horvan told him. "We rented the cabin from Mr. Lane. You just missed him."

"Did they check on my brother?" Dellan blurted out. It wasn't an act. Part of him hoped against hope there'd been nothing to find, that it had all been a nightmare.

Officer Logan opened his notepad. "Can you tell me exactly what happened, leading up to your call to Chicago?" He gave a slight smile. "I know you've already gone through this with the Chicago PD, but I have to check."

Dellan swallowed. "This morning after breakfast, I placed a Skype call to my brother, Anson Prescott. My half brother, if you want to be exact."

"Why did you call him?"

"To say I was coming home. I've been away for over a year." His stomach clenched at the lie.

"Was Mr. Prescott surprised to hear from you?" Officer Logan made notes.

"I think he was surprised my sabbatical was finally over."

Officer Logan frowned. "Sabbatical? If he knew that, then why did Mr. Prescott have you declared missing last year?"

Dellan did his best to feign astonishment. "That's news to me, officer. We discussed my taking time away from the business after New Year's last year. I have no idea why he'd do such a thing."

"I'll come back to this in a second. So… you placed the Skype call. What time was this?"

Dellan glanced at Hashtag, who peered at the laptop. "Ten this morning, officer. Dellan made the call on this laptop." Hashtag turned it around, and Officer Logan looked closely at the screen, scribbling in his notepad.

"The call didn't last long," he noted. "Just over three and a half minutes."

Dellan nodded. "I told him I was coming back to Chicago within the week, and that I was ready to take back the reins. He's been running the company in my absence."

"How did he react to that?" Officer Logan gazed at Dellan. "Was he unhappy about the news?"

Dellan shrugged. "I couldn't tell. He knew when I left he'd be the CEO temporarily, until my return."

"Then what happened?"

Dellan fought to maintain some degree of calm. "He said he heard a noise, and he got up from the laptop." He shivered. "That was when the screaming started."

"Then who disconnected the call? Did you see anyone else?"

Dellan shook his head. "The screen went blank. I called the Chicago police." He leaned forward. "*Now* can you tell me about Anson?"

Officer Logan put down his notepad. "I'm not at liberty to reveal any details about the case. I can only tell you that Mr. Prescott is dead." His face tightened. "You have my condolences."

Dellan closed his eyes. "It sounded so awful from here. And when the call got disconnected...." He swallowed again and opened his eyes. "Is there anything else you need to know?"

Officer Logan glanced at his notepad. "Can we go back to where you've been for the last year?"

Dellan recalled his conversation with Hashtag. "I make regular large donations to several conservation groups, located in different states. I decided to get away from it all and spend some time checking on my investments."

"Conservation groups?"

Dellan gestured to the window. "National forests, for example."

"Did you inform any of these groups that you'd be visiting?"

Dellan smiled. "I didn't want to make a fuss. I kept my visits quiet. That way, I got to see how my money was really being spent."

"You can prove these visits?"

"Yes, there will be credit card receipts showing where I went. Do you want to see them?" Dellan reached into his pocket for the phone Hashtag had gotten for him, praying he'd read the man correctly.

Officer Logan smiled. "Not at this time, sir. You told my colleagues in Chicago that you would be going to your office. They might ask to see your records." He tilted his head to one side. "Can I ask why you decided to take a sabbatical?"

Dellan didn't have to lie. "We'd just lost Tom Prescott, my stepdad. Then my mom died too. I lost my own dad when I was seven. It felt like I'd lost everyone I'd ever loved. I'd been Tom's manager since I was in my late twenties, and losing him was...." He yearned to feel his mates' arms around him, but that would have to wait.

Says who? No sooner had Dellan heard Horvan's words than a feeling of warmth and comfort flowed over and through him, and he knew it came from his mates.

Dellan took a deep breath. "Anson assured me he was more than capable of running the company if I decided to take a break, and I knew if there were any problems, he would contact me. When no frantic messages came, I assumed all was well."

"Then you have no clue as to why he would declare you as missing."

"None at all, Officer Logan. It's a complete mystery." Dellan frowned. "What confuses me, however, is if he declared me missing, why didn't it make the news? The CEO of a successful pharmaceutical company disappears? That's a national headline right there. And seeing such headlines would have brought me right back to Chicago." He was amazed at how easily the lies rolled off his tongue.

"It is a mystery," Officer Logan admitted. "Mr. Prescott was only twenty-three. Wasn't he a little young to be left in control like that?"

"The board obviously didn't believe so."

Officer Logan closed his notepad, and Dellan heaved an internal sigh of relief. "When do you plan on returning to Chicago?"

"We're all booked on the first flight out of Missoula tomorrow morning," Hashtag said smoothly.

The officer frowned. "All of you?"

Dellan nodded. "These are my friends. They've kindly agreed to accompany me."

Officer Logan got to his feet. "It sounds like they're a good bunch of friends." He gave Dellan a single nod. "Thank you, sir. I'll inform Chicago PD to expect you sometime tomorrow. I'm sure they'll be able to give you more information about Mr. Prescott's death." He held out his hand. "Again, my condolences."

Dellan rose to his feet and shook. "Thank you, Officer Logan." He waited until Logan had left the cabin, gotten into his vehicle, and pulled away before dropping onto the chair, all his energy gone.

"Wow. You were amazing." Crank applauded him. "You even had me believing you."

"But did *he* believe me? That's what matters." Dellan wasn't convinced.

"You played it just right," Horvan said, slipping into the empty chair next to him. "You didn't hesitate about providing proof. Your reasons for taking off were totally understandable. And you spoke calmly and clearly, looking him in the eye."

"Horvan's right." Roadkill nodded approvingly. "You came across as honest. Upset about Anson. And he was just making sure what you told him matched up with what you told the Chicago cops."

"So I get to do this all over again tomorrow?" Dellan wanted to be sick. "I don't think I'm cut out for all this."

"Just wait until the Chicago police are satisfied with your story. They can't believe you're involved, not unless you conspired with a gorilla to… you know." Hashtag went into the kitchen and returned with a glass. "Here. Drink this. I think you need it."

Dellan took the whiskey gratefully. The fiery liquid warmed his belly.

"Okay." Horvan glanced around the table. "Roadkill has tied up the loose ends, Mr. Lane is picking us up in the morning, and the police have confirmation about the Skype call. Let's pack up, and then Roadkill and I will run into Salmon for pizza and beer. No cooking tonight, boys."

Crank beamed. "Now *that* sounds like a good evening." His eyes gleamed. "Hey. We could watch porn."

Roadkill arched his eyebrows. "Really? So you'd be okay with gay porn, if that's what Horvan wants to watch?" His lips twitched.

Crank shrugged. "Wouldn't be the first time. A hole is a hole, right?" He headed for the bathroom.

Roadkill flicked a glance in Horvan's direction. "Gay," he whispered. "Or bi. But straight?" He waved his hand in a kind of "meh" gesture. "That boy would bust Maury's lie detector in a heartbeat." Beside him, Hashtag was holding his belly, clearly trying to muffle his laughter.

Rael stood behind Dellan, rubbing his shoulders. *Try to turn your mind off for one night? I know that's asking a lot with everything that's happened, but you need to relax.*

Dellan reached up and covered Rael's hand. *I just want to curl up on the couch with you two.*

Rael kissed the top of his head. *Sounds like my kind of night.*

Think of it as the calm before the storm, Horvan told him.

Dellan's instincts told him the storm was going to be bigger than any of them anticipated.

CHAPTER TWENTY-FIVE

THE UBER pulled up outside the Global Bio-Tech building, and Roadkill, Crank, and Hashtag got out. Dellan hesitated, his pulse racing and his stomach churning. The time since their flight landed had passed quickly. They'd dropped their bags off at Horvan's apartment, done a quick change of clothing, and then headed for the office. But now they were there....

It'll be fine, Horvan assured him. *We'll meet with the police as arranged, they'll ask more questions, and that will be it. We can get out of here and take you home.*

Dellan swallowed. *I don't want to see inside that office.* Time had done nothing to dim the memory of that final call. Right then he wasn't sure if he ever wanted to step foot in there again.

They probably won't let you anyway. Rael took his hand and held it. *It's a crime scene, remember?*

Dellan froze. *He... he won't be here, will he?* Dellan could still see his cruel smile as he watched Anson's slaughter.

Unlikely. Rael squeezed his hand. *And even if he were, I don't think he'd come out of it well. Not with this bunch and in their present mood.*

You know it. Horvan covered Dellan's other hand with his own.

The Uber driver coughed loudly.

I think that's our cue to get the fuck out of here. Horvan pushed the seats forward and squeezed through the gap, Dellan and Rael following.

"Here we are again," Roadkill said cheerfully, staring up at the glass-fronted building.

"Yeah, but this time without the mob in the lobby," Hashtag added.

"Aw, crap."

Dellan glanced at Crank. "What's the matter?"

"I just realized what yesterday was. Yet *another* year when I missed out on my St. Patty's Day corned beef."

Roadkill narrowed his gaze. "And like I tell you every year, you can have corned beef anytime."

Crank jutted out his lip. "But it *tastes* better on St. Pat's."

Hashtag pointed to the building. "Eyes on the prize, numbnuts. Newsflash—today is not about you and your stomach."

They followed Dellan through the main doors, Horvan and Rael flanking him.

Dellan smiled to himself. *I have the best set of bodyguards.*

You know it. Horvan's pinkie brushed against his, and the slight contact warmed him.

You say that a lot, you know. Not that Dellan was complaining. He loved Horvan's confidence. Then another thought came to him, sending warmth surging through him. He loved Horvan, period.

"Mr. Carson?" One of the security guards stepped out from behind the desk and strode over to him, hand outstretched. "Wow. It's good to see you, sir."

Dellan shook hands with him. "It's Rick, isn't it?"

Rick beamed. "You remembered." Then his face fell. "You know what happened, right?"

Dellan nodded. "I'm here to meet with the police. They know I'm coming."

Rick shook his head. "A terrible thing."

"I suppose the top floor is out of bounds," Dellan remarked, suppressing a shudder.

"Yeah. The police have it all taped up." Rick pointed to the three leather couches on the far side of the lobby. "Why don't you sit down, and I'll order some coffee for you and your guests while you wait for the police."

"Coffee would be great."

Rick held out his hand once more, and Dellan clasped it. "I'm glad you're back, sir."

Dellan's throat tightened a little at the sincerity in Rick's voice. "I'd like to say I'm glad to be here, but in the circumstances…."

Rick released his hand, and Dellan led the group over to the couches.

"Looks like you were a good boss," Hashtag commented as they sat down. "I know respect when I hear it."

"Tom always said it was good practice to know the names of your employees." Dellan could still hear Tom's voice, quiet, calm, and firm.

You really loved him, didn't you? Rael took his hand and squeezed it.

Dellan smiled. *He was an easy man to love. Yeah, I loved him.*

"And he still *is* a good boss," Horvan added. "Because it's his company, right?"

"When he's ready to run it again," Rael said quietly. Dellan gave him a warm glance.

"Er, guys?" Crank nodded toward the main door. "Cops are here."

"Just in time for coffee," Roadkill commented dryly.

Two officers came over to where they sat. "Mr. Carson?"

Dellan got to his feet. "Good afternoon."

"Can we see your ID, sir?"

Dellan handed it over, not daring to breathe. The older officer examined it before giving it back. Dellan heaved an internal sigh of relief. *God bless Hashtag.* He prayed Anson had taken his real ID and stored it at the house.

They shook hands, and then everyone sat down. Dellan indicated the silent group. "These are my friends who were with me at the cabin. They're helping me out here because I didn't want to be alone right now."

The older-looking officer gave them a polite nod, then focused his attention on Dellan. "I'm Officer Franks, and this is Officer Dalton. I wouldn't normally interview someone in surroundings like this, especially in a murder case, but you're obviously not a suspect."

Dellan frowned. "Obviously? Because I was in Idaho at the time?"

"No, Mr. Carson. Because your brother's killer is already known to us."

Officer Dalton peered closely at Dellan. "Did you know your brother kept a tiger in his office?"

"Yes, but only when I saw its rescue on the news. Anson must have got it after I'd left for my sabbatical. It was one of the things I wanted to discuss with him during our Skype call." He swallowed. "Not that I got the chance."

"You don't sound like you approve," Officer Franks remarked.

Dellan shrugged. "I'm not a fan of keeping wild animals in captivity, especially not in such an environment. That poor tiger must have been going out of its mind. I'm grateful to whichever activist group got it out of there." *So grateful, they would never believe it.* He sighed. "I'm sure Anson wouldn't have agreed with me."

"He seems to have been keen on having an exotic animal as a pet. Apparently he replaced the tiger with a silverback gorilla almost immediately," Officer Dalton told him. "Which then escaped from its cage...." He focused his gaze on Dellan, who stilled.

"Then that was what I heard? It was the gorilla that killed him?" This time there was no way he could hold back on the shudder that rippled through him.

Officer Franks nodded, his face solemn. "But not before he was able to shoot it. I'm afraid we haven't finished with your office yet." He gave Dellan a speculative glance. "You are intending on running the business again?" When Dellan nodded, Franks cleared his throat. "The officer in Salmon was able to confirm the Skype call. We were unable to do so from here because your brother's laptop is missing."

There was silence for a moment.

"But... how can that be, when I called him on it?" Not that Dellan was under any illusions as to the laptop's location: Anson's "associate" had obviously removed it.

"That's where we're at a loss too," Franks admitted. "We were at the scene maybe twenty minutes after you called, and there was no one around, not even your brother's secretary. It appears Mr. Prescott had given her the day off, which was not a rare occurrence. She says it happened a couple of days every month, regular as clockwork."

237

"And Mr. Prescott was in no state to disconnect the call," Dalton added. "So there had to be someone else present. Or someone who came into the office afterward and removed it. The problem with those scenarios is that in both cases, they would have seen Mr. Prescott's body, yet no one called the police."

Dellan's stomach rolled over. *Tying up loose ends, my ass.* The unknown associate had left one very big loose end.

"While it *is* suspicious, there is no doubt concerning Mr. Prescott's death. However, the case will remain open for the time being." Franks clammed up as Rick came over with a tray of cups and a pot of coffee. He deposited it on the table, then withdrew.

"Will you gentlemen have some coffee?" Dellan asked them.

Franks shook his head. "Where can we contact you, Mr. Carson, should we need to speak with you again?"

Dellan rattled off the number for the house, and Dalton took note of it. "I'll be staying there for the present. It's only thirty or so miles from here." A thought occurred to him. "Is the company helicopter on the roof pad? That was how we traveled to and from the house."

"No, sir. We checked up there." Officer Franks got to his feet, Dalton with him, his hand extended. "We're sorry for your loss. We'll be in touch with any developments."

"Thank you, officers." Dellan shook hands with them and watched as they left the building. He sagged into the couch, his breathing shaky.

"Police officers refusing free coffee? Now I've seen everything." Hashtag's eyes widened. "They *were* real cops, right? Did anyone take note of their badge numbers?"

Horvan sighed. "Give that steel trap mind of yours a day off. They were cops. And yes, I looked at their badges." He poured Dellan a cup and handed it to him. "Well, that went better than I expected." He regarded Dellan with obvious approval. "You were great. Again."

"Are we thinking Anson's 'associate' has the chopper?" Crank asked, hooking his fingers in the air. "Because if it's not here…. And that's how Anson would've gotten here, right?"

Dellan nodded. He glanced at Horvan, his chest tightening. "I want to go home."

Horvan's hand was gentle on his. "Then that's what we'll do. Let's go back to my place, pack some bags, and then I'll rent a car to take us to—where is your place anyway?"

"Homer Glen. It's less than an hour's drive, depending on traffic."

Crank huffed. "Am I gonna be sharing a room with these two again?" Hashtag whacked him on the arm, and Crank glared at him. "Hey, quit hitting me."

"I will when *you* quit bitching," Hashtag told him, his eyes flashing. "*We're* the ones who have to put up with you moaning in your sleep."

Crank became very still. "Do… do I say anything?"

Roadkill smiled. "Oh yeah. Very illuminating."

Before Crank could respond, Dellan cut in. "Crank, I don't think Hashtag needs any more blackmail material, so you'll have your own room, I promise."

Crank beamed. "Aw, thanks." A second or two later, he scowled. "Hey!" Everyone chuckled.

Hashtag patted Crank's cheek. "You know I love ya, right? And I promise not to post any video where your mom can see it."

Rael cocked his head to one side. "How big is this place? I know you said large, but…."

Dellan patted his hand. "I don't want to spoil the surprise." He couldn't wait to see their faces. Then he thought about the house. "Guys? I have to make a call so Mrs. Landon knows to expect us."

"Who's Mrs. Landon?" Rael asked.

"The housekeeper. She'll want to get the rooms ready."

Rael peered at him. "You need a housekeeper?" When Dellan didn't respond, he glared. *You are* such *a tease.*

Dellan grinned. *You're only just working that out now?*

The thought made him smile. *We have so much to learn about one another.* He couldn't wait to find out more about his mates.

ROADKILL PEERED through the windshield. "Nice neighborhood, Dellan. How long have you lived here?"

Dellan stared at the familiar landscape of abundant trees and lush green grass. He loved how the only indication in some cases that there were properties along the narrow lane were the mailboxes at the roadside. "Tom had this place built about sixteen years ago." He smiled. "He built it for my mom." He caught his breath as the house came into view.

God, I've missed this place.

"Holy fuck." Crank let out a long whistle. "He really loved your mom, huh?"

"That's not a house, that's a fucking mansion," Roadkill exclaimed. "How many bedrooms does it have?"

"Five. Eight bathrooms. Plus there's a set of rooms in the basement for Mrs. Landon." Dellan enjoyed their shock. He still recalled Tom bringing him to the site when the house was being built, showing him the plans and discussing what they would do with the grounds.

"Is that a lake over there?" Rael asked, his eyes wide.

"Yup. The house backs onto it." He loved to swim in it, only wishing he could do it in tiger form. The neighbors across the water would have had heart attacks. He'd had to find other places where he could shift.

"What are we talking, seven or eight thousand square feet?" Hashtag asked.

"Ten," Dellan replied with a smile. "And it's set on five acres."

Horvan shook his head. "Makes my apartment look about the size of a postage stamp."

Which brought Dellan to the thought he'd hidden from his mates all day.

Before he had time to reveal it, Roadkill pulled up in front of the garages and switched off the engine. "Looks like I get to choose where to park," he joked. "You got spaces for how many cars?" There was one other car.

"Five."

Everyone piled out of the rental car, and Dellan stood for a moment, gazing at the house that had been home since his early twenties.

"Crank was right about one thing," Horvan murmured. "There's no sign of the chopper."

"Wow. Was that praise?" Crank rolled his eyes heavenward. "End of fucking days, I'm telling ya. Well, don't just stand there. Give us the five-cent tour." He lugged bags from the trunk, and Hashtag helped. Dellan led them around to the right, where the main door was located. It opened as they approached, and Mrs. Landon stood there, smiling.

"Mr. Carson. It is *so* good to see you." She hadn't changed much. Her hair was still as white as ever, and her face as lined.

He greeted her warmly before indicating the others. "These are my guests, who'll be staying for a while." Right then he had no idea how long that would be.

"I've prepared all the rooms, as you requested." She swallowed. "When you said you'd need all the rooms, I took the liberty of clearing Mr. Anson's things away. Everything is in boxes and stored for safekeeping, and his room has been cleaned."

Tom always said she was a treasure. "Thank you, Mrs. Landon. I didn't think about that."

She glanced at the group and then frowned. "Will one of them be sleeping on the sofa bed in the den?"

Dellan cleared his throat. "Two of them will be sharing my room." There was no point trying to hide the truth from her. He'd learned that long ago. He gestured to Horvan and Rael, introducing them.

Mrs. Landon's cheeks flushed. "Very good, sir. I'll make sure you have sufficient towels in your bathroom." Her smile faltered, and the light in her eyes died. "I still can't believe it. Mr. Prescott really is dead, then?"

Dellan nodded, taking her hand in his. "I still can't believe it either." It wasn't a total lie.

She sighed. "When you've settled in, we can have a chat over some tea. And I've made a batch of your favorite cookies, maple and pecan."

K.C. WELLS

Dellan gave her a brief hug. "I've missed you too," he whispered.

She peered at Horvan and Rael. "They look nice. You've done well there." Before he could react, she gave them all a warm smile. "Dinner will be at seven. Then I'll leave you all to it. Mr. Carson said you were more than capable of looking after yourselves and that I wasn't to fuss." Her gray eyes twinkled.

Dellan chuckled as she headed for the kitchen. "Mrs. Landon is a character."

"She knows you're gay?" Horvan asked.

"Ever since she discovered the place where I hid my gay magazines. Mom said she didn't want Anson to find them. He was only little." His chest tightened, and tears pricked his eyes.

Horvan put his arm around Dellan's shoulder. "Whatever he did later in life, that doesn't alter the fact that he was your little brother. There was a time when you loved him, right?"

Dellan nodded. "He was a sweet kid." *Where the hell did he go wrong?*

We'll probably never know. Even in his head, Rael sounded sad.

"Can we go look around now?" Crank was almost buzzing.

Dellan laughed. "Go explore. But no skinny-dipping in the lake. You'll scare the fish."

Crank's eyes bulged. "Are you fucking kidding? I'd freeze my nuts off. To say nothing of my dick." He patted Roadkill on the arm. "Come on. I wanna explore."

Roadkill followed him, laughing. "You big kid." Hashtag was behind them.

"We can take a look around later," Horvan said. "Right now I need to make a call, and *then* I need to hold my mates."

Dellan was only too happy to oblige.

CRANK SAGGED against the couch seat cushions. "That Mrs. Landon sure can cook," he remarked, rubbing his belly. "I haven't eaten that well in ages." He yawned, stretching his arms high above his head. "I'm bushed."

"We *have* crammed a lot into today," Hashtag commented. "I meant to get to work on the computers, to see what I can find, but I can't keep my eyes open. And it's only nine o'clock."

"Then let's call it a day," Horvan declared. "We'll start work tomorrow. We could all do with an early night."

Dellan wasn't fooled for a second. *Don't think I'm unaware of what you'd like your early night to entail.* Not that he hadn't been thinking the same thing. Besides, he wanted to put a proposition to them.

"I've given Mrs. Landon a few days off," Dellan told them. "She and Anson were close at one time, and I want her to be able to grieve properly. Besides, I thought that was best while we search for more information."

Roadkill grinned. "Great. That means Crank can fart in comfort." That earned him a glare.

"Doesn't she have a set of rooms in the basement?" Horvan inquired.

"Yes, she does, but her daughter and granddaughter live about a mile away. She wanted to go spend some time with them."

"Don't tell me she looks after this place on her own." Roadkill seemed horrified by the prospect. "That's way too much work for one person."

"Mrs. Landon sees to the laundry and cooking, and there's a service that cleans the place," Dellan told him. "Plus there's a gardener who comes once a week."

"I can't get over this room," Hashtag murmured, staring up at the vaulted ceiling with its dark oak beams. "It's as big as a barn. Seriously, you could hold a dance in here."

Dellan smiled. "This was where Tom and Mom entertained. It was such a different life for her. She went from scraping to make ends meet to living in luxury. I think that's why Tom built the house. He wanted to make up for the hard years after Dad disappeared."

"Did they really meet in a coffee shop?" Horvan inquired.

He nodded. "Tom said he didn't usually frequent such places, but he was in the vicinity, it was pouring rain, and he needed shelter.

Only he kept going back. He said he was captivated by her. And she had no idea who he was or what he was worth."

"That probably made for a refreshing change," Rael commented.

"It sounds like a fairy tale," Roadkill said softly. "I'm glad she found happiness again. And it sounds like Tom was a great stepdad."

"He was." *God, I miss him. I wish he were here.*

Rael got up off the couch and extended a hand to Dellan. "I'm off to bed. You coming?"

"Nah, he always looks like that," Crank quipped, before both Roadkill and Hashtag piled on top of him, cushions flying.

Horvan laughed. "You know where your rooms are. Leave the place tidy. And we'll see you in the morning."

"Bye, boys. Have fun storming the castle," Crank called out. Then he laughed. "And by castle, I mean—" Hashtag slapped a hand over his mouth, cutting off whatever he'd been about to say.

Roadkill rolled his eyes. "Yup. Gayest straight man ever."

They trooped up the stairs to the third floor, which contained only one room. It had been Tom and his mom's bedroom until Tom's death. After that, she'd chosen a smaller room, and Dellan had taken the master bedroom. He loved the space, not to mention the huge bathroom with its walk-in shower, and the three dormer windows set into the roof.

I can't imagine Anson not appropriating it once I was captured. Judging by its cleanliness and minimalist appearance, it seemed Dellan was correct. He made a mental note to inquire the following morning as to the whereabouts of his own possessions. *Anson must have stowed them somewhere.* He hoped.

Once they were inside with the door shut behind them, Horvan stripped off. "I don't know about you two, but that shower has been calling me all night."

"Want some company?" Dellan asked, removing his own clothing.

Rael snickered. "Oh, I'm not sure there's room." He tugged his sweater over his head and shoved his jeans down to his ankles. It wasn't long before the three of them were standing beneath the jets, kissing and touching, moving their hands gently over soapy skin, washing away the last traces of their day.

As far as Dellan was concerned, it was bliss. No frantic fumblings, no sighs of lust, just the three of them connecting in sensual pleasure. As the water sluiced away, it took with it Dellan's last remnants of tension, leaving in its place a newfound confidence.

"There's something I'd like to put to you," he said as he toweled his hair dry.

"Something you've kept locked away from us," Horvan said with a smile. "I've had this feeling all day you've been preoccupied, but I put it down to the stress of coming back to Chicago and meeting with the police. But it's not that, is it?"

"I'm glad you said that, because I was about to," Rael added, tossing his towel onto the floor.

Dellan sat on the ottoman at the foot of the bed. "How attached are you to your homes? What I mean is, would it be too much of a wrench to give them up?"

Rael stilled. "You want us all to live here."

"Got it in one." He gazed at them earnestly. "There's plenty of room here. And we can give ourselves more privacy by judicious planting. That way, if we want to shift, no one would see. There are *five freaking acres*, for God's sake."

Horvan peered at Rael. "Your thoughts?"

Rael shrugged. "My place is a rental. I only live there because of its proximity to the forest. It's not like I'm attached to it." He gazed thoughtfully at Horvan. "And you?"

Horvan stroked his chin. "I can give up the apartment. That's rented. But the place in Indiana...." He sighed. "That's all mine. And I love those forests. I know we'd have space here, but it wouldn't be the same."

Dellan was prepared for this. "Then how about a compromise? We live here, and once a month we go to your place. It's not exactly far, right? We'd be a two-home family."

When Horvan smiled, the light in his eyes unclenched Dellan's stomach. "I like the sound of that."

"Me too." Rael looked toward the window and shivered.

What is it? Dellan was instantly on the alert. *What do you sense?* Horvan raced toward the window and peered out into the darkness.

Rael sighed. *Nothing. It's just... he's out there somewhere.* He didn't need to say who. *And he's going to find us, isn't he? Maybe not tomorrow. It could even be a year from now, but he will come. And he won't be alone.*

Dellan got up and walked over to where Rael stood. "It would be easy to succumb to fear," he said softly, "but you know what? I'm not going to do it. I refuse to live like that." He leaned in and kissed Rael on the lips. "Besides, there are better ways to spend tonight than worrying about him."

The hitch in Rael's breathing as Dellan kissed his neck, then moved lower, was delightful.

"I think I've been very patient, don't you?" Dellan whispered, brushing his lips against the fragrant skin of Rael's neck. "But I don't want to wait anymore."

Rael shuddered and closed his eyes. "Then don't."

Horvan moved to stand behind Rael, and they closed in on him, Horvan planting a trail of kisses over his shoulder. Rael's shivers multiplied as Horvan lifted him into his arms and carried him to the bed.

Dellan loved Rael's wide-eyed stare as they climbed onto the bed, moving toward him with stealth. Rael licked his lips. "I... I feel like I'm being hunted." Another shudder rippled through him as he lay on his back, slowly tugging on his already stiffening cock.

Dellan smiled. "Well, you *do* have something I want."

"And what's that?"

He grabbed Rael's knees and pushed them roughly to his chest, before shoving a folded pillow under his ass. "This," he said, spreading Rael's asscheeks and homing in on that enticing pucker.

Rael held his legs and let out a low cry as Dellan warmed Rael's hole with his tongue. "I've been waiting for that," he croaked.

"And I've been waiting for this." Horvan was at Rael's side, leaning over to take Rael's dick in his mouth.

The noises that spilled from Rael's lips were music to Dellan's ears. Dellan gazed at Horvan as he sucked Rael deep, his own cock hard. They kept up their sensual assault, driving Rael to the edge again and again but never over it, pausing occasionally to kiss him, pouring their urgent need into every intimate embrace.

Then they changed position, Dellan flipping Rael onto his belly and tugging his hips higher until Rael's ass was in the air, before diving back to tongue-fuck his hole. Then it was his turn to groan as Horvan pulled Dellan's cheeks apart, stretching him wide, readying him for Horvan's tongue. The physical sensations mingled with the internal groans and cries of joy as their minds connected, the three of them locked into a circle of spiraling pleasure.

How they got from the bed to standing in front of the full-length mirror, Dellan had no idea. But it felt like time had been suspended as he guided his dick into position, ready to slide into Rael, Dellan's gaze focused on Rael's reflected eyes.

"Please," Rael whispered. "I want you inside me." His hands were flat to the mirror, his body bent over, his gaze locked on the three of them.

Dellan slid home, and their mingled cries added to the exquisite tightness that encased his shaft. Then he stilled as behind him, Horvan slowly pressed the head of his cock into Dellan's body, inching his way in, finally making them one flesh.

This was home.

Dellan kept his gaze locked on their reflection. Sandwiched between Rael and Horvan, his fingers dug into Rael's shoulders as he pistoned back and forth, shuttling between filling Rael to the hilt and impaling himself on Horvan's thick shaft. The sight alone was enough to bring him perilously close.

Horvan gripped him around the waist, yanking him back, the sharp slap of flesh against flesh growing louder and more frequent as Dellan plowed into Rael, his hips in constant motion. And through it all, Dellan heard them in his head, felt every sensation that thrilled them, and shuddered with every pulse of exquisite rapture that spiked through their bodies.

Oh God, I love you both so much.

It was as if Dellan's words unlocked the release they sought, and Horvan cried out as he filled Dellan with his load. *Love you. Love you, my mates.* The throb of Horvan's dick within him forced a groan from his lips, and Dellan trembled as he shot hard inside Rael, not easing his grip on Rael's shoulders.

Rael arched his back and cried out, his come spattering the mirror, his shaft jerking as he came hands-free. Dellan shook as his orgasm jolted through him, making his legs tremble, but he held on to Rael, conscious of Horvan's cock still inside him, his hands still encircling Dellan's waist. Horvan bent over and kissed down Dellan's spine, their thoughts a nonsensical mix of sensual joy and fulfillment and internal murmurings of love.

They found their way back to the bed, where Horvan took the center, pulling them both to him, as if unwilling to let them go. *I never dreamed it could be like this.* He held them close as they exchanged kisses and caresses, unable to lie still, their bodies moving against one another in a gentle undulation.

Dellan clung to them, opening his mind to their thoughts, exulting in each touch and embrace, lost in a joy so fierce, it made his heart sing.

You saved me. Both of you.

Rael brought Dellan's hand to his lips. *And we are never going to let you go. You're stuck with us, forever.*

Dellan thought that sounded goddamn perfect.

DELLAN HAD no idea what time it was. Darkness pressed against the small dormer windows, and no light intruded into the room. Yet his heart raced.

Something is wrong. Then he realized what had awoken him. Horvan was sitting up in bed beside him.

"What's wrong?" Dellan whispered.

Horvan reached over him to switch on the lamp, flooding the room with warm light, jerking Rael into wakefulness. Rael blinked in the sudden brightness. Then he was wide-awake, bolting upright in bed.

"You feel it too." Dellan's heart was still pounding.

Horvan threw back the covers. "I hear it. There's someone downstairs."

CHAPTER TWENTY-SIX

HORVAN WAS out of the room and racing down the stairs before his mates were even out of bed. As he passed the rooms on the second floor, the others emerged, hot on his heels. Horvan said nothing but ran down the last flight.

In the hallway, illuminated by the moonlight that flooded in through the open front door, was the hulking form of a large man, and he was fighting with a—

"Fuck, that's a black leopard," Roadkill shouted.

The man had his hands locked around the cat's throat, doing his best to keep it—and its claws—away from his body.

"I'd appreciate a little help here, Horvan," the guy gritted out.

What the fuck?

Horvan snapped on the lights, and the dueling pair stilled for a second. Then the leopard wrestled itself free of the guy's hold and headed straight for Horvan.

There was no time to shift, and Horvan knew this was going to hurt. From behind him came twin roars, loud enough to rattle the chandelier. The leopard jerked its head toward the sound and froze, its fangs bared, as one very pissed-off lion and an equally enraged tiger crossed the floor toward it, moving slowly with menace, their hackles raised.

That was apparently more than enough for the leopard. It turned and fled through the open door.

The guy straightened, brushing hairs from his jacket. "You took your time." He gazed with interest at the lion and tiger who were circling him. "Well, hello there. Pretty kitties." When Rael and Dellan growled, he hastily pulled back his outstretched hand. "Er, Horvan? Wanna make with the introductions? And fast?"

250

Horvan expelled a breath. "Guys, it's okay. This is Robert Johnson, affectionately known to us as Brick." He pointed to his mates. "Brick, these are Rael and Dellan."

"Hey, Brick." Crank greeted him with a wave. "Long time no see. And to bring you up to speed, Rael is the lion and Dellan is the tiger. They're shifters. Horvan is a bear shifter, and these two are his mates." He grinned.

Rael shifted back into human form with all of his usual speed, and Dellan shimmered back a little more slowly. "I'll go upstairs and grab us some clothes," Rael said quickly before heading up the stairs.

Dellan stared at Brick, sniffed, and smiled. "Well, hello."

Satisfied any fur-flying incidents had been averted, Horvan glared at Crank. "What the fuck? You don't think you could've put a brake on your fucking mouth?"

Crank rolled his eyes. "Dude. He fought a leopard in Dellan's hallway. Then a lion and a tiger came charging down the stairs. Please, tell me how you were planning on explaining that." Next to Crank, Hashtag smirked.

Horvan arched his eyebrows. "Uh, I was *about* to say they're my mates. Brick knows about me, you dumbass. He's a polar bear shifter."

"All right!" Crank clapped Hashtag on the arm. "See, now *that* is a real bear. Not like H's teddy bear."

Before Horvan could smack Crank upside the head, Roadkill sighed. "Hey, Brick. Not that we aren't happy to see you, but what the hell are you doing here?"

"Horvan called me yesterday when you guys got here. Said this place was too big to secure with just you four, so he wanted to know if I could come and keep an eye on the perimeter." Brick gave a smug smile. "Seems like he had the right idea. I was patrolling the grounds when I saw a guy at the front door. Figured he was up to no good. When no alarms or motion-sensing lights went off, I got my answer." He arched his eyebrows. "Any idea what the little black kitty wanted here?"

Crank snorted. "I suppose next to you, a leopard *is* a little black kitty."

Horvan ignored him. "No clue. Maybe he was here to clean up anything incriminating Anson might have left." He glanced at Dellan, who waved his hand.

"It's okay. You're only stating what all of us are already thinking," Dellan said quietly. He addressed Brick. "We were going to start going through Anson's computer tomorrow." He stifled a yawn.

Brick gave him a firm stare, before gazing around at the circle of men. "Okay. You lot go back to bed. I'm gonna do my thing and make sure the alarm system is functioning again, and I'll see you in the morning. We can talk more then." He gave Dellan a warm smile. "I am really freakin' happy to meet you." Rael appeared at the foot of the stairs, a pair of sweats in his hand, and Brick nodded to him before glancing at Horvan. "You had to have two mates, right?" He shook his head. "The rest of us don't get so much as a sniff at a mate, and you get two."

Horvan gave Brick a hug. "Thanks for getting here so quickly. Sorry I didn't react fast enough when I saw you and the leopard, but I didn't expect you to get here until tomorrow."

"Hey, you called, I was in the neighborhood, I came." Brick gave them all a stern glance. "Bed. Now. Because it sounds like you've got work to do in the morning. Someone sent that guy here on a mission, and you need to figure out what it was. Now, point me in the direction of a kitchen. I'll sort myself out a coffee—then I'll be back out there." His eyes twinkled. "Gotta make sure you have no more surprise visitors."

Roadkill patted Brick on the back. "Glad you're here, dude. I'll sleep soundly now in my nice, comfortable bed, knowing you're out there in the cold wind."

Brick gave him the finger. "Polar bear shifter, remember? The cold doesn't bother me like it does you daisies."

Horvan trudged back up the stairs, calling out good night as he and his mates left the boys on the second floor. By the time they were back in their room, the three of them curled up in that wide bed, he was more than ready to get some more sleep.

Brick was right. They had some figuring out to do.

"HEY, YOU okay?" Horvan bent down and kissed Dellan's forehead. "That sigh sounded pretty huge." He sat down beside Dellan on the couch. Rael was fixing lunch, Hashtag was working in the office on Anson's computer, and Roadkill and Crank were conversing with Brick on the patio while they smoked.

Dellan threw the sheaf of papers he'd been reading onto the coffee table. "There's nothing here. Well, nothing untoward." He'd taken folders from the office filing cabinets and had spent the morning poring over them. "Nothing about the drug. Or any indication who that man is. Just what I'd expect to find, related to the company." He glanced in the direction of the office. "I gave Hashtag some space. I know he works best when it's quiet."

Horvan had taken him some coffee. "He was fairly disgusted how quickly he cracked the password. Made noises about how lax Anson was when it came to security." He chuckled. "He went quiet when he hit the encrypted files, though."

"Does he think he can get into them?"

Horvan laughed. "To quote him, 'This might take a while.'"

"What was the password, by the way?"

Horvan stilled. "Your name. And I find that intriguing."

"Halle-fucking-lujah!"

They both gave a start at the loud cry. Horvan ran to the office, Dellan behind him.

Hashtag was staring at the monitor and grinning. "You ain't better than me, you piece of shit." He looked up at them, his eyes shining. "I'm in. And you'd better believe there are a ton of files in here." He started tapping the keys, his gaze locked on the screen. "How about we start with this one?" Hashtag glanced at Dellan, then dragged a chair across. He patted its seat. "I could use you here. You might know what to look for."

Dellan sat beside him. Horvan stood behind Hashtag's chair, peering at the screen.

Rael came in, carrying plates of sandwiches. "If Mohammed won't come to the mountain... I figured getting you away from work was a nonstarter." He put them on the desk. "Have you made headway?"

Hashtag groaned. "For Christ's sake, I just got in. Gimme a sec, all right?"

Dellan pointed to the screen. "Open that one." Hashtag clicked on it, revealing a spreadsheet. Dellan peered closely at it, his lips moving as he read silently.

"What is it?" Horvan's scalp was prickling, and that was never a good sign.

"Shipments," Dellan murmured. "A *lot* of shipments."

"Of what?" Rael demanded.

Dellan sagged back into his chair. "A product I don't recognize. There's only a code for it, which is strange in itself. And another thing. There are figures dating back a year but only relating to the size of the shipment. No sales figures." He shook his head. "It's like... whatever this is, it's either being shipped free of charge or he simply hasn't recorded the figures." Dellan looked up at Horvan. "Like it's a secret."

"Any idea where these shipments are going?" Hashtag asked.

Dellan shook his head. "The destinations aren't in here. Just codes."

"And what are you thinking?" Horvan had a feeling he already knew the answer.

Dellan sighed. "That this is the drug they used on me. Anson was producing it and sending it out. But to whom? And why in such numbers?"

"If you're correct, there'll be evidence in the labs, won't there?" Hashtag asked. "I mean, if that's where they made this stuff. *Someone* had to make it, right? And there might be more files in here that relate to it. I'll do a search for that code."

"Any clues in those files as to who our friend is?" Horvan badly wanted a name for that guy.

"I don't think I'm gonna find a photo labeled Bad Guy," Hashtag remarked with a wry chuckle. "But you never know. Anson doesn't appear to have been some great criminal mastermind." He pointed at the screen. "There are several images in here. Let's see if one of them is of our friend." Hashtag snorted. "Friend. Yeah, right." He clicked the first one, then rotated through to the end. "Nope. It's not him. They all seem to be of one guy, though. Anyone have any idea who he is?"

Horvan was instantly aware of the change in Dellan. *You're so cold.* It was as if he could feel the ice that crawled over Dellan's skin. Rael shivered violently.

Dellan didn't say a word but stared numbly at the screen.

"Dellan?"

Slowly, Dellan turned to look at him. "I... I don't understand."

Rael knelt at his side, his hand on Dellan's knee. "I'm only reading profound shock. What's wrong?"

Dellan swallowed and pointed to one of the images. Horvan leaned in to take a closer look. It was a photo of a man who appeared to be in his sixties, but he wasn't posing for the picture. It was like someone had taken a quick snap of him. Behind him was a fence with barbed wire along the top. There were several people in the background, of differing ages, and Horvan was struck immediately by the similarity of their expressions. They all seemed tired or ill. One thing stood out, however.

No one was smiling.

"Do you know him?" Horvan asked softly. Stupid question, because Dellan's reaction screamed recognition.

Dellan nodded. "That's my dad." His voice was flat.

A stunned silence fell over them before Rael broke it. "But... isn't he...?"

Dellan nodded. "Declared dead when I was fourteen. Hasn't been seen since I was seven." He drew in a shaky breath. "His... his hair is grayer than the last time I saw him, and his face is more lined, but that *was* more than thirty years ago." Dellan's brow furrowed. "It can't be him." He grabbed hold of the mouse and hovered over the image. "No. This isn't possible. This file was created last year."

"Hashtag." Horvan spoke quietly. "Look at the photo. Tell me what you see."

Hashtag said nothing for a moment but enlarged the picture, looking at every part of it. Finally, he expelled a long breath. "Okay. Wanna know what it reminds me of? Those old photos of concentration camps. I half expected to see a tower with an armed guard. But most of all, it's their expressions. Like there's no hope."

Hashtag's words mirrored Horvan's thoughts.

"Hey, what does a guy have to do around here to get fed?" Crank called out, his voice nearing. "'Cause my stomach thinks my throat's been—" He fell silent as he stepped into the room, Roadkill and Brick behind him. Crank straightened, all traces of humor vanishing. "Okay, what's up?"

Horvan sighed heavily. "Nothing much. Just a photo of Dellan's dad, who is looking very much alive."

Rael met Horvan's gaze. *What the fuck have we gotten into here?* He put his arm around Dellan's shoulders. Dellan's mind was a mess, a convoluted jumble of shock and distress.

Horvan reached into his pocket for his phone and speed-dialed a number.

"What's up?" The voice on the other end was calm as always.

Horvan cleared his throat. "This business just got way more complicated."

"What do you need?"

"Possibly the whole team. I wanted to put you on alert."

"Gotcha. I'll have them on standby. Keep me informed." The call disconnected.

Horvan pocketed his phone and turned to face the others.

Roadkill stared at him. "All of us?"

He nodded. "This isn't over. In fact, it could be barely the start."

"Of what?" Hashtag demanded.

And there was the problem. Horvan had no clue. He just knew his gut was telling him this wasn't good.

I have to find him. Dellan gazed at him with anguished eyes. Rael tightened his arm around Dellan.

Horvan nodded. We *will find him. I promise.*

Whatever it took.

The End

Well… for the moment.

K.C. WELLS lives on an island off the south coast of the UK, surrounded by natural beauty. She writes about men who love men, and can't even contemplate a life that doesn't include writing.

The rainbow rose tattoo on her back with the words 'Love is Love' and 'Love Wins' is her way of hoisting a flag. She plans to be writing about men in love—be it sweet and slow, hot or kinky—for a long while to come.

If you want to follow her exploits, you can sign up for her monthly newsletter: http://eepurl.com/cNKHlT

You can stalk—er, find—her in the following places:
Email: k.c.wells@btinternet.com
Facebook: www.facebook.com/KCWellsWorld
KC's Men In Love (my readers group): http://bit.ly/2hXL6wJ
Twitter: @K_C_Wells
Website: www.kcwellswrites.com
Instagram: www.instagram.com/k.c.wells
BookBub: https://www.bookbub.com/authors/k-c-wells

UNDER
THE COVERS

K.C. Wells

Will they find their HEA in Romancelandia?

Can they find their HEA in Romancelandia?

Chris Tyler loves his job. He photographs some of the hottest guys on the planet, but none stir him like Jase Mitchell. He'll never let Jase know – he values their friendship too much to spoil it.

Jase is looking forward to the Under The Covers Romance convention. It's a great opportunity to connect with readers who want to meet their favorite cover model, but more importantly, with agents who could advance his career. Too bad the only person he yearns to connect with is Chris.

What Chris wants is Jase in his life, but he's afraid that's sheer fantasy. What Jase desires is a Hollywood dream, but that will mean leaving Chris behind. What both crave is a real-life romance and their own Happily Ever After.

www.dreamspinnerpress.com

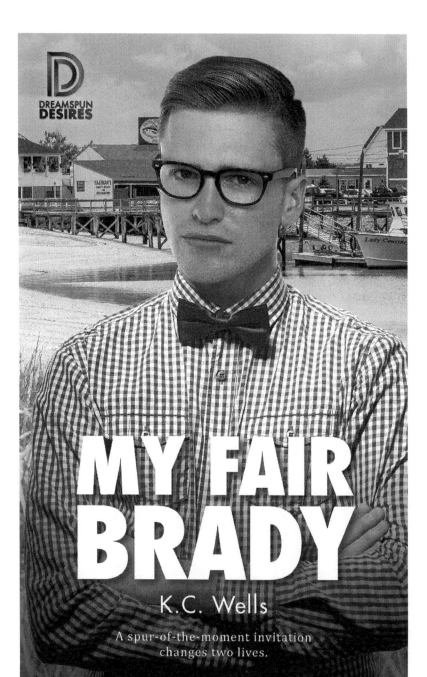

DREAMSPUN
DESIRES

MY FAIR BRADY

K.C. Wells

A spur-of-the-moment invitation
changes two lives.

A spur of the moment invitation changes two lives.

Jordan Wolf's company runs like a well-oiled machine. At least until his PA, Brady Donovan, comes down with the flu and takes sick leave. Then Jordan discovers what a treasure Brady is and who really keeps his business—and Jordan in particular—moving like clockwork. So when Jordan needs a plus-one, Brady seems the obvious choice to accompany him. After a major shopping trip to get Brady looking the part, however…. Wow.

Brady has a whole new wardrobe, and now his boss is whisking him away for a weekend party. Something is going on, something Brady never expected: Jordan is looking at him like he's never seen him before, electrifying Brady's long-hidden desires.

But can the romantic magic last when the weekend is over and it's back to reality?

www.dreamspinnerpress.com

K.C. WELLS

TRUTH WILL OUT

A Merrychurch Mysteries Case

Jonathon de Mountford's visit to Merrychurch village to stay with his uncle Dominic gets off to a bad start when Dominic fails to appear at the railway station. But when Jonathon finds him dead in his study, apparently as the result of a fall, everything changes. For one thing, Jonathon is the next in line to inherit the manor house. For another, he's not so sure it was an accident, and with the help of Mike Tattersall, the owner of the village pub, Jonathon sets out to prove his theory—if he can concentrate long enough without getting distracted by the handsome Mike.

They discover an increasingly long list of people who had reason to want Dominic dead. And when events take an unexpected turn, the amateur sleuths are left bewildered. It doesn't help that the police inspector brought in to solve the case is the last person Mike wants to see, especially when they are told to keep their noses out of police business.

In Jonathon's case, that's like a red rag to a bull....

www.dreamspinnerpress.com

Made in the USA
Middletown, DE
08 December 2024